Where there's smoke...

"Fire!" somebody yelled, and as one, we all turned and fled.

My heart raced, and my palms broke out in a sweat. I took off for Mom's office. She must have heard the commotion, because she met me at the doorway. "What the hell's going on?"

"Mom, we've gotta get out of here! It's—"

"A smoke bomb!" Tiffany yelled. I turned to see her emerge from the fog now creeping down the hall. Her eyes were watering, and she had a hand over her mouth while she coughed and gagged. "This is your fault!"

"My fault?" I asked, astonished anyone would think I'd stoop to something so juvenile and mean.

Thrusting a sheet of crinkled paper at me, she coughed and spluttered but managed to say, "Whoever opened the door and…threw the smoke bomb tossed this in first. Says right there, 'Back off…Pink…or next time it'll be a helluva lot worse than…smoke!'"

So much for my plan of keeping my stalker on the Q.T.

Dear Reader,

What's hot this spring? Silhouette Bombshell! We're putting action, danger, romance and that exhilarating feeling of winning against the odds right at your fingertips.

Feeling wild? *USA TODAY* bestselling author Lindsay McKenna's *Wild Woman* takes you to Hong Kong for the latest story in the SISTERS OF THE ARK miniseries. Pilot Jessica "Wild Woman" Merrill is on a mission to infiltrate the lair of a criminal mastermind—but she's been thrown a curveball in the form of an unexpected partner....

The clock is ticking as an NSA code breaker races to stop a bomb in *Countdown* by Ruth Wind, the latest in the high-octane ATHENA FORCE continuity series. This determined Athena woman will risk her career and even kidnap an FBI bomb squad member to save the day!

Indiana Jones and Lara Croft have nothing on modern legend Veronica Bright, the star of author Sharron McClellan's *The Midas Trap*. Veronica has a chance to find the mythical Midas Stone—but to succeed, she's got to risk working for a man who tried to ruin her years ago....

Meet CPA Whitney "Pink" Pearl, heroine of *Show Her the Money* by Stephanie Feagan. Blowing the whistle on a corporate funny-money scam lands her in the red, but Pink won't let death threats, abduction attempts or steamy kisses from untrustworthy lawyers get in the way of justice!

Please send your comments to me c/o Silhouette Books, 233 Broadway, Suite 1001, New York, NY 10279.

Sincerely,

Natashya Wilson
Associate Senior Editor, Silhouette Bombshell

STEPHANIE FEAGAN

$HOW HER THE MONEY

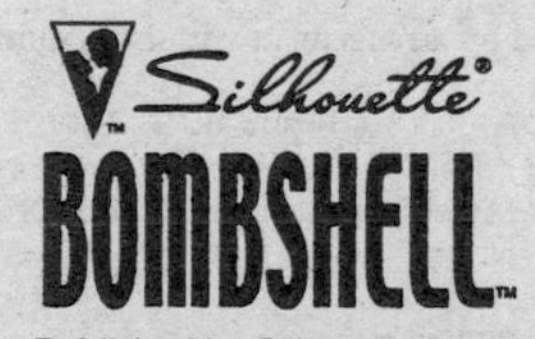

Published by Silhouette Books
America's Publisher of Contemporary Romance

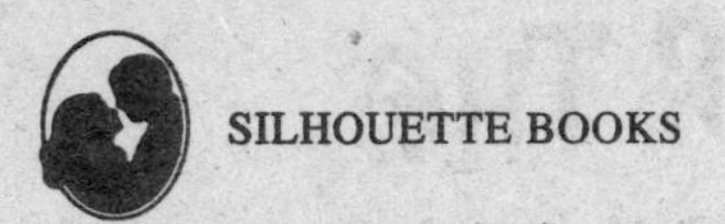

ISBN 0-373-51354-2

SHOW HER THE MONEY

This edition published by arrangement with Harlequin Books S.A.

www.SilhouetteBombshell.com

Printed in U.S.A.

STEPHANIE FEAGAN

didn't grow up dreaming of becoming a CPA. She planned to be a park ranger so that she could live in the mountains of Yellowstone National Park, marry a good-looking guy who liked bears and spend her evenings by a cozy fire, writing novels. But a funny thing happened on the way to college. Instead of a forestry degree, she graduated with a BBA in accounting and became a CPA. Instead of marrying a mountain man, she married an oilman. And instead of living amongst mountains and pines and bears, she lives in the flatlands of West Texas, amongst mesquites and jackrabbits. That's okay for Stephanie—she happens to love the mesquites and the jackrabbits. She especially loves her oilman. And she does spend her evenings writing novels, although instead of a cozy fire, she opts for an air conditioner. Stephanie would love for you to visit her Web site at www.stephaniefeagan.com.

This book is dedicated to the memory of
Edward Cotner.
We miss you, Eddie.

****

Acknowledgments

My undying gratitude belongs to the following people: Jo George, CPA extraordinaire, aka Mom, for answers and inspiration. Callie and Leslea, for the gift of time. Kay Sirgo and Cheryl Cotner, for the first reads. Dan Fogelberg, for keeping me company in the wee hours, via headphones. Pam Payne, Nancy Kleinkopf and the Wet Noodle Posse, without whom this book never would have happened. Karen Solem, for believing in Pink. Natashya Wilson, every writer's dream editor, for your patience, help and friendship. And most of all, my thanks to Mike, for the oil-field expertise, your love and support, and your unwavering faith in me.

Chapter 1

Sitting in front of the senate finance committee was like sprinting down Dallas Central Expressway, naked. If I didn't get run over and killed, I was bound to become the butt of everyone's joke first thing in the morning when the newspapers came out.

Either way, I'd rather get a root canal, have lunch with Aunt Dru, who could bore God into a premature Armageddon or remarry my lying, cheating mongrel of an ex-husband than face a row of senators bent on ferreting out the truth behind one of the worst accounting hoodwink jobs in history. Never mind that they got the first scent of blood from me. Less than a month ago, I thought I could set things straight, Marvel Energy would get their hand slapped and all would be well. How was I to know that what I discovered was only the tip of the iceberg?

I'd finished giving my prepared statement, and now it was

time to run through the rack line with all those fun and happy senators who vaguely reminded me of a movie I once saw about the Salem witch trials.

"Ms. Pearl, I'd like some clarification on a few points."

Eyeing Senator Santorelli, a romantic-looking Italian with perfect hair, I nodded.

"What was your position within the accounting firm before you were dismissed?"

"I was promoted to senior manager last December, with the understanding I was being groomed to make partner within three years. This was my first year to head the Marvel Energy audit. I reported directly to Lowell Jaworski, the partner in charge of the firm's Dallas-based energy and petroleum clients."

"When you initially discovered the irregularities in Marvel's accounting methods, were you aware how deeply your own firm was involved?"

"I had no idea." That all came later. It broke my heart to discover the firm where I'd worked for over eight years was rotten at the core. But I didn't say that. I was pretty sure the finance committee could care less about my heart.

"What sort of discrepancies, in particular, did you find while working on the Marvel audit?"

Oh boy. This was the fun part. "Based on the dollar amount of oil reserves Marvel claims to hold, they own close to a sixteenth of the world's supply of petroleum. Marvel is a large company, sir, but not that large. My staff was only able to track down a fraction of their claim. Marvel has less than sixty million dollars of debt on the balance sheet, but I believe they owe various banks upwards of four hundred million. All of this debt was carried off the books, within a maze of partnerships and offshore trusts. As I dug deeper, I found out the company overstated their quarterly income for the past five quarters by almost twenty million."

"When you asked about these discrepancies, what was Mr. Jaworski's reaction?"

I cleared my throat and shot a glance at my hired gun attorney, Mr. Dryer. He nodded slightly, indicating I should go ahead. Returning my gaze to Santorelli, I caught an odd look on his face, one I couldn't decipher. "Mr. Jaworski told me my chances of making partner would fall to zilch if I didn't back off and leave it alone."

Santorelli paged through the copies of documents I'd provided to the committee, then looked at me with that weird look again. He almost looked like he wanted to smile. There was a bit of a twinkle in his dark eyes. Or maybe it was just the awful fluorescent light in the hearing room. At any rate, I had the sense he found all of this amusing in some way, and that pissed me off. After becoming a CPA, landing a job at the most prestigious firm in the universe, then working ungodly hours, week after week, year after year, all so I could make it to the top, I was now on unemployment. And Santorelli thought this was funny? I couldn't believe it. Maybe he just had that kind of face that always looks like it wants to smile.

"Ms. Pearl," he began in a solemn voice that belied his expression, "I see workpapers and documents here, along with the preliminary findings of the Securities and Exchange Commission investigation, that go a long way toward backing up your claim that Marvel grossly understated debt and overstated assets, but nothing in here gives us any proof that the irregularities weren't the result of error, or miscommunication, or negligence. You say the Marvel execs and the partners of your firm knowingly hoodwinked investors, that all the misstatements were on purpose, but we can't begin investigating anyone unless we have some sort of evidence. All we can do with these documents is allow the SEC to file suit against Marvel and the firm for what amounts to setting up a maze of companies so complicated, it would take Einstein a year to figure it out. It's no wonder there are so many mistakes."

The sole woman on the committee, Barbara Clemmons from New Hampshire, piped up then. "Isn't it true that you approached the SEC *after* you were let go from your position at the firm?"

Again, I glanced at Mr. Dryer. He leaned over and whispered, "Tell the truth. They're going to try and say you did all of this for revenge, and without the memos, it doesn't look good. Just do the best you can."

Do the best I could? Oh, Lord. Turning back to face the row of senators, I said, "Mr. Jaworski told me, if I was determined to take my suspicions to the SEC, he'd fire me. In light of what I found, I didn't see I had any choice."

"If you're so certain this was a conspiracy, where's the evidence?"

Time for some major ass-covering. I mentally slipped into my iron underwear. "The Marvel executives sold every share of Marvel stock they were legally allowed to sell the day I took my findings to the SEC, and at the same time, put a freeze on the employees and wouldn't allow any of the retirement fund Marvel stock to be sold. Then they announced an adjustment to earnings and the stock price fell by fifty percent."

"All that proves is the Marvel executives were running scared because they knew you were opening the company up for an SEC investigation. There's no law against someone looking out for their own interests. Perhaps they froze the retirement fund to avoid a further drop in the price, which would protect the investors. As for the earnings adjustment, they no doubt wanted to set the record straight in their own way, rather than allow for the perception of wrongdoing among their shareholders."

Un-freaking-believable. She was painting the execs at Marvel as the wounded party in all this. They'd lied, cheated and ripped off the investors by selling out before the stock price tanked. But Barbara Clemmons had the nerve to insinuate that I was Chicken Little, causing a panic when clearly, it was all just a big misunderstanding.

She said in a tone now almost hostile, "I was given to understand we would see evidence at today's hearing. Instead, all you have are theories." The other senators nodded agreement, looking annoyed. Except Santorelli.

He was frowning at Ms. Clemmons, but she didn't appear to notice. Instead, she was frowning at me, as though I was the bad guy in all of this. Dammit! If only I had the freakin' memos. Time to lay out The Big Confession. "Almost two weeks ago, I obtained copies of several memos between Lowell Jaworski and the CEO and CFO at Marvel. They prove the complicated partnership scheme was designed for the express purpose of hiding debt and losses that would affect Marvel's bottom line, and therefore the price of their stock. The memos also prove that the firm agreed to look the other way in exchange for very lucrative consulting work."

"The SEC informed us of the alleged memos," she said, her middle-aged, jowly face set in stern disapproval, "but where are these memos? Why didn't you turn what you had over to the SEC investigator?"

Okay, this was it. The moment I'd dreaded since the instant I realized I no longer had my ace in the hole. "The memos were scanned and saved onto several disks, one of which I stored in a safe deposit box at my bank, some I hid in my home and one was earmarked to be taken to the SEC. Before I could get the disk to the SEC, it was stolen, along with all but one of the hidden copies. The disk in the lockbox was accidentally taken by my ex-husband." Who still had a key because I was so busy working my ass off, I didn't think to have it changed. Because the only things in the damn box were our marriage license—yeah, like I wanted to keep that safe—and my mother's will. Because I forgot George even had a key. Huge mistake on my part. I was convinced someone had paid George big bucks to swipe the disk, but I wasn't going to say that. I already looked like a fringe lunatic, paranoid and grasping at conspiracy theories. No way I wanted to get into it about George.

"Did you contact the police about the theft?"

"Yes, but they weren't able to reach any conclusion as to who might have broken into my home." So much for the boys in blue upholding the law. They'd acted as though they'd like to arrest me for being such a pain in their ass. Floppy disks didn't register on their radar as any consequence. That the disks represented all that stood between me and very hot water never seemed to register. They'd taken a report and I hadn't heard from them since. "I thought I'd be able to retrieve the memos before today's hearing. Regrettably, I could not."

"So," she said a bit smugly, "there will never be any evidence to prove your claim. Is that right?"

"Respectfully, no, that is not right. There is one disk remaining, but I don't have access to it."

Santorelli spoke before Clemmons could ask another snarky question. "Where is it?"

I panicked, and Mr. Dryer leaned close. "You have to tell them." He raised one graying brow, reminding me of my father. This wasn't a good thing.

Taking a deep breath, I looked at Santorelli. "Inside a box that was taken by someone who misunderstood which box I intended to get rid of."

"The solution seems simple, Ms. Pearl. Get the box back."

"I can't get the box back because it was sold." In a garage sale, by my aunt Fred, who's the Garage Sale Queen, always hunting for inventory. But no way I was telling the senator, or anyone else. Someone had taken five of my copies, and I was determined to hang on to the sixth. It held everything the justice department needed to charge the Marvel Energy executives and the partners of my ex-employer CPA firm with felony counts of fraud, gross negligence and perjury.

The only people who knew where the box was now located were me, Aunt Fred and my third grade teacher, who'd bought the box. Me and Aunt Fred weren't talking, and Mrs. Bohannon was currently rolling across the Serengeti in the back of a Land Rover, shooting pictures of giraffes, completely unaware she had the key to my fate stored in one of her closets. "I can retrieve the disk within three weeks, as soon as the person who bought the box returns from out of the country."

Santorelli glanced at his fellow senators, then leveled a look at me. "I assume no one purchased an empty box, Ms. Pearl. What was in the box?"

A sharp look at Mr. Dryer. He only nodded, and his already thin lips completely disappeared. We'd been all through the box issue. If I lied, if I said something was in the box, other than what really was in the box, it could harm my credibility if the investigation ended with criminal charges against Marvel Energy. It didn't seem reasonable that anyone would ever be the wiser, but Mr. Dryer assured me they had ways of finding these things out. Not wanting to arm the Marvel defense team with any ammunition, I decided to tell the truth, even if it meant laying my pride at the feet of the senate finance committee—and the rest of the United States. At least, the ones who watched C-SPAN. I looked straight at the senator and said clearly, "Mister Bob."

"Mister Bob?"

"A blow-up doll."

The army of press congregated behind me, along with a smorgasbord of others, including the head honcho of the SEC, chuckled and guffawed. The senators all smiled. All except Barbara. I tried to save face. "It was a gag gift, given to me on my thirtieth birthday."

Santorelli stopped grinning, barely, and said in a pseudo-forceful tone, "I believe we've covered everything, Ms. Pearl. Thank you again for coming forward and we'd like to reconvene this hearing when you have the memo copies in hand."

"Yes, sir. I will be here."

He leaned forward a bit, his dark eyes trained on mine as though he really wanted me to get what he was about to say. "Ms. Pearl, it takes a lot of courage for a person to do the right thing, then suffer the consequences as you have. However, I must advise you of the precarious position you're in. Although this was the first year you were in charge of the Marvel audit, you were involved with the audit over the past five years, in a lesser managerial capacity, but still in a position of authority over the audit staff. If further investigation by the SEC reveals malfeasance or negligence on the part of your firm, you are now under the umbrella of immunity this committee has extended to you in return for your testimony. You will avoid prosecution, civil or criminal. But I remind you, immunity was granted based on your full cooperation."

"Sir, I've told you everything I know, provided all the documents and evidence needed to proceed with the investigation."

"Ms. Pearl, your immunity can be revoked in the absence of all requested information. You said you had the memos. Now you say you don't. Without them, it looks as though you blew the whistle to cover yourself in the event Marvel's house of cards caved in. It comes down to a you-say–they-say situation. From the look of what you have provided, Marvel is very close to defaulting on a large amount of their debt. That may force them into bankruptcy, which would cause a lot of questions to be asked, perhaps putting you in the line of fire."

I leaned toward Mr. Dryer. "Can they revoke immunity?"

He nodded. "I think they only offered it because they want those memos. Without them, he's right and it looks like you sang just to cover yourself."

"Does the fact I knew nothing about any of it have no impact at all?"

Mr. Dryer shot me a look that said he wasn't buying any of it, either. Even my own attorney didn't believe me. For eight hundred bucks an hour, the least he could have done was fake it. "Like the man said, it's your word against theirs. I suggest you do all you can to get your hands on that disk."

A mental picture of Mrs. Bohannon popped into my head. She was a ditzy old girl when I was in third grade. Dear Lord, please, please let her still have the box, and the disk I'd stuck in the bottom of it.

"Ms. Pearl, do you understand what I'm saying to you?" Santorelli asked in an even voice.

"Yes, sir. I will get the memos." Or die trying.

As soon as we were dismissed, I wasted no time firing Mr. Dryer. Why give him eight hundred bucks an hour for getting me immunity that wouldn't hold up? I could get the same service with a back-alley attorney who charged a hundred bucks an hour. Just what I'd do about an attorney, I wasn't sure, but I'd think of something. I supposed I had to have one. Muddling through the process of hearings and handing over sensitive documents wasn't in my repertoire. Digging for facts is more my calling. Legal-eagle stuff blows my mind. Without an attorney, I was bound to say and do all the wrong things and wind up in prison, or at the very least, owe a ginormous amount of dough after I was sued by the SEC.

When I got back to my hotel room, I had a surprise waiting for me. Another note, threatening a slice-and-dice job on my private body parts, along with a lovely gift of dog doo.

Somebody had it in for me, and the threats were arriving more frequently. The notion that someone was following me and watching every move I made was creepy enough, but the dog doo took my anxiety to a higher level. I figured, anyone who took the time to find dog poop, scoop it up, preserve it, transport it and artfully arrange it in some strategic spot where I'd be sure to find it, whether with my eyes, my nose or the heel of my foot, was severely twisted. The notes I could almost understand. Someone had a major problem with me ratting out the firm and Marvel Energy. Maybe that someone was in danger of losing their job, or even facing possible indictment.

But the poop took it to a new level. A very scary one.

Still, I wasn't going to back off. Not that I'm a modern day superhero, or Joan of Arc, or anything. I just don't like getting shoved around, and I really have a problem with fat cats taking investors for a ride, then swiping their cash. Dog doo or no, I wasn't backing off.

While me and the housekeeping lady worked at cleaning up the mess, I sent a silent prayer, asking God to forgive me for having murderous thoughts. That's the great thing about God. He's so forgiving. Man, I wished I could do that.

But I couldn't. I despised the Dog Doo Stalker for terrorizing me with poodle bombs and sick notes. I hated Senator Santorelli and Barbara Clemmons for forcing me to humiliate myself in front of the entire nation. And I especially despised my ex-boss, Lowell, for firing me.

The next morning, I caught the early flight out of D.C. and arrived in Dallas before lunch. Not that it mattered. My days of power lunches at places like Beau Nash and The Mansion were over. I could still afford a plate of food that cost more than a new tire, but I had way too much pride to waltz into a fancy-schmancy restaurant and eat lunch alone.

Which is how I felt. Very alone. Being a whistle-blower might earn a girl a place in heaven, but it's hell on a social life.

I spent an hour wandering around my ransacked loft, half-heartedly picking things up and putting them in their places. Lord, but I loved the loft. It was two-thousand square feet of upscale, modern architecture. I had splurged and bought beautiful Cantoni furniture and the result looked like something out of *Architectural Digest.* I'd never actually wanted a home that more closely resembled a Starbucks than a cozy place to live, but it grew on me. From the bathroom's black ceramic bowl and brushed steel faucet that poked out of the granite wall, to the kitchen's stark wood cabinets and stainless steel appliances, to the narrow balcony that looked out over Central Expressway, the loft screamed success. And I was successful. Very. *Was* being the operative word.

With the sofa and chair cushions slashed, my books strewn all over the floor, the rugs ripped up and the dishes all broken, the loft was uncannily a mirror of my career, once again. Whoever had broken in to hunt for the disks did a bang-up job. They'd not only destroyed my home, they'd slashed the tires on my car and ripped out the upholstered leather seats, leaving the poor thing's guts hanging out. I'd had the seats and tires replaced, but it almost seemed to me that the car was wounded. Sad and dejected. It didn't run quite as well as before.

But then, neither did I. My spirit was so low, I kept asking myself if it was all worth it. Then I'd think of all the people who would suffer because of what Marvel and Lowell had done, and I knew I couldn't roll over and give up.

As I packed up my portfolio and left for my fourteenth job interview, I wondered why I bothered. No one would hire me. I was a whistle-blower, and despite my honorable intentions, I'd come to realize that most people saw it exactly as Barbara Clemmons and the rest of the finance committee saw it—I'd done it for purely self-serving reasons. Until I had the evidence to prove otherwise, I was as guilty of creating the problems at Marvel as any of the top brass in the company and at my firm. I was a bad guy. It wasn't fair, but what could I do? Every single interview ended the same. "Your credentials are perfect, Ms. Pearl, but until you've settled your affairs with the federal government, we don't feel it's in our best interest to offer you a position." Which was a nice way of saying, "You may be hanging out in the joint soon, so buzz off."

Nevertheless, I spent the next week looking for a job. By the end of the road, I was down to inquiring about a bookkeeping position with an elderly woman who had a lot of oil and gas interests. I'd office in her laundry room, account for her money and when things got slow, I would need to run a few personal errands. Dry cleaning. Weed the beds. Maybe address invitations to her monthly supper socials.

The real killer? I couldn't even get that job. The old lady said she'd seen me on C-SPAN, and the only reason she'd agreed to interview me was so she could see me in person. Then she asked if Mr. Bob was anatomically correct.

I came home that night to a message from my mom. "Pink, baby, come home. You're running through your money so fast, you'll be on the streets before long. Now I know you think moving back to Midland is the worst thing in the world, and working for me is a last resort, but I have news for you, baby. You're down to your last resort. Besides, I could really use the help. Call me."

Most people think I followed in my mother's footsteps and became a CPA like she did. They're wrong. I was a sophomore in college when Mom decided she'd had just about enough of my dad and enrolled herself in summer school. She tested out of a gazillion hours, buzzed through in two years and graduated with an MBA about the same time I wrapped up my five-year plan and got my bachelor's degree.

We each went to work for top-dog accounting firms, me in Dallas, her in Midland. I stuck with it. She didn't. After a few years of taking orders from managers twenty years younger, she ditched the firm and went out on her own.

She's wildly successful, and it was really very nice of her to offer me a mercy job. I was appreciative, but moving home and working for her was honestly, truly, the worst possible thing I could imagine.

Too bad I had absolutely no choice in the matter.

I called and said I'd do it. The next morning, I put the loft up for sale, packed what I could into the Mercedes SUV and headed west, waving to Dallas in my rearview mirror.

As I drove back to the town I'd sworn never to live in again, all I could think was what a miserable failure I'd turned out to be. In spite of my devotion, my marriage had crashed and burned. I'd lost a great job because I tried to do the right thing. And I was about to take a mercy job with my mother. How pathetic was that?

To top it all off, I had a notice from the IRS in the day's mail. I was going to be audited.

I didn't mind so much. It gave me something different to obsess about.

Midland sits three hundred miles west of Dallas, rising twenty-four stories out of the flattest land on the planet. The twenty-four stories is the tallest building downtown and it's joined by other wannabes that make the skyline pretty impressive, from ten miles out on the highway. It's called the Tall City, at least by locals. Everyone else calls it the armpit of Texas, or "that town where Baby Jessica fell down the well." After George the Second got elected, they hung banners from the downtown light poles with a photo of George W. giving the thumbs-up, and a line beneath him that says, "Midland's Rising Son." They are real proud of George and Laura in Midland. Even the three Democrats.

I couldn't stop thinking of Dallas's trees and lakes and lush, green grass as I drove that last ten miles into Midland. The landscape around the Tall City is anything but lush. In fact, I've often wondered if they did a little bomb practice around Midland before they dropped the Big One on Hiroshima. The loftiest plant life is maybe four feet tall. Mesquite. Lots and lots of mesquite. Some cactus, a little sage and a very wee bit of some thin green stuff that looks like the hair on Charlie Brown's head. Midland is not scenic.

Still, it has a certain charm, especially within the city limits. All that oil money buys a nice town. Mom told me once, there are more rich people per capita in Midland than anywhere else in Texas. Maybe America. I believe it.

I drove into town and went straight to my mother's house, a zero-lot line in a small, gated community. It pained her to spend the money, but she had a certain image to uphold. Or so she said. I think she secretly craved a real house, in a ritzy part of town, and that's exactly what she got. The place was big, with four bedrooms, decorated in luxurious fabrics, dark mahogany and old-world paintings. Very British Indies. She has a pool in the back, and with the August heat rising off the road, I'd been thinking of that pool since Abilene.

It wasn't until I got to the door that I realized I didn't have a key. So I got back in the car and drove downtown, to Mom's office, located in the old First National Bank building, the one that's the tallest. It's had so many owners and names over the past twenty years, ever since the oil bust of '85, nobody knows its actual name. Everyone just calls it the Old First National Bank Building.

Mom's office is on the fifteenth floor, and her reception area is similar to her house, with beautiful mahogany, plush fabrics and recessed lighting. Mom can be so tight, she squeaks when she walks, but she spends the bucks when it comes to her professional image. Mom says, look successful and you'll be successful. Guess she's right. Mom makes a lot of dough.

I walked into the office and saw a pretty, young woman with light brown hair and pouty lips manning the reception desk.

"May I help you?" she inquired cordially.

"Hi, I'm Pink," I answered, walking close to her desk, glancing at her name plate, "and it's nice to meet you, Tiffany." I stuck my hand out and she shook it, then said a little breathlessly, "I think your mom's been expecting you. Go on back."

"Thanks." I turned and headed down the short hall toward the big hall that houses a small conference room, five offices on each side, then opens up into the bull pen, where the lower staffers have cubicles. Mom's large office is at the end, generally a mess, with stacks of files all over the place.

I was halfway there when she popped out of one of the side offices and waylaid me. "Pink! You're here!"

She pulled me into the conference room across the hall, we hugged, then she held me away from her and did a quick inventory. "You've lost weight."

"I've been a little stressed."

"Of course you have. I'm sorry, baby."

Sympathy from Mom has never been ample. Much like rain in Midland; infrequent, longed for, but given sparingly. I swallowed back the giant lump of Pity Party tears in my throat and managed to smile. "Thanks, Mom. And thanks for the job."

She waved away my thanks and said pragmatically, "You need a job and I need someone to work in my new forensic accounting department. It's almost cosmic, the way things worked out."

"Forensic accounting? I thought your practice was solely tax prep."

"It was, up until a month ago. I hired an MBA named Sam Weston. He was with the FBI, and I hired him as soon as he retired."

"The FBI?" My voice sort of squeaked on the "FBI" because I was so surprised. An FBI guy, working for my mom? "What's he going to do, exactly?"

"Trace assets in divorces, testify in court, look into bad oil deals, and things like that."

I was beyond surprised and almost shocked. Mom is hip and modern in a lot of ways, but old school when it comes to business. Forensic accounting sounded very glam for someone like my mother. "And you want me to work for Sam?"

"That's the plan." Mom looked like she did the year she gave me a calculator for Christmas, when I was thirteen. I wanted a padded bra and I got a calculator. "Isn't it exciting?" She looked ready to whoop it up and start clapping.

Compared to her penthouse enthusiasm, my excitement was in the basement, but I was definitely grateful she didn't expect me to do tax returns, because I'm not a tax accountant. I'm an auditor. Not the sort of auditor the IRS hires to scare the hell out of people. Not the sort who pokes around a company, looking for pilfering employees. Most people think companies hire us to seek and destroy embezzlers.

They're wrong.

All we do is look over the financial statements and make sure the company isn't lying their ass off so people will be suckered into buying their stock and the price will go through the roof and all the Big Dog executives can make off like bandits when they sell their stock options. Companies can't claim to have oil reserves worth eighty bajillion dollars when really they have maybe forty or fifty million bucks worth. They can't claim to have a few measly million dollars of debt, when in fact, they owe so much to every bank on the planet, even God couldn't bail them out.

As an auditor, it was my job to make sure everything was clean and tidy at the companies I audited. If things weren't clean and tidy, Lowell Jaworski put his foot down and demanded things get fixed, or he'd write a bad opinion and every investor out there would dump their stock. All in all, a pretty good system. Until the Marvel Energy fiasco.

Nothing was clean and tidy at Marvel Energy, but for fifty million dollars worth of consulting income, Lowell decided he didn't care. Which unfortunately signaled the ending buzzer for my career as said auditor.

Now, Mom was opening a new career opportunity for me, and maybe I wasn't as over the moon about it as she appeared to be, but I was glad to have a job doing something useful, something I had a prayer of understanding. The myriad tax laws were my worst nightmare. "I'll do my best," I told her.

She hugged me again, which surprised me. Mom seemed more sentimental than usual, and her usual doesn't lean toward mushy.

"I've never wanted anything but for you to be happy, Whitney, and I feel bad for you because this has all been so awful. You deserve a break, and a fresh start." Dropping her arms, she stepped back and gave me a funny look. "You don't seem very fired up about this."

Sighing, I shoved my hair behind my ears. "I'm sorry, Mom. This is really great of you, but it's a crummy feeling to know the only job I can get is a mercy job with my mommy. It's humiliating. And it makes me so mad, because I don't think I've done anything wrong, yet I'm being punished."

"It won't always be like this. When you're all done with the finance committee and everything's over, people will begin to see you in a different light. You'll be able to get back the respect you're missing right now."

I mustered a smile and leaned over to kiss her cheek. "Thanks, Mom. I love you, too."

She patted my arm, then nodded toward the doorway. "Come on and meet Gert. She's the senior manager in charge of staffing and human resources."

We walked across the hall and she introduced me to a dumpy woman who didn't smile and stared at me like I was something she'd scrape off her shoe.

"Gert will get you all set up," Mom said as she turned to leave. "Come see me when you're done and we'll talk more."

The woman continued to stare at me hostilely and I sat down, trying to think of something personal to say to make the awkward moment go away.

I was forming a few questions in my mind, like "Hey, Gert, how long you lived in Midland?" or "Yo, Gert, love that blouse, you clever thing, and I've always wanted a blouse with little numbers printed all over it," when she asked in a husky, manly voice, "What do you know about forensic accounting?"

I looked at Gert, in her pathetic blouse, with her pathetic glasses and mousy hair and grim reaper face, and thought, no way in hell she was gonna treat me like a first year staff, like a newbie, fresh out of college, without a clue.

Sitting up straighter, I cleared my throat and gave Gert my very best I'm A Professional With Balls Of Steel look. "Having worked as an auditor the past eight years, I can't think forensic accounting will be much of a stretch."

Gert made an odd noise, a cross between a grunt and blubbery thing with her lips. Obviously, she had no faith in my abilities. "Jane needs someone to work with Sam who is dedicated, fair and *honest.*"

Her emphasis on the word "honest" made me mad, but I had a feeling she intended it to, so I calmly nodded and agreed with her. "No doubt, that's why she hired me."

"All of her reasons to the contrary, I believe she hired you because you can't get a job anywhere besides Burger King."

"Why is my employment here any of your business? Did my mother make you a partner in this firm?"

That hit a nerve, and it dawned on me, she was afraid Mom would eventually make me a partner and leave her in the dust. A part of me felt sorry for her because she saw me as such a threat, but another part of me thought Gert needed a few lessons in diplomacy, politics and the subtle application of cosmetics. No doubt she was freaking brilliant, or Mom wouldn't hold her in such high regard, but if she wanted to run with the Big Dogs, she was going to have to make some changes.

I'd known lots of accountants just like Gert. Miserable, bitter people, always clawing for a leg up, never getting that old saying that one wins flies with honey, not vinegar.

With her lips pursed together as if she'd just swallowed a cup of vinegar, she stared at me with blatant dislike. "We have a very strict policy about time. Jane doesn't like to eat time. If we can't bill it, she eats it."

"Yes, I'm aware of billable time."

"And we expect you to be punctual. Office hours are eight in the morning until five in the evening, except during tax season, when everyone stays until eight and works Saturdays."

Remembering some audits when me and my staff stayed at a client's office for four days straight, around the clock, I almost laughed at Gert, sounding so, "Hey, this is a tough job and you're obviously a wuss and a Mama's girl, so you better get ready for some long hours." Almost laughed. Maybe I would have, if I hadn't been ready to chuck an eraser at Gert's head.

"And lastly, you're to have no contact with clients unless you okay it with me first. You may say something that the firm could be held liable for."

Okay, that was it. I'd had enough. Standing, I looked down at Gert and said, "Should I raise my hand when I want to go pee? Do I need a permission slip to leave for lunch?"

Gert narrowed her already squinty eyes and looked up at me through slits. "There is no one on earth I respect more than Jane Pearl, and I'm not going to sit by and let you take advantage of her. I'll be watching, and if you screw up, even once, I have permission to fire you. Now, do you want to have a seat and let me go over the procedure, or would you care to give up now and go look for another job?"

Sinking down to the chair, I thought about my ex-boss, Lowell, and the Marvel execs, and wished I could line them up in front of a firing squad. They were all still lunching at The Mansion, taking off for a weekend in Santa Fe, enjoying life in Dallas, where there was live music and art films and bars that served nothing but martinis, while I was taking orders from a battle-ax named Gert. It was so unfair and everything in me railed against it. How was it that I did the right thing but was the one to suffer?

I slumped back in the chair and wished I'd majored in something like basket-weaving. Of course, knowing my luck, I would have gone to work for a guy who smuggled drugs in his baskets, and still been faced with the whole whistle-blower thing.

"Okay, Gert. Lemme have it."

For the next thirty minutes, Gert droned on about workpaper referencing and professional etiquette and office procedure and some other accounting stuff that I pretty much tuned out. I will admit, even though I hated Gert, the CPA, I felt really sorry for Gert, the woman. I wondered why she dressed that way, and wore her hair in that awful bun, and had on no makeup. Makeup was invented for women like Gert. She looked to be maybe midthirties, and she wore no wedding ring, so I assumed she was a lonely old maid whose work was her life.

I refused to think of myself that way. It scared the hell out of me.

Finally, she wound it up, then took me around to meet the other staff, who all seemed friendly enough, whether because they were sincere, or because the Big Cheese was my mom, I couldn't be certain. I supposed it didn't make much difference.

Although I wasn't able to meet my new boss, Sam, because he was in court all afternoon, that was fine by me. Dressed in a wrinkled skirt and a navy cotton top, I was not at my best.

While I got the nickel tour with Gert, a client came to see Mom, so I was told to wait in one of the empty cubicles in the bull pen until she was available. Gert looked happy to be rid of me and left me there without another word.

Very tired and thirsty after a six-hour drive and a run through the rack line with Gert, I went to the break room for a Coke. On the way back to the cube, I noticed the light was on in what I'd thought to be an empty office. I walked past and glanced inside and saw a tall, meaty guy who was a dead ringer for Sammy Hagar.

He had to be a senior, or a manager, since he was in a real office with real walls, but he was dressed in jeans and a Hawaiian shirt. Not standard Midland CPA issue slacks, dress shirt and tie. He was tan and his blond hair was long and wavy, in a ponytail. I'm serious when I say he looked like Sammy Hagar.

I went to the break room a couple more times during the next hour and always shot a look at Sammy, but I couldn't ever get a good enough look to decide if he was hot, or just interesting because of the Sammy Hagar thing.

Finally, Mom's client left and she waved me into her office. I shoved some files aside and took a seat on her small sofa. "Who's the guy in the Hawaiian shirt?"

"That's Sam. Didn't Gert introduce you?"

"She said he was in court this afternoon."

Mom frowned. "She must be mixed up. He's due in court tomorrow." She reached for the phone, punched in some numbers and said into the receiver, "Sam, can you spare a minute? I've got your new hire in my office." When she hung up, she glanced at me and narrowed her eyes suspiciously, like she always does when she thinks I'm up to something. Mom Radar is more finely honed than anything the defense department can put out. "I'm sure you think he's cute, but don't get any ideas. I have a very strict policy about inter-office dating."

"The very last thing I'm interested in right now is a date. I only wanted to know who he is, and why he looks like he just got off the bus from Laguna Beach."

"Sam's a little...different. But the guy's so smart, and detail oriented, I try and overlook his odd choices in clothing. He does wear a suit to court."

I was still bemused with Mom's laid-back attitude toward Sam's professionalism when the man himself walked into her office. As I stood to shake his hand, I realized he was even bigger than I'd thought. I also noticed his eyes, unlike the dark brown of Sammy Hagar's, were as blue as the Pacific. "How do you do?"

"*You're* my new hire?" he asked in maybe the sexiest male voice I'd ever heard. He dropped my hand, gave me the once-over, then dismissed me as inconsequential. He looked to Mom. "I told you I wanted a man."

Before Mom could respond, I said, "In spite of my lack of a penis, I can actually count to twenty-one."

He frowned at me. "It's got nothing to do with how smart you are. I need a man for this job."

"Why? Are you threatened by females?"

"Only when they whine, which you're bound to do, a lot. This job entails getting out in the field, maybe getting your hands dirty, and most of all, dealing with men in the oil business. Your mother told me you grew up here, so you know exactly why it's a major handicap to be a woman, looking for information from guys in the oil business."

"Hmm, yeah, I did forget this is the land before time."

"Jane, I understand sticking by family, but this has disaster written all over it."

Mom looked disappointed and it dawned on me, she was going to go with Sam. She was going to make me do taxes! No way could I let that happen. "Sam, you can look at this like I'm bound to be ineffectual, or you can look at it like I'm a CPA with eight years of audit experience. The fact that I grew up here is a point in my favor. I know a lot of people, and I can open a lot of the same doors a guy could. At least give me a chance. Isn't that fair?"

"I'd consider it a big favor," Mom said, looking hopeful.

What was up with Mom? She's a barracuda when it comes to business and her pansy attitude was blowing my mind.

Sam stared at me for a long time, and I had the feeling he expected me to look away, or squirm, or otherwise cave under his direct eye contact. I therefore stared back. Finally, he said with a hint of a growl in his deep voice, "Aw hell, I know damn well I'm gonna regret it, but okay. One chance. Screw this up and you're gone. Understand?"

I didn't like his patronizing tone, but I admired his honesty. I decided to overlook the tone. "Understand."

He glanced at my clothes and shook his head. "Do you always dress like that?"

"Only when I'm moving out of my house, then driving for six hours in one-hundred-degree temperatures."

His blue eyes crinkled at the edges when he smiled at me. "You're a real smart-ass, aren't you?"

"Usually."

"Good. You're gonna need a smart mouth." He headed for the door. "Follow me, and pay attention."

I glanced at Mom and noticed she looked a little smug, as if she knew all along it would turn out this way. Knowing Mom, she probably did.

Chapter 2

In Sam's office, I watched his arm stretch when he spread some document copies across his desk, and noticed a tattoo of an anchor on his forearm, above his skin diver watch. "Nice tattoo," I said. "Did you get it in the Navy?"

"Uh-huh."

"When were you in the Navy?"

"Pink, I like to keep business and personal separated. Understand?"

"Got it."

He pointed to the documents lining the top edge of his desk. "These are bills of lading for Domino Pipe Company. They're a primo pipe supplier and our client buys from them on a regular basis. His name is Ollie Shanks and his partner is his cousin, Bert. Ollie and Bert are each fifty percent partners in Shanks Resources, a small oil company they started back in the eighties. Ollie thinks Bert is switching the primo pipe for some crap pipe, selling the good stuff and pocketing the difference."

"Why does he think that?"

"Because every well they've drilled and completed in the last six months has sprouted casing leaks and they're losing a lot of barrels back to the hole."

Looking over the division order, I asked, "Is Bert a moron? He has to pay half the cost of the new pipe, which he can't sell for what they paid for it if he's doing it on the sly. And he'd probably make twice the money off the oil he's losing to the hole."

"He's dumb like a fox. He has to split the oil with Ollie, but by selling the pipe he only had to pay for half of, pocketing one hundred percent of the profit, and buying crap pipe on the cheap, he comes out ahead."

"So what are we supposed to do?"

"Prove that Bert is switching the pipe. Ollie needs solid evidence that his cousin is cheating him because he wants Bert out of the company."

"Because he's a crook?"

"Among other reasons." Sam gathered up the documents and the bank statements and handed them to me. "Go get 'em, tiger."

I walked toward his door. "No problem, but if you ever call me tiger again, I'll hurt you. Understand?"

"Got it."

I spent some time getting acclimated to the Shankses' information, but had barely begun to work out a plan before five o'clock came. Almost as though a silent alarm sounded, the bull pen became a hive of busy activity, the staff tidying up desks, closing files, gathering up purses and briefcases. I joined the frenzy, anxious to get to Mom's and float in the pool, a cold Corona in hand.

Faster than a herd of crazed cattle, we all stampeded down the hall, but as we got closer to the reception area, I caught a whiff of something so vile, so nasty, I covered my nose and mouth to keep from gagging.

Then I saw the smoke.

"Fire!" somebody yelled, and as one, we all turned and fled back to the bull pen.

My heart raced, my palms broke out in a sweat and my only thought was to get Mom. I took off for her office, but she must have heard the commotion because she met me at the doorway. "What the hell's going on?" Her dark eyes were wide with worry.

"Mom, we gotta get out of here! It's—"

"A smoke bomb!" Tiffany yelled.

I turned to see her emerge from the fog now creeping down the hall. Her eyes were watering and she had a hand over her mouth while she coughed and gagged.

Sam came out of his office and immediately took control, which effectively calmed everyone down. The shrieks and shouts stopped in favor of Sam's stern commanding voice. He barked an order for someone to call 9-1-1 and directed one of the seniors to take everyone down the exit stairs.

Turning to follow, anxious to get Mom out of there because she looked so frightened, it hadn't yet occurred to me to wonder why anyone would set off a smoke bomb in the office.

Not until Tiffany came up behind me and said in a choked voice, "This is your fault!"

The group stopped before passing through the stairway door and stared at me with giant question marks in their eyes.

"My fault?" I asked, astonished anyone would think I'd stoop to something so juvenile and mean.

Thrusting a sheet of crinkled paper at me, she coughed and spluttered, but managed to say, "Whoever opened the door and…threw the smoke bomb, tossed this in first. Says right there, 'Back off…Pinkie, or next time it'll be a helluva lot worse than…smoke!'"

My earliest memory is when I was three years old and my dad ran over the cat. Mom loved that cat. I wouldn't know that by observation because as I said, my first memory was when the cat went to the big litter box in the sky. I know Mom loved the cat because she talked about Blix for the next twenty-eight years of my life. Part of my hazy memory is Mom wigging out in the driveway, crying and accusing Dad of doing it on purpose, so maybe she just talked about the cat because it reinforced her opinion of my father. I don't think he did it on purpose because he has a real soft spot for animals. A mean son of a bitch to people, but no way he'd run over poor Blix on purpose, even to piss off Mom.

All the same, I don't think she ever forgave him. And I don't recall Mom ever wigging out like that again.

Until Tiffany read the note from the Dog Doo Stalker.

While me and Mom and the rest of the staff, except for Sam, who stayed behind to check out the smoke bomb, tromped down fifteen flights of stairs, she hysterically asked questions in a shrill voice that was beyond unnerving. I answered all of them as truthfully as possible, well aware the staff was listening to every word. So much for my plan of keeping the Dog Doo Stalker on the q.t. I was already persona non grata to most people—the Dog Doo Stalker would reduce me to leper status.

Outside, in the late afternoon heat, we had to wait for the

fire department and the Midland bomb squad to check the building. Being a captive audience, I had no choice but to take it while Mom hounded me for details, railed against me for keeping it from her, insisted I had to destroy the disk so "that maniac" would leave me alone.

I patiently listened and let her go off on me, until she said I had to destroy the disk. "Mom, you can ask me to do just about anything, but not that. As soon as I get the disk, I'm handing it over to the finance committee."

Finally aware of our audience, Mom gave the staff the evil eye and they slowly moved away, although they couldn't go home because the fire department had the parking garage blocked off.

"The disk isn't that important!" she said in a stage whisper the firemen could probably hear on the fifteenth floor. "The SEC has enough for an investigation. Let them take care of it."

"They can prove Marvel has a lousy accounting system, maybe even prove there's some funny money involved, but it will all fall on the grunt people, the little guys who had to follow orders. I'm certain the Marvel execs and my firm have already destroyed any documents that could prove they set the whole thing up, that none of it was due to stupidity or carelessness. If I don't turn over the disk, not one of the lousy bastards at the top will pay for what they've done."

"Pink, you've always been so damn righteous! Is this whole Marvel mess worth getting yourself killed? It's only money, for God's sake!"

Anger threatened to overtake rational thought, but I managed to keep it under control. I'd like to say it's because I'm calm, collected and handle myself with reasonable gracefulness, but the truth is, I knew I couldn't win an argument with Mom if I got too pissed. The woman is amazing. I took a deep breath, let it out slowly and explained why I wasn't going to mind her. "To you, it's only money. To thousands of investors, it's their life savings, their college funds, their retirement packages. Last year, the CEO at Marvel bought an island. An *island,* Mom! And the greedy crook bought it with other people's money. If I witnessed a guy robbing a bank, would you want me to say nothing and let the guy go free? Because this is no different."

"I might, if the bank robber was threatening to kill you!"

She looked ready to blow a gasket and I began to worry she'd pass out from heat and fury.

Sam came out the front door of the building and headed toward us, a policeman in tow.

"We'll just ask Sam what he thinks," Mom said. "He was with the FBI for almost fifteen years. He'll tell you how dangerous this stalker person is."

Lucky for me, Sam wasn't personally involved. Unlike Mom, who clucked after me all the years I was growing up, who was now roaring like a mother bear, Sam couldn't care less what happened to me. Well, that's not really fair. I'm sure he cared, but obviously not like Mom does.

While the cop stood by and listened, nodding as though he agreed completely, Sam said to Mom, "This guy wants to scare Pink into giving up, but I don't think he'll cross the line and hurt her, or anyone in the office. He's bluffing."

"How do you know? Are you a mind reader?" Mom turned her anger and frustration toward Sam and I felt for him.

He shot a look at me, then focused on Mom's very red face. "Because, Jane, if he wasn't bluffing, she'd already be dead."

After answering police questions for over an hour, I was finally able to leave. Mom said she had to pick up some tax information from a homebound client, so I had a brief reprieve from her nervous, worried looks and angry grumbles.

Relaxing a little, I drove to her house, anticipating a float in the pool. And the Corona. Maybe two. Or three.

It wasn't until I drove up to her house that I realized I'd never gotten a key. Dammit. I parked in back, in the driveway, climbed through a window and hurried to shut off the security alarm before time ran out and the cops were called. But when I got to the control box, I realized the security alarm wasn't on. The hair on the back of my neck rose up when I heard someone whistling. Stepping close to the door so I could haul ass if it turned out to be a burglar, or the stalker, I called out, "Hello! Who's there?"

A medium-built man with a small beer belly and thick, brown hair stepped into the living room and smiled at me. "I'm Harry, the air-conditioner guy."

Breathing a sigh of relief, I smiled at him. "Hi, Harry. Mom having trouble with her air conditioner?"

"Just needed a little Freon." He narrowed his brown eyes. "So you must be Pink."

"Yes."

"How'd you get a name like that?"

"Remember Pink Pearl erasers?"

"No."

"Well, they're erasers that are pink and they're Pink Pearl brand and lots of accountants used to use them. When I went to work as an accountant, I got the nickname because my last name is Pearl and it just sort of stuck."

He still looked confused, but I wasn't going to discuss my stupid nickname any further.

"You don't look like your mother."

I sighed and leaned against the column. "No."

"Does your dad have blond hair and blue eyes?"

"Yes."

"Because your mother is dark, with dark hair and eyes. She almost looks Italian."

I resisted being sarcastic and thanking him for telling me what my mother looked like. "Indian."

"How's that?"

"Her grandmother was Cherokee. She's dark because of the Indian thing." I turned away and said as politely as possible, "If you'll excuse me, I think I'll unload my car now."

"Sure, sure. Do you need some help?"

"I've got it, thanks."

Forty-five minutes later, Mom got home and came outside. "Whitney Ann!" She walked to the edge of the pool and stared down at me with one of those You've Been A Naughty Girl looks.

"If you say *one* word, I swear to God, I'll leave and never speak to you again. And I am *not* kidding." I held my second Corona next to my face, loving the feel of the cold glass.

"I wish you wouldn't be so—"

"Mom, I'm warning you."

"Fine," she snapped in a voice that indicated it was anything but fine. She glanced at her watch. "Already past seven. You hungry?"

"Starving."

"Then go get some clothes on. I brought fajitas home and we're having company."

"Aw, Mom, gimme a break! I'm so tired, I'd have to wake up to die. And I'm half-looped. Who's coming for dinner?"

"A lawyer named Ed."

"A lawyer? Are you dating him?"

"Of course not! You know I don't date. Besides, he's young enough to be my son and that would be weird."

"Well, I know you wouldn't be trying to fix me up, so what's with Ed?"

"He refers a lot of his divorce clients to me for tax advice, and I send him my tax clients who're getting divorced. Now, he and Sam work together on our mutual clients. He's a good attorney, I think, but besides that, he owes me a big favor." Mom took a seat at the end of a teak chaise lounge and watched me float around with the beer. "Since you got rid of that overpriced Washington attorney, you need another one, so I coaxed Ed into helping you for a discounted fee."

"How much discounted?"

"Two grand, plus expenses."

"And he's a lawyer? You musta done one helluva favor for him. What'd you do? Spring him out of prison?"

"Ed won a very large case last year and failed to make his estimated payments to the IRS. I got all of his penalties abated."

"What's with this guy not paying his taxes? Is he a deadbeat?"

"No. Ed's just…well, he's sort of a free spirit."

"Which means he's a bum. Your only daughter, about to be crucified on the altar of the U.S. government, and you find me a bum of a lawyer."

She stood and walked toward the back door. "Don't be so dramatic. You'll like Ed. Trust me."

After dragging my exhausted, half-drunk ass out of the pool, I showered and dressed in a loose, cotton sundress, one of my better Target finds, and went to the kitchen to help Mom get supper on the table. She was just pulling the fajitas out of the oven, saying, "I love Rosario's fajitas, but I guess maybe they're better when you eat them there."

A deep voice responded, "They'll be okay."

I moved farther into the kitchen and spotted a tall guy leaning against the opposite counter. In a faded red T-shirt, he was buff, with longish, dark hair that didn't look like he wore it long on purpose. It looked like he either forgot to go get a haircut, or blew it off. Glancing at the hole in his jeans, I voted for blew it off. Ed was not a guy who cared what he looked like.

He definitely looked like the type of guy I'd love to have hot sex with, then send home right after. Not relationship material. Bad boy material. And I knew all about bad boys. I married one.

Mom spotted me and said, "Pink, this is Ed."

I stuck my hand out to shake his and smiled politely. At least I think it was polite. Feeling his huge, warm hand wrap around mine was very stimulating. I may have leered at him, but I'm not sure. The hot sun and the Coronas and my complete lack of a love life over the past year and a half all added up to a few lightning-bolt zings in the vicinity of my hootus. So maybe I did leer at him and probably held his hand too long. He smiled back and mumbled something like, "Nice t' meet you."

I finally let go of his hand and we stood there, eyeing each other like moose in mating season. Hmm. Nice body. Good teeth. Smells awesome. For a minute, I wished I was a moose. Then we could go get it on and no one would think anything about it.

But alas, I wasn't a moose. And Mom was right there, noticing all the animal attraction and clearing her throat, as if to say, *Back off you two and save the drooling for later.*

I turned to glance at her and noticed her eyes, those dark, flashing Mom eyes, said, *See, I told you so.*

Mom loves to say "I told you so." Most times, I don't care. It gives her a charge, so why not? Other times, it really ticks me. This was one of those times. I decided not to like Ed, just to show her she wasn't always right. Looking up at him, I asked casually, "So, Ed, what's with you not paying your taxes?" I ignored Mom's sharp breath.

He never so much as blinked. "I forgot."

"And the IRS bought that?"

"No. They bought that I've never made that much money before and didn't realize I needed to pay in quarterly."

"So, how much did you make?"

"Whitney Ann!" Mom said in a take-no-prisoners voice, "Stop asking such personal questions and behave yourself!"

Ed still didn't look away, or appear one bit concerned. "A little over five million."

"Musta been a good case. Who'd you sue?"

"Marvel Energy."

Just like that, he got me, right between the eyes. "You enjoyed that, didn't you?"

He smiled then. Grinned, actually. "Loved it. Wanna go for round two?"

"Maybe later. I'm starving."

Mom looked ready to wring my neck, but she didn't say anything else, or call me Whitney Ann! again. We sat down in her elegant dining room and ate fajitas out of a foil pan and talked about the Midland school board and their latest attempts to pass a gigantic school bond. Ed wasn't as dumb as he was a slob. In fact, he seemed very intelligent.

By the end of supper, I knew I needed to steer clear of him. He was an accident waiting to happen, and I was doomed to be the sole casualty. My ex-husband, George, was just like Ed. Well, except that George was a mechanic and Ed was a lawyer. But other than that... And I suppose Ed did have better manners. George would never have asked if Mom and I would like more iced tea as he got up to pour himself another glass. George would have grunted, pointed his fork at his glass and waited for me to jump up and get it. He got away with that exactly once. After that, he waited so long, his ice melted.

Ed poured more tea into my glass, then Mom's, and retook his chair. "Tell me about Marvel Energy and the senate finance committee."

"What? Don't you watch CNN? I'm the flavor of the week. Me and Senator Santorelli. They've got me sleeping with him."

"Well, he is very attractive," Mom said. "And he's single now, since his wife passed away. You know the media loves him, and they really get off on pairing him up with single women."

"I don't even know the man. And I don't think he's the least bit attractive."

"Why?" Mom frowned at me over her fajita stuffed tortilla.

"Gee, let me count the ways. Could it be because he made me tell the entire United States about Mister Bob?"

"He meant well. How could he have known about Mister Bob?"

She had a point, but I was not in the mood to be understanding. I refocused on Ed's face. His very attractive, manly face, with a five-o'clock shadow and really nice brown eyes. "What do you want to know that isn't already out there?"

He swallowed his drink of tea, set the glass down and said easily, "I want to know how you knew about the memos and how you got them."

Sitting back in my chair, I stared at him for a long time.

"You're going to have to trust me," Ed said.

I took a long drink of tea. Would he believe me? Or would he be like Mr. Dryer and Barbara Clemmons and assume I was as guilty as the partners at the firm? I supposed there was only one way to find out. "When I discovered the enormous amount of debt Marvel carries off the books, and how close the company was to defaulting on those loans, I went to Lowell and told him. He said I should forget the loans, that I should just conduct the audit and make sure I had workpapers to back up clean financials."

"He told you to lie?"

"Only a lot. That's when I knew he'd set me up. He promoted me and put me in charge of the audit so when the news broke that Marvel is basically bankrupt, I'd be in the hot seat. I'd get my license jerked for gross negligence while Lowell stood back and acted like he had no clue. The firm would stay in business and my career would be history. I was the sacrificial lamb."

"He didn't count on you blowing the whistle."

"Not hardly. Or maybe he just thought I wasn't smart enough to figure it all out. The day I suggested we should go to the SEC with what I'd found, he went ballistic. I told him I was gonna do it, and he fired me. The next day, I turned over copies of Marvel's debt instruments to the SEC, thinking they'd investigate, fine the company and demand they clean up their act. Instead, they asked me a lot of questions about how we'd conducted the audit in the past, about how much debt Marvel had during those years and how we missed it. That's when it dawned on me, Marvel had been hiding debt at least three years before the current year, and Lowell must have known all along. That's when I knew we weren't just talking about losing a CPA license. We were talking about criminal charges against any of the management who worked on the Marvel audit during the past several years, including me. By blowing the whistle on Marvel, I'd basically set myself up. No way anyone would believe I wasn't aware of the cover-up."

Ed gave me a funny look and I held my breath. He had to believe me. If he didn't, how could I hire him to represent me, to help me get through the next hearing?

"If you'd realized the hidden debt was there in years past, would you still have gone to the SEC?"

"Yes," I answered without hesitating. "It all would have come out eventually because Marvel didn't have the income they needed to pay off the loans, but I hoped I could get things straightened out before they had to declare bankruptcy. I hoped I could keep the stock from losing all of its value."

"Even if it meant putting yourself on the line?"

"Even then, but I didn't realize my position until I went to the SEC and they started asking a lot of questions. I was scared to death, and figured my only hope was to find something that proved the deal was between Lowell and the CFO and CEO at Marvel, which would go a long way toward proving me and the others who worked on the audit had no clue about the debt."

"The memos," Mom said, her dark eyes wide.

"As it turned out, there were memos, but for all I knew, it could have been on the back of a cocktail napkin. I went to the office late one night, got in with a key card I swiped and hit pay dirt. I called the SEC the following morning and set up an appointment to deliver one of the disk copies a couple of days later. They asked if I was willing to testify in front of the finance committee and I said I'd have to consult an attorney. I hired Mr. Dryer, and he set up a deal that I'd have immunity from any prosecution, if it came to that, in exchange for my testimony. When the disks were ripped off, I didn't want to admit it, thinking I might still be able to get my hands on the Mister Bob copy."

"Do you think they offered the deal because of the memos?"

"Mr. Dryer said so. He says if I don't get the last disk,

they'll withdraw immunity and I can be prosecuted along with Lowell and the other principals at the firm."

"Santorelli made it sound like they can't prosecute anyone without the memos," Mom said, her face pale. "If you don't turn them over, they can't prosecute you, so why does it matter? You don't need immunity."

I hadn't counted on Mom being so difficult. "I lucked out when I found those memos, and I'm sure they've been destroyed by now, but there may be other letters, or e-mails or something they can use to bring charges against the firm. It may even become obvious that the firm signed off on fraudulent financial statements. I have no idea, Mom."

"You can't be prosecuted if you're innocent!"

"I'm afraid she can," Ed said in a deep, calm voice. "Guilt by association. She might not be found guilty, but she can certainly be prosecuted."

Mom rubbed her hand across her forehead. "What a nightmare." She looked at Ed and said, "And as if it's not bad enough, she's got some maniac after her."

"Maniac?" He turned a questioning look toward me.

I explained about the loft, the car and the missing copies of the disk, but before I could finish, Mom went off about the Dog Doo Stalker.

I ate my fajitas and didn't add anything. I didn't need to.

"...and after she went to the SEC, he started calling in the middle of the night, threatening to kill her if she gives the disk to the finance committee. I told her, she should get rid of the disk, but she insists..."

I tuned her out by wondering if Ed was married, or had a girlfriend. I wasn't interested in starting a relationship or anything like that, but I'd been alone a long time, and something about Ed really punched my buttons.

When Mom was on the verge of foaming at the mouth about the danger I was in, Ed held up his hand and stopped her. Turning to look at me, he asked, "Do you have any clue who he is?"

I slanted a "duh" look at him. "Because of me, at least fifteen men are about to lose their jobs, and some of them may be starting new careers making license plates in the joint."

"You think one of the Marvel executives, or a partner at your firm may be behind all this?"

I shrugged. "Stands to reason, doesn't it? They have the most to lose."

"Yes, I suppose that's true." He narrowed his eyes. "I'll represent you, Pink, but you have to agree not to talk to anyone at Marvel. They have a branch office here in Midland, so you're likely to run into some of the employees. And do not tell anyone where Mister Bob is right now. After what I discovered during the lawsuit against Marvel, I don't trust any of them. This is the big leagues. The dog shit dude is a nuisance, but these guys mean business. One wrong move, one small leak of information, one hint that all you've got can be taken, and you could be playing a harp."

He managed to scare me spitless. I shot a look at Mom and felt an enormous guilt trip for freaking her out so badly. Her food forgotten, she sat back in her chair and stared a hole through me, a couple of fat tears rolling down her pretty cheeks. "Jesus, Mom, don't cry."

"How can I help it? This is like getting mixed up with the mob."

Ed took a drink of his tea and set the glass down carefully. "Worse. This is worse. At least with the Mafia, you know who the bad guys are."

* * *

Early the next morning, I stopped by the donut shop on the way downtown to buy a couple dozen for the office. In spite of their outward friendliness the day before, after the smoke bomb, I was afraid they all either hated my guts, or were scared to death to be anywhere close to me. So I thought maybe donuts would make everyone happy. Hell, I wasn't above buying friends.

With that in mind, I pulled into the parking lot next to the Donut King and went inside, my mouth immediately watering from the yeasty scent. As I stood at the case, deciding which round pieces of fried dough I should get, I heard a man behind me say, "Glory be, look who it is! Pink, is that you?"

I turned and smiled, and even though I remembered Ed's warning about not talking to any of the employees, there was no way I could turn away from one of the nicest guys at Marvel. "Roy! How are you?"

"Never better." We shook hands. "I came from Dallas to Marvel's Midland office for my monthly meeting, and I had to stop off at the Donut King. Really love their donuts."

Making myself not look down at the evidence of his love affair with the Donut King, I simply said, "Who doesn't?"

Roy chuckled, then slowly sobered. "You know, Pink, we're all rooting for you at Marvel. Took a lot of guts to do what you did, and even though it'll shake things up at the company, it's a good thing. I think the only ones who're upset with you are the execs, and the way I see it, they were about due for a comeuppance."

"Thanks, Roy." I smiled again, and wanted to throw my arms around him, I was so grateful for any morsel of support. Roy Kipper had always been amiable, and a big help to me and the staff during the audits. He managed the revenue distribution division at Marvel's head office in Dallas. "Can I buy you lunch today? It'd be like old times."

Reaching up, he smoothed back the patches of hair growing on either side of his otherwise bald head. "No can do, but thanks for the offer. We're having a big powwow about maybe closing the Midland office, and since I'm gonna have to be the bad guy, I need to stick around."

My spirits sank again and I nodded my understanding. "I'm sorry, Roy."

"Hey, that's the way it goes. I'm not an executive, but I'm upper management, and a year from retiring, so bein' the bad guy sort of fell on me. Hate to do it, but the company needs to tighten its belt if we've got a prayer of stayin' up." He smiled at me and patted my shoulder. "Good to see you, Pink."

I watched him leave and it was another five minutes before I could order my donuts because I was so choked up. It made me furious, Lowell and the Marvel brass's greed and complete disregard for anyone else. People would lose their jobs, and investors would lose their savings. It all made me sick, and I felt guilty because I was the one who started the fall of their house of cards.

By the time I got to the office, it was about eight-twenty. I came in balancing the boxes of donuts and a few of my desk things and said hello to Tiffany. Her pretty blue eyes widened like she was afraid and I thought, geez, they're only donuts. "You want a donut?"

"Goodness, no," she said, "I never eat donuts."

Of course she didn't eat donuts. She was skin and bones. I turned and headed toward the break room, where I left the donuts, then went to get started on the Shankses' project.

Within an hour, I had several things figured out, but most of it only led to a longer laundry list of questions. For one thing, there were quite a few checks to a company called Birds in Flight. Sixth sense told me there was something behind those checks, that they had something to do with Bert's shady dealings. The endorsements on the back were no help, simply a stamped For Deposit Only, followed by an account number. The Birds in Flight bank was in Miami, which I thought was peculiar. I couldn't think of any oil-related companies based in Miami.

With my methodical approach to the project, I came up with ten different ways to prove Bert Shanks was cheating his cousin. Problem was, all but one of them required information I didn't have and wasn't likely to get, because it was all information Bert would have. Even if Bert wasn't the sharpest tool in the shed, I didn't think he'd hand over information that would prove he was a crook.

So I'd have to go with the tenth plan, which involved staking out the pipe yard and waiting to see who bought the new pipe from Bert. The buyer wouldn't hire a trucking company to drive out and pick up a load of what amounted to black market pipe, so chances were good they used their own vehicle to transport the pipe. Once I had a license plate number, I would go from there. If I was really squirrelly, the truck might have a company name painted on it.

I decided to go check out Shanks Resources' equipment yard, but on the way out of the office, I thought I'd snag one of the donuts I'd yet to eat. As I walked toward the break room, I passed Tiffany and noticed what looked suspiciously like cinnamon sugar stuck to her lip gloss. I was polite and pretended not to notice. Then I got in the break room and saw both boxes of donuts were empty and wished I'd said something to her like, "When you said you never eat donuts, you meant before ten, didn't you? Once ten o'clock rolls around, it's a free-for-all, right?" I was so hungry, even Mom's raspberry infused sawdust diet bars started to look tasty. Resigned to my fate, I grabbed one and left the office.

I drove out the Rankin highway, to the south side of Midland, where a lot of oil companies have yards. Most of them are several acres of scrubby land, enclosed by metal fences, and at any one time, there might be a couple of pumpjacks, a few tanks, extra pipe or wellhead equipment scattered around, looking rusty and old. When a well depletes and stops producing economically, it has to be plugged, but all the equipment is saved for whenever a new well is drilled and proven to be productive. Or the old equipment is sold off. Either way, it ends up in somebody's yard until it's needed again.

The Shankses' yard was farther out, actually outside of the city limits, away from the highway by a couple of miles. It was the perfect setup for a cheating partner. I drove around, looking for a spot to park when it was dark, where I could see what was going on, but no one could see me. I was glad the Mercedes was black and that it was an SUV, although it groaned a lot when I ran over a stump, and I had the sneaking suspicion it wasn't really made for off-road. But how could I have known I'd need an off-road vehicle when I bought it a year ago? The farthest off-road I ever got was the parking lot at Northpark Mall.

I found a good spot behind a cluster of mesquites and made a mental map so I'd know how to get there in the dark, without headlights. Driving back around, I cruised through the Shankses' yard, scoping out their equipment, particularly the pipe. There were several strings of brand-new pipe, already strapped and ready for delivery to a rig.

From the bills of lading, I knew the pipe had been delivered the day before yesterday, so it was a good bet Bert would be selling it off soon. If I was lucky, that very night.

After congratulating myself for being so clever about the whole thing, I headed off to look for an apartment. I knew Mom would go ballistic and tell me it was too dangerous, not to mention I was silly to pay rent when I could live with her for free. But I had to have some space, sans Mom.

I saw five apartments before I found one, and it wasn't anything to write home about, but it would do. On the second floor, it was a one-bedroom, furnished with cheesy, cheap furniture, including a scratchy couch with wooden arms supported by half wagon wheels. The grounds were well tended, and although there was no pool, there was a small duck pond, complete with a cutesy sign that said Duck Xing. I never did see any ducks.

After signing a six-month lease, I paid the deposit, then went to get my hair cut. I headed for Mabel's House of Beauty to see if anyone could squeeze me in.

Mabel's is one of those old-time beauty parlors, housed in a tired shopping center storefront, with avocado-green linoleum floors and faded photographs of the nineteen-sixty-five Junior League Charity Ball marching around the walls. Every picture features some of Midland's leading ladies in their glory days, all with Mabel's House of Beauty bouffant hairdos, thick eyeliner and elbow-length evening gloves.

When I stepped inside, I was greeted by the whirs of multiple hair dryers, female chatter, a ringing telephone and Buck Owens on the stereo. It was like stepping back in time. I'm pretty sure I was the only woman under fifty.

The receptionist, a short, stout woman with a name tag that read Bessie, smiled warmly. "Can I help you, hon?"

"I don't have an appointment, but I need to get my hair cut."

Bessie nodded enthusiastically. "We've got a new gal, Dot, and she just happens to be free right now."

I followed Bessie to the back of the shop, toward Dot's station. Dot was maybe the skinniest woman I'd ever met, with a deep smoker's voice and coal-black hair, the kind of dyed black that looks blue in fluorescent lighting. We chatted a bit while she washed my hair, and I discovered Dot was from Big Spring, that her husband died and left her no money, so she had to go back to work, and even though she was "right mad at him" at first, now she figured he'd done her a favor because she'd made so many new friends at Mabel's.

While she snipped my hair, she rambled on about her grandkids and her Buick and George W. and the best recipe for King Ranch chicken. I didn't pay close attention, but I was listening, sort of zoning out with the buzz of the sounds in the shop and Dot's smoky voice.

I guess that's why I started so violently when someone shouted, "Lord a Mercy! It's *pink!*"

"Sugar, you shouldn't jump like that," Dot said from behind me. "I cut a bit too much when you moved."

Her words didn't fully register, I was so fascinated with the scene unfolding two stations away. The woman I'd thought yelled my name was actually talking about her hair, a big, fluffy mass of cotton-candy pink. She was righteously pissed off.

"Goodness," Dot said, "looks like Miz Colder's on a tear again. Reckon she'd learn her lesson after last time."

"Last time?"

Dot leaned close and whispered, "She's a stubborn old thing and insists on picking out her own color, even though she don't know nothin' about it. Last time, her hair was blue as the sky, and I'm not lyin'. She got mad and swore she wouldn't come back, but there she is."

Mrs. Colder was ancient. At least a thousand years old,

with serious wrinkles and a hunchback. Dressed in a colorful silk blouse and red knit pants, she stood behind the operator chair, her spidery hands clutching the grips of her walker, her sharp, blue eyes staring at the mirror and her thin lips pressed into a straight line. *"I want my money back!"* she yelled, making me start again. Amazing that such a small person could pack so much punch into a shout.

Her hairdresser, a harried woman who didn't look much younger than her client, murmured something I couldn't hear, which appeared to send Mrs. Colder over the edge.

"Been comin' here for nigh on *forty years,* paid Mabel *scads of money,* and this is the *thanks* I get!"

She had a big, black leather bag, big enough to carry a month's supply of Depends. Or a 747. It was huge, and bulky. With an incredible show of strength, despite her thin, scrawny appearance, she hauled the bag up and rested it on her walker. Reaching inside, she thrashed about for a bit, then withdrew a cell phone. "I'm callin' *my lawyer,* you hear?"

"Miz Colder," her hairdresser said in a firm voice, "we can't give your money back because you haven't paid yet!"

Ignoring her, Mrs. Colder made her call.

The entire shop had gone quiet, even the ladies under the hair dryers switching them off so they could hear what was going on. The only sounds were Buck Owens' twangy tune and Mrs. Colder's intermittent shouts.

We were all so focused on the old lady, I never noticed the presence of a sinister figure until something dark caught the corner of my eye and I glanced in the mirror. In the place where Dot was supposed to be stood a man in a black jumpsuit with a ski mask over his face. Before I could do anything, like run, or scream, he clamped one hand over my mouth, grabbed me with his other arm and hauled me out of the chair. Looking wildly about for help, I saw that Dot had moved close to Mrs. Colder, and the rest of the shop was focused toward the front. No one was looking, no one knew I was being abducted in broad daylight!

I was so frightened, I guess my body went on autopilot, and without consciously thinking about it, I kicked out and my toe connected with Dot's little cart. It crashed to the floor, scattering rollers and hair pins and cans of Aquanet.

Everyone turned toward me, including Mrs. Colder. *"Let her go,"* she shouted, still holding the phone.

The man only held me tighter, squeezing the wind out of me, causing sparkles in my vision, forcing me to stop kicking and squirming. If I live to be a hundred, I will never forget just how Mrs. Colder looked as she reached into her black hole of a bag and pulled out a small, silver gun. An old lady with a walker and a pistol. Jesus, that blew my mind.

"Let her go, *swine,* or I'm gonna *blow a hole* in you!"

I don't think the guy believed her. He never slowed down.

He should have believed her. She fired the gun and the small fax machine on the counter at the back of the shop exploded into a thousand flying pieces. I heard him mumble, "Holy shit!" But still, he kept going.

While I watched in horrified fascination, Mrs. Colder aimed the gun right at the man, which meant the gun was pointed directly at me. Jesus God, I was going to die! An old lady with pink hair and a shaky hand was about to end my life, and there wasn't a damn thing I could do about it.

She fired again and I flinched, then hit the floor when the man dropped me. Had she shot him? Was he dead? A little dazed, I glanced behind me and all I saw was the exit door as it closed. The man was gone.

Drawing in a deep breath, I noticed three drops of blood on the avocado linoleum. Wide-eyed, I turned my head and looked at Mrs. Colder. "You shot him!"

"'Course I did, but *he'll live* 'cause I only nicked him. Been shootin' since I was *knee-high to a grasshopper.* Reckon I could pick the wings *off a fly* at fifty feet, if I was of a mind to." She shuffled over with her walker and looked down at me from piercing blue eyes. "You okay, little missy?"

I was scared and shaky and completely freaked out, but I'd get over it. Offering the old lady as much of a smile as I could muster, I nodded. "Thank you, ma'am."

She was about to say something, but before she could speak, I heard Ed's voice. "What the hell's going on here?"

"Ed?" I peeked around Mrs. Colder's red pants and saw him rushing toward us. He was dressed in another pair of faded jeans and a black T-shirt that was exactly like the red one. He looked like a guy who rode a Harley and had sex with girls with gigantic breasts. Ed looked mighty fine. He didn't look anything like a lawyer.

"You know Ed?" Mrs. Colder shouted.

I decided she had a speech problem and that's why she spoke with intermittent shouts. "He's my attorney."

She slapped the handle of the walker. "Mine, too!"

"I was in the car when Mrs. Colder called, and heard everything, but I had no idea what was going on." Ed bent to lift me to my feet and held on to me when I swayed. "What happened?"

Before I could say anything, Mrs. Colder gave him the blow-by-blow, her voice rising and falling with her odd, shouting cadence. I noticed the rest of the shop was staring, eyes wide, mouths hanging open in stupefied shock. No doubt, Mrs. Colder's showdown with the bad guy was destined to become a legend at Mabel's House of Beauty.

Ed insisted on taking me to lunch, so after the police came, asked a lot of questions, took some of the blood off the floor, and Dot finished my haircut, we took off in his old 4-Runner.

He turned to look at me when he stopped at a red light. "I talked to Santorelli this morning and advised him I'm now your counsel." His voice was low and solemn. "He told me the Marvel legal team filed a request for injunction to keep your disk from being admitted as evidence. They're claiming it's inadmissible because you obtained it illegally."

"What will happen if they get the injunction?"

Ed stared at me for a moment before answering. "Santorelli says he'd have no choice but to withdraw your immunity because it's based on you turning over the disk."

"If there's an injunction, that's not my fault. Besides, I was the one who went to the SEC. Doesn't that mean anything?"

He shook his head, sending my heart into my shoes. "It might be a mitigating factor if they prosecute, but just like a crook who turns himself in, your honesty after the fact doesn't alter your involvement."

How stupid I'd been to naively believe I could do the right thing, that I could be open and honest, and the bad guys would pay. I read the writing on the wall, and it told me I was going down. Lowell and the Marvel guys could afford enough legal muscle to weasel out of any charges the government could lay on.

I, on the other hand, had Ed. He was bright and good-looking, and probably enough of a shark to make the big time. But he was inexperienced and unconnected to anyone in Washington. Looking across at him, I swallowed hard. What choice did I have? No way I could afford a lawyer like Mr. Dryer. I'd have to take my chances with Ed.

"Cheer up," he said as he reached out and rubbed a tear from my cheek with the pad of his thumb. "I'm gonna help you."

I know it's awful, but that only made me cry harder.

Chapter 3

Midland is known for oil and rich white men and Baby Jessica, but it should also be known for Mexican food. There are forty-seven Mexican food restaurants in Midland, and the population is right about ninety-five thousand. That's a Mexican restaurant for every two thousand people. That's a lotta enchiladas and tamales and tacos. That's a Mexican food lover's wet dream.

I have personally eaten at all forty-seven, and do have a few favorites. Bettina's House of Enchiladas is one. So is El Corazon, which means The Heart, and makes no sense, because they don't serve any kind of heart, and nothing in the place is a heart, or resembles a heart, but a white guy who spoke no Spanish opened it in the fifties and I guess he thought El Corazon sounded cool.

Ed took me to Bettina's and I nearly had an orgasm right there in the corner booth, beneath a piñata shaped like

SpongeBob SquarePants, because the hot sauce was so good. That's another thing. In Midland, in all of west Texas, nobody calls hot sauce, salsa. That's a foreign, sissy word. It's hot sauce, and we have chips and hot sauce. Not chips and salsa.

Bettina outdid herself and I practically ignored Ed while I dived into the awesome food. There are undoubtedly a lot of women who'd have lost their appetite after what happened at Mabel's, but I wasn't one of them. It was almost as though I enjoyed it more, could fully appreciate being alive.

That's not to say the guy planned to kill me. The part of my mind that keeps the fires of hope burning wanted to believe he'd only intended to rough me up a little, to convince me to lose the disk.

Ed talked while he worked through the Plato Grande, which means Big Huge Plate of Everything in the Kitchen. "Is there any way at all to get your hands on that disk before Mrs. Bohannon gets back home?"

"Not unless I break into her house, and even if I did, I can't be sure the box is there."

He shook his head as he polished off his taco. "I really thought the guy was just bluffing, but now I think he's serious about hurting you. Your mom has a good security system, doesn't she?"

"The best, but it's not going to do me much good while I'm living in an apartment."

"Pink, you can't move to an apartment. It's too dangerous."

"Maybe so, but I'm moving anyway. Besides, I already rented one." Seeing an argument forming in his expression, I said quickly, "Living with Mom is not an option. After what happened this morning, she'll follow me everywhere I go and fret about it and keep harping on me to blow off the disk. It'll be bad enough at the office all day, but listening to her around the clock will make me a raving maniac."

He conceded the point, but he still didn't look too happy about it. Then he asked, "What's it like to work for your mom?"

"I can't say for sure since this is technically my first day, but based on how I grew up and the relationship we have, I'd say it's going to be great sometimes, difficult sometimes and absolutely awful the rest of the time. I love Mom and I'm so proud of what she's done with her life, but she's very different from most moms. When I was four, she wanted to teach me to swim, and because she's a big believer in just doing it, she tossed me in the deep end and shouted, 'Swim!'"

"And you swam, I bet."

Looking across the table at him, I realized he was a member of Mom's Fan Club. Not that I thought that was a bad thing. It just made it harder for him to see, well, certain realities about my mother. "No, Ed, I didn't swim. The lifeguard pulled me out and did mouth-to-mouth, then threatened to call the cops on Mom for child endangerment. I know you wanted me to say, yes, I swam, and all was well and Mom did the right thing by shoving her four-year-old into the deep end of the Midland Country Club pool. But all was not well, and I was too afraid of the water to go swimming again until I was twelve, when Brandy Hernandez had a pool party and invited Lucky Barnes. I was hot for him and didn't want to embarrass myself, so I took lessons, but even now, I'm not real hip on bodies of water any bigger than my bathtub if I don't have a flotation device."

"You were hot for Lucky Barnes? The guy's a loser."

"Maybe now he's a loser. In sixth grade, he was hot. Besides, he had a cool bike and listened to Def Leppard."

"Did you go out with him?"

"Not a chance. He went with Brandy because she jumped in the pool and lost her top and he was wowed by her boobs."

"He wasn't wowed with yours, I take it."

"Well, no, because I didn't jump in and lose my top like Brandy did. That's not to say he would've been wowed if I had lost it, because I was only twelve."

"So was Brandy."

"True. But she was obviously a wild child, losing her top like that, and Lucky being Lucky, he went for the wild thing."

"You weren't a wild child?"

"I had my moments, and I probably would have jumped in and lost my top and given old Brandy a run for the money, but I was too afraid of the water, so I just stood there and watched Lucky take her around the side of her house to make out where her parents wouldn't see."

"You wanna know what I think? I think Lucky was probably a lousy kisser and you'd have been disappointed."

"Why would you think that?"

"I've seen the guy eat and it's not pretty. He's probably one of those wet kissers. You know, the slobbery kind."

"Ed, how sensitive of you," I said with a smile. "I bet you're right. And he probably tried to cop a feel off Brandy."

"No doubt about it." He returned my smile, making his handsome face look good enough to eat. Or kiss. "So you see, your fear of the water turned out to be not such a bad thing. In a strange way, what your mom did turned out okay."

My smiled died. "No wonder you're an attorney. That was friggin' amazing."

"Thank you."

"I didn't actually mean it as a compliment."

His smile morphed into a grin. "I know."

The man was just way too good-looking for comfort.

He stood and handed me his keys. "You can go on out to the car if you like. I'm going to stop off in the men's room."

A little bemused by him, I watched him walk away, then got to my feet and headed for the door. I was halfway there when the Marvel CFO walked in, followed by the COO and a guy who's the corporate attorney, but looks more like a bald bodyguard in a pinstriped suit. Roy Kipper brought up the rear. He looked as awkward and uncomfortable as a nun in a whorehouse, and when he caught sight of me, he turned bright red, all the way to the top of his bald head. He mumbled something about taking a leak and scurried off to the men's room.

Panic set in. I wasn't sure whether to ignore them, be polite and say hello and keep moving, or stop and speak like the friends we used to be.

In the end, what I wanted didn't make any difference. The CFO, a tall, lanky guy named Larry Sparks, but whom everyone knows as Sparky, stepped in front of me before I could get to the door.

"Hello, Pink," he said in a neutral voice.

"Hi, Sparky." I nodded at the COO and the lawyer, then looked at Sparky, waiting for him to say something.

"Saw you on C-SPAN."

I nodded again.

"Just curious, Pink, how does it feel to fuck a senator?"

Oh-ho, so that's how it was gonna be. "Just curious, Sparky, how does it feel to be a greedy bastard, commit fraud and ruin thousands of people's lives?"

Sparky took a threatening step closer, his nostrils flaring and his cheeks pink with either anger or too many of the martinis I could smell on his breath, which was hot on my face. "If you turn over that disk, you'll be the one who ruins their lives."

"I have no choice. Even you can see that."

"We all have choices. You just seem to be inclined to make

all the wrong ones." His angular face formed into a dark frown. "Like sleeping with Santorelli."

"If you believe everything in the news, then you must believe that you and Lowell Jaworski set up a plan to defraud the state of Texas out of millions of dollars of past oil and gas overrides."

"You know that's not true."

"Yeah, Sparky, just like I know it's not true I sleep with a senator." I caught his look of pure hatred before he schooled his features into mild dislike. I admit, it unnerved me and I decided I needed to leave. Immediately. "I have to go," I said, stepping aside to move around him.

He stepped aside at the same time, blocking my way.

"Look, Sparky, you're not going to intimidate me. No matter what you say or do, I'm handing that disk over to the finance committee." With a firm grip on my nerves, I stepped aside again and made to walk out.

Again, he blocked my way. Then he went one worse and grabbed my arm. "Not so fast, sister. I just want to hear you explain how it is you never caught any discrepancies last year, or the year before that."

"Get real," I said, now thoroughly furious and disgusted. "You know I was promoted to senior manager in December, and this was my first year to head the Marvel audit. I didn't have access to the memos and spreadsheets before this year."

"Do you seriously expect anyone to believe you? Don't you get it? By squealing to the feds, you're digging your own grave. They'll throw you in jail same as the rest of us."

His hand on my arm tightened painfully and I flinched, wanting to kick him, knowing I couldn't cause a scene. I cast about for some kind of a comeback, anything to make him let go of my arm. For once in my life, I was at a loss.

While the COO and the refrigerator-size attorney mumbled something from behind him, Sparky took advantage of my muteness. He leaned closer. "Here's a little advice, for old time's sake. Don't hand that disk over, or something very, *very* bad will happen to you."

Every hair on my head stood on end. I glanced down at his hand, still holding my arm in a bruising grip, and saw a white bandage. Mother of God! Was Sparky the Dog Doo Stalker? He didn't seem the type, but he'd just threatened me, and his hand was wounded. Maybe from a gunshot?

Shocked and tongue-tied, beyond freaked, I was about to cry out and get someone's attention when I heard Ed say, "I suggest you let go of my client before something even worse happens to you, Mr. Sparks."

Looking as though he'd just awakened from a trance, Sparky's eyes widened, he let go of my arm and stepped back. Jerking his head to his companions, he walked toward a table and they all took a seat, smiling and talking as though he hadn't just been a major asshole.

Ed nudged me and I walked outside, sucking in the dry, hot air. I was more shaken than I wanted to admit. "Ed, his hand was bandaged. I think he's the guy who grabbed me at Mabel's."

"I doubt it, Pink. The police think the guy was hit in the arm, and I happen to know, Sparks was in a meeting all morning. A lot of the Marvel execs are in town to go over their Permian Basin holdings."

"Does that mean the Dog Doo Stalker isn't connected to Marvel?"

"No, it just means I don't think Sparks is your man."

"Then the guy's still out there."

"True, but he's got a bum arm now, so maybe it'll keep him quiet for a while."

"Wonder what happened to Sparky's hand?"

"I'd like to think he closed it in a car door, or sliced it open on a meat cutter, or something equally painful."

"I still can't get over how he acted, Ed."

"Just be careful, Pink. If you see him, or any of the others, don't talk to them."

"But, Ed, I tried to walk away!"

He stared at me with a worried frown. "Next time, try harder."

Mom was out for meetings all afternoon, so I spent the remainder of the day working on my spreadsheets of Shanks Resources' bank statements. I found several more checks to Birds in Flight and spent some time on the phone and the Internet, looking for information, but came up empty.

At five, I joined the cattle drive and left the office, headed for Mom's to tell her about what happened at Mabel's, and to drop the bomb that I'd leased an apartment. I dreaded it, but figured it was best to bite it and get it over with. Besides, I needed to get out to the Shankses' yard as soon as night fell, which would be close to nine o'clock since it was late summer.

Mom wasn't home yet, so I took the opportunity to float in the pool. I'd been there half an hour when Harry showed up.

"Hey, Harry," I said as he came outside, "Mom need more Freon?"

He looked at me and shook his head. "No. She said there's a noise, or something, so I came to check it out."

Thinking it sure was late for an air-conditioner guy to be working, I said, "This must be a really busy time of year for you."

"Uh, yeah...yeah it is. Real busy. Been at it since seven this morning." He stepped back, said he'd talk to Mom later and left.

He'd looked sorta uncomfortable and I checked to see if I

was coming out of my bathing suit, but I wasn't. I wondered if Harry was casing the joint, but decided he wouldn't have come out to say hello if that was his purpose.

Mom finally came home and set to work making chicken and dumplings. She said she thought I could use some comfort food, which had the effect of making me feel even more guilty for renting an apartment and dissing her.

I dropped a kiss on her cheek and inhaled deeply. Mom smells good, always. Don't know what it is. Just Mom. "Thanks, Mom. You need some help?"

"No, I've got it." She slanted a look at me as I settled on a barstool on the opposite side of the kitchen island. "I hear you got a haircut today."

Yikes. She'd already heard about it. "Who told you?"

"Ed. He was at a meeting I went to this afternoon. Are you okay?"

"I'm okay."

While she stood there, all Mom-like and domestic, making dumplings, she casually said, "Let's go over to old lady Bohannon's tonight, break in and get the disk out of Mister Bob's box."

It took me a minute to recover from my shock enough to speak. "Uh, Mom, that's known as breaking and entering and can get us ten years in the Big House."

"Only if we get caught."

"You're not serious." She couldn't be. Could she?

She glanced up from the dough. "I'm dead serious. Let's get the disk, get it to the boys at the SEC, and this maniac won't have any reason to stalk you."

"It's tempting, Mom, but too risky."

"Not as risky as a stalker who tried to haul you off in the middle of the day, from a crowded place."

"Maybe not, but I'll take my chances and avoid prison."

"Well, okay," she said with disappointment edging her voice, "but let me know if you change your mind."

With a cup towel in her hands, she turned toward me. "Where were you at ten-thirty? I came to ask you to lunch."

Oh, man, this was it. I'd hoped I wouldn't have to tell her until later. I sucked in a deep breath. "I went to look for an apartment."

"Did you find one?"

"As a matter of fact, I did. It's a one-bedroom on the west side of town. The Windmills."

"I've seen those before. Not too dumpy, but kind of old."

"This one has turquoise appliances." I was waiting for her to start the lecture about the danger of living alone and the foolishness of wasting my money.

"When do you move in?"

"Anytime I want. I signed the lease effective today." Any time now, she was going to get wound up.

"Let me know if you need some help. My air-conditioner guy does some other stuff for me, and he'd be available."

"Okay, sure, Mom. Thanks." I waited for her to say it.

"I think I'll go take a quick shower before dinner." She turned and walked out of the kitchen.

Watching her go, I coulda caught several flies, my mouth was so wide-open in shock. Where was the lecture? Where were the hangdog looks? Where was her favorite martyr routine?

Something was up with Mom, and I intended to find out what it was. Shoving off the barstool, I trailed her into her bedroom and confronted her in the bathroom. "Mom, aren't you going to say anything about me not staying here with you?"

She tossed her skirt into the hamper, then turned my way. "No, why would I?"

"I don't know. I just figured you'd be upset about it."

"Why would I be upset?"

Looking down, I nearly had heart failure. "Where'd you get that bra?" It was a black lace thing, a push-up. Mom's breasts were way, way out there, her cleavage so deep, she could hide a television in it.

"Picked it up on sale at Missy's Lingerie. You like it?"

"Yeah, but, Mom, it's kind of sexy," I said, thinking maybe she didn't realize that bras like that were designed for appearance, not comfort.

She turned and preened in the mirror. "It's not kind of sexy. It's real sexy."

"Why do you care? You hate men."

"So? Doesn't mean I don't want to feel sexy. I'm only fifty-five, Pink. Not hardly ready for the home."

It finally dawned on me. "You're dating someone, aren't you?"

"Heavens, no! After your father, I'd rather be shot than date someone. Men are such a pain in the ass. Can you imagine me living the life I do with a man hanging around, expecting me to cook and clean and wash his underwear? No thanks. I like being single. I can go where I want, work when I want, spend my money how I want."

"Mom," I said pointlessly in an age-old argument, "not all men are like Lurch. There are some real nice guys out there."

"Maybe, but not after I get hold of 'em. I'm just no good with men."

That was true. Mom has iron ovaries when it comes to work, but around men, she reverts back to a doormat. I don't know why. She doesn't, either. "Speaking of Lurch, how is he?"

"I haven't talked to him since he moved up to Lake City, right after his divorce from Nelda. That was maybe four months ago. I expect he'll call when he gets sick of fishing."

"You know, of course, it's totally weird that you helped Dad divorce his second wife, and you still talk to him."

"It's not out of any great benevolence on my part. I've got a vested interest in him hanging on to his retirement fund. I get a thousand bucks a month off him until he croaks, and he can't pay me if he loses his whole wad to some idiot like Nelda. The very idea, buying pink phones for her Mary Kay business. She was a piece of work, that one. And your father was stupid enough to let her run through half his retirement fund before he woke up and smelled the disaster."

"Good ol' Lurch. He just stays clueless." At the best of times, my relationship with my father is lousy. At the worst of times, it's closer to war. I don't get along with my dad. No one gets along with my dad. He's gruff, rude, arrogant and just not a very nice guy. One of my cousins called him Lurch once, years ago, and it stuck. We've called him that ever since, but not to his face. I slipped up a couple of times and he asked me, 'Why do you call me Lurch? Who's that?' That sums up Dad to a tee. Who the hell doesn't know who Lurch is? Nobody, that's who. Nobody except my dad.

Mom unhooked her bra, then stepped out of her panties. She got in the shower and continued talking, her voice coming over the glass door, along with clouds of steam. "I still don't know why you thought I'd be upset about you not living with me. It's maybe more dangerous, but it's not as though I'd be much defense against this nutcase who's stalking you. The thing is, Pink, you're thirty-one years old, and living with your mama would be kinda pathetic. For another thing, and don't take this the wrong way, I do actually have a life, and you living here would cramp my style."

"Cramp your style? What style? All you ever do is work."

"How would you know? You've lived in Dallas the past eight years. Maybe I'm a real swinger and you just don't know it."

My mom, a swinger? Yeah, right. She was only trying to make me feel better about ditching her. "It's okay, Mom, really. I'm sorry I rented an apartment, but I just have to—"

"Pink!" The door opened and she poked her head out. "Has it occurred to you that my whole life doesn't revolve around you? I love you, baby, but you're a grown woman, and you need to fly on your own. Besides, I've gotten used to living here alone." She closed the door again.

Okay, I admit it, my feelings were hurt. I thought she *wanted* me to live with her. Then I found out, she wanted me to get a place of my own, and was *glad* I wasn't living with her.

I said I was going to stir the dumplings, but she stopped me before I could get out the door. "Would you get me a pair of panties and a sundress before you go?"

In her closet, I opened the drawer where she kept her lingerie. Mom musta had two hundred pairs of panties in there, and I am not kidding. My mom has a panty obsession.

Not that I blame her. She grew up with nine brothers and sisters on a dirt farm and never had any underwear. She told me a story once about second grade. A girl pooped her pants and left them in the bathroom. The teacher demanded to know who they belonged to and no one would fess up, so the teacher threatened to check beneath each little girl's dress. Mom was terrified because she had no underwear. The poopy girl finally caved, but Mom was scarred for life.

I felt kind of sad, all of a sudden, because Mom was such a great person, and deserved to be happy, and she'd gotten such a bum steer with her childhood, her panties and Lurch.

As I laid her things across the vanity stool, I vowed to be a little more understanding, and to be extra nice to her.

After I ate enough chicken and dumplings to sink a Navy battleship, I went to the apartment and spent a while unpacking. Close to nine, I stopped to get ready for my stakeout of the Shankses' yard and changed into some old jeans and a dark shirt.

By nine-fifteen, I was driving down Rankin highway, toward the cutoff that led to the Shanks Resources' equipment yard. When I turned onto the dirt road, I squinted in the darkness, looking for any sign of life. Other than a few jackrabbits and a coyote, there was nothing. At the yard, I could see the strapped pipe, still resting on the pipe racks, which are nothing more than steel sawhorse-looking things, designed to keep the pipe off the ground. I drove to the hiding place I'd picked out earlier in the day and parked behind the mesquites, then settled back to wait, hoping this would be the night Bert's buyer would show up to claim the pipe. I had a thermos of coffee, a stash of pink marshmallow snowballs, a blanket—because Midland is technically in the desert and it gets chilly at night—a set of binoculars and a machete I found in Mom's garage. Figured if I had to pee, I'd do it wielding the machete and chop off the heads of any rattlers who wanted to bite me. I listened to Carlos Santana, turned up loud so I would stay awake.

It was almost midnight when I saw lights in the distance. While I watched, they came closer, eventually moving into the Shankses' yard. It wasn't a pipe trailer truck, but a Suburban.

A short man I assumed to be Bert Shanks got out and stood at the back of the vehicle, looking down the caliche road in the very pale moonlight.

Within ten minutes another set of headlights approached and a large flatbed truck pulled into the yard and parked. I looked through the binoculars to see the door of the truck, sitting at an angle to where I was parked, but it looked as though there was no lettering or company name there. Damn. So much for it being easy. Three large men climbed out of the truck and began loading the primo pipe off the racks and onto the truck, using the forklift Bert and Ollie kept at their yard.

I stopped Carlos's guitar, rolled down my window and tried to catch any of their conversation, thinking it would give me a clue what company they were with. Unfortunately, the noise from the forklift and the pipe banging about drowned out their voices. I waited for the pipe to be loaded, binoculars, pen and paper in hand, ready to write down the number of the license plate as soon as they turned around to leave. But when the time finally came, I couldn't read the license number because half of it was covered in mud.

Saying a lot of cuss words I'm sure earned me a reservation in hell, I waited until Bert started his Suburban before I started the Mercedes. I inched my way around the mesquites and followed at a safe distance, leaving my headlights off, which wasn't a problem because the moon was so bright.

When we got to Rankin highway, Bert turned right and the truck turned left. I hesitated for a bit, debating what to do. If I followed the truck, I could see where it went and get the license plate number after it was parked for the night. But I ran the risk of the guys in the truck seeing me, and I had a pretty good idea they wouldn't like me following them. What to do? Across the highway, I saw a pumpjack in the middle of mesquites, its giant horse head steadily moving up and down. That's when it dawned on me, if I could see a pumpjack in the moonlight, I could see the road. No way the truck guys would notice the black SUV if I drove without the lights on. And it wasn't like there was much traffic. At the moment, there was no traffic at all.

I pulled out and followed the truck's taillights, tiny specks of red in the distance. As we sped through the night toward Rankin, a small oil field town an hour south of Midland, I thought about Bert and wondered why he was cheating his cousin. If they were partners, they must have been friends as well as cousins. How did a guy get to a place where he'd steal from his kin? From his friend?

The truck sailed right through Rankin, headed for Iraan and Terrell County, a vast no-man's-land that looks like those arroyos and cliffs and scrubby cactuses John Wayne always rides through in westerns. The ones that are supposed to look like Mexico, but are really in California and look like Texas.

Fifteen miles south of Rankin, my tire blew out. How the little SUV didn't turn over, I'll never know, but I managed to get over to the side of the road without any problems.

While I watched the truck's taillights disappear in the distance, I cussed a lot more, confirming my hell reservation.

I spent close to an hour trying to get the tire changed, and I'm no dummy, but it was like rocket science. More than anything, I wished someone would come along and help me, but the possibility of that was about as good as a group of extraterrestrials landing out in the pasture and offering to zap a new tire on. During rush hour, there might be three cars on the road from Rankin to Iraan. At one-thirty in the morning, there were zero. Zip. Nada.

For maybe another fifteen minutes, I paced and cussed

and weighed my options. In the end, I did what I was afraid I'd have to do all along.

I called Ed.

He was sound asleep, because duh, it was two o'clock in the morning. "Ed, I am really, *really* sorry to wake you up, and I hate to ask, but could you come and get me? I have a flat tire and I can't change it."

"Sure, Pink," he mumbled. "Just tell me where—" he slowed and yawned, "—you are."

"South of Rankin about fifteen miles."

"Rankin?" He wasn't groggy anymore. That was probably because of the huge rush of angry adrenaline pumping through his body. "What are you doing in frickin' Rankin?"

"I'm not in Rankin. I'm fifteen—"

"Okay! Just tell me why you're out at 2:00 a.m. on the Rankin highway, headed for Iraan?"

I explained, slowly because I knew he was angry and tired, never a good combination for the male of our species. "I thought about walking back to Rankin, to the gas station and waiting for them to open, and I suppose I could, if you'd rather not come."

He was very quiet and I thought maybe he'd gone back to sleep when he said in a deep, menacing voice, "Stay right there, Pink. Don't walk back to Rankin, don't flag anybody down, don't do anything but sit right there in your car and wait. If you're not there when I get there, I will find you and I'll wring your neck. Understand?"

Not liking his autocratic, Lurch-like tone, I said, "Ed, honestly, will you save the—"

"Do you *understand?*"

"I understand. You don't have to shout."

"Jesus, Pink, how do you get into things? It's like you're a giant magnet for trouble."

"I'm sorry," I said, but realized I was talking to no one. Ed had hung up.

I must have dozed off while I waited because the next thing I knew, Ed was hauling me out of the car, asking about the jack. I pointed toward the other side of the car and he stalked off to fetch it. The whole time he changed the tire, he explained how to do it and gave me a lecture about being more careful and not following trucks in the middle of the night.

"Don't you realize, those guys were probably hired by whatever company is buying the pipe, that they're not the usual drivers? I bet they found those guys in some smelly beer joint and offered 'em a hundred bucks to haul the pipe. This is the part where you use the tool to loosen the lug nuts. And for God's sake, Pink, don't ever do this again. Does Sam know you're out here chasing down renegade pipe?"

"No."

"I oughtta beat the shit outta him, giving you a pipe case. Everybody knows pipe guys are about as close to the Mafia as the oil field gets. Now you take the tire off." He did and rolled it away, to the back of the car, then went back to the front right wheel. "You put the spare on like this, and you need to tell Sam, no more pipe cases. Tell him you want a safe little divorce where all you have to do is trace some cash and IRAs and maybe a stock or two. Now tighten the lug nuts."

"Do you know Bert and Ollie?"

He glanced up at me and scowled. "Why?"

"Because you're way more pissed than this calls for. I think you know one or the other of them and I'm stepping on your toes by trying to get the goods on Bert."

I could tell by the look on his face, the one he couldn't quite hide quick enough, that I was dead on the money. "Are you getting one of them a divorce?"

"No. I'm not doing anything with either of them."

I hated to call him a liar, but I knew he was lying and it made me real mad. "This is no way to start a relationship, Ed."

Again, he scowled at me. "What relationship?"

"We're friends, aren't we? Friends...with benefits."

"Yeah, we're friends," he said as he stood and handed me the Mercedes tire tool, "but the benefits haven't accrued yet."

"The point is, you're lying to me and I resent it. If you're involved with the Shankses, you should tell me now. I'm bound to find out and won't you feel like a heel that you didn't tell me?"

"Pink, you may as well know, I never feel like a heel."

I knew then, he wasn't telling. Didn't matter. I'd weasel it out of Sam tomorrow. "Thanks for your help," I said as graciously as possible.

"Don't mention it," he said sarcastically as he walked away. "Next time, call Triple-A."

That hurt. "Next time, I'll call Sam."

Ooh, that got him. He stopped in his tracks and turned around. My feminine intuition was right. Mom said Ed and Sam worked together on mutual clients, but they were also virile males with way too much ego and testosterone. No doubt, whatever they worked on together was a constant battle for one-upmanship, and whatever they worked on apart was a pissing contest. Maybe that was why Ed was so put out with my investigation into Bert Shanks's dirty pipe deal. He saw it as a threat to himself from Sam, via me.

"Don't call Sam."

"Why not? He's my boss now. Seems like he's the logical one to call."

Ed's hands wrapped around the top of my arms and he pulled me close, until my boobs were squished against his hard chest. "There are things you don't know about Sam, that your mom doesn't know. I advised her not to hire him, but she did it anyway. If you're hell-bent on working for him, you need to be careful."

I didn't think there was anything about Sam that was dangerous or weird or menacing, but I let Ed think I believed him. I even went so far as to ask, "What about Sam?"

"Never mind. Just steer clear of him when you're not in the office."

Now I know this is incredibly goofy of me, but I was actually happy to hear Ed give me a lecture like that. If he wanted me to stay away from Sam, it had nothing to do with any perceived danger to my person. It was all about his perceived claim to my person. Men are so territorial. No way did Ed want me and Sam hooking up. Not when he thought he was front and center. "Okay, Ed, if you say so."

He kissed me then, sort of hard, like he was mad, but he had to kiss me so I'd remember he was staking a claim. I almost laughed at the thought, but I didn't. Ed probably wouldn't appreciate me laughing after he kissed me.

Then he got in his 4-Runner, started the engine and waited for me to get the Mercedes turned around. He followed me all the way back into Midland and didn't turn until I was on the street where the old, dumpy apartments welcomed me home.

I didn't sleep well. Anxious and jumpy, I kept dozing off, then starting awake, my heart racing with fear. At least three times, I got up and prowled the tiny apartment, a pair of scissors in my hand. All three times, I found nothing out of the ordinary, felt foolish and went back to bed.

At six o'clock in the morning, my cell phone rang. I figured it was Mom, checking to see if I was okay, or maybe just to see if I was out of bed yet.

After I answered, I wished it was Mom, calling to rag on me for still being in bed. Instead, it was the Dog Doo Stalker.

"Give up?" he asked in his whispering, gravel voice.

"How's the gunshot wound?"

"Hurts like a mother. Still can't believe the old lady shot me."

He actually sounded like his feelings were hurt, and believe it or not, that made me smile. Leave it to me to get a sensitive guy for a stalker.

"I wasn't gonna hurt you. I just wanted to talk."

"Why not call? Hauling me out of a beauty shop in broad daylight's a little risky."

"Okay, so maybe I thought it'd scare you. Dammit, won't you just blow off the disk? I'm not cut out for this."

"Me neither, and no, I won't blow it off. Why don't *you* give up?"

He didn't answer. Just breathed into the phone like a pervert with asthma.

"They're going to find you. They have your DNA now."

"Doesn't matter. They'd have to know who I am before they could do a match, and trust me, they'll never know who I am."

Throwing my legs over the side of the bed, I put my feet on the floor and cringed at the squeaking bedsprings. The bed had to be as old as the turquoise appliances. It was foolish of me, I know, but before I could think much about it, I bluffed the hell out of him. "Maybe I know who you are."

I swear, he sounded like he laughed, then turned it into a cough. "Come on, Pinks, you can do better than that."

"How can you be so sure that I don't know?"

Like my dad, he said in a patient, patronizing way, "Because if you knew who I was, I wouldn't be talking to you on the phone right now. I'd be in jail, now wouldn't I?"

Good point, but no way I was gonna say so. "Look, I got the message, and I know what you want, but you can't have it."

"How 'bout if I come over there and slit your pu—"

"Not even then." I can't explain it, but intuition told me the guy was harmless. And maybe what Sam said about him added to my lack of serious concern. I was concerned, and hugely aggravated, but I wasn't really frightened. "Even if you killed me, it wouldn't matter. I've got a plan in place to get that disk to Washington, whether I'm the one who takes it or not."

"Maybe I don't believe you."

I sat down again and sighed. Good God, I was so tired. "Maybe it won't matter. If the injunction goes through, the disk is useless anyway."

"I'm not counting on that. Give up, Pink."

"I can't give up."

He was quiet again, but his breathing was harsher than before. I expected him to keep on about the disk, but he stunned me when he whispered, "You should know, there's somebody that doesn't like you nosing into those pipe sales."

Pipe sales? How the hell did the Dog Doo Stalker, somebody who had to be connected either to my old firm, or Marvel Energy, know anything about what I was doing in my new job? "What do you know about that?" I didn't get an answer. The guy hung up and all I heard was a dial tone.

Chapter 4

The day only got worse. When I got to the office, tired, depressed and nervous as a cat in a rowboat, Tiffany said an IRS agent was waiting for me.

There are some who say that the IRS only audits certain individuals; either the ones who are randomly drawn by the huge, monstrous IRS computer, or the ones who have major income and deductions of a questionable nature. I'm convinced there is another group the IRS chooses to audit, and those are the ones who somebody snitched on. Right or wrong, facts or lies, if somebody calls the IRS and says, "Hey, I know this chick who cheats on her taxes," it's a good bet that the IRS will have somebody look into it. I was convinced the IRS's interest in me was precipitated by the Dog Doo Stalker.

The IRS agent assigned to my audit was named Ronnie Maloney, a short, fat, know-it-all, arrogant toad. I hated him on sight. But he was an IRS agent, so I did my best to make nice. Even when he kept staring at my breasts. They're not really anything to write home about, but maybe Ronnie worked with men all day and he wasn't used to seeing breasts. Or maybe he was just a perverted, chauvinistic asshole. Either way, his constant attention to my boobs set my teeth on edge and I had a very difficult time keeping my fingers from gouging out his eyeballs.

After I brought him a cup of coffee, we sat at the conference table and he asked a lot of questions and looked through all of my receipts and bank statements and such. He asked about Busy Bee Bookkeeping, where I'd had my taxes done the past several years. "If you're a CPA, why don't you do them yourself?"

"It's not an 'if,' Mr. Maloney. I *am* a CPA, and I don't do my own taxes because I'm an auditor."

"I looked into this firm before I came over, and they don't do audits here." He said this while staring at my breasts.

Crossing my arms over my chest, I replied, "After I was fired from my previous position, I had some difficulty finding a new one. This firm offered to hire me in their new forensic accounting division."

Looking disappointed because I hid my boobs from him, he sighed and raised his gaze to mine. "Why were you fired?"

"Is that relevant to my tax situation in the prior year?"

"It might be. Just answer the question."

Did the moron never watch CNN? Did he not read the paper? Did he live under a rock? My answer to these questions was, not likely. He knew exactly why I was fired, and his question went all over me like a cheap suit. So I chose not to answer. I stared at him and made myself not blink.

"I'm waiting," he said in an arrogant tone.

"You can wait until the cows come home, and I'm not

going to answer. My employment, or lack of it, is none of your business and has zero relevance to my tax return."

That seriously steamed Ronnie. His pudgy face turned red and his beady little eyes bugged out. He went back through my receipts, pulled one out and said, "This dinner is extravagant." He pulled several more out of the stack and tossed them on the table. "So is this one, and this one, and this one, and so on. In fact, Ms. Pearl, I'm disallowing all of these meals."

He was *not* going to intimidate me. "You can't disallow them. My firm reimbursed me for legitimate meals, which took place for the sole purpose of entertaining clients. I picked up the reimbursements in my income, and those receipts are an offset to that income."

Looking like he enjoyed being a slimeball, he smiled. "I'm an IRS agent, Ms. Pearl. If I say the meals are extravagant, they are. They're all disallowed." He ripped through the receipts and pulled out the ones for my travel expenses to Houston, to Midland, to San Angelo and to Oklahoma City. "These were all pleasure trips and therefore disallowed."

Really pissed by now, I forgot about shielding my boobs, dropped my arms, grabbed the edge of the table and leaned forward. "Those trips were taken by directive of my firm, on official audit business for one of our clients."

"No, they weren't. They were for pleasure. You stayed in luxury hotels and took cab rides." He slapped his fat, dimpled, white hand on the stack of rejects and exclaimed, "Disallowed!" He grinned evilly and looked down at my breasts again.

"Mr. Maloney, no one in their right mind would come to Midland for pleasure. And if all those trips were for pleasure, it would mean I took eight weeks of vacation last year."

He dropped his smile and leaned forward, his bug eyes still

staring at my breasts. "I wouldn't be surprised if you took eight weeks of vacation. It's people like you who give CPAs a bad name, always billing exorbitant fees, raping your clients who work hard to show a profit, ruining their reputation and—"

"You own Marvel stock," I said, collapsing back in my chair. It all made sense then. "That's what this is all about, isn't it? You're here to get your pound of flesh because I squealed to the SEC and your stock's lost half its value."

"Are you insinuating I'd perform a biased audit?" Ronnie looked more than mad. He looked murderous.

I stood and gathered up my paperwork. "I'm not insinuating, bucko. I'm outright accusing you of being a lowlife bastard, out for revenge. If you'll excuse me, I'm going to call Senator Santorelli and tell on you."

I guess he didn't believe me, because that was when he made a gigantic, huge mistake. He grabbed my arm and jerked me around to face him. I've got a thing about being manhandled, and to say I was pissed would be like saying King Kong was a bit on the large side for a gorilla. "Get your hand off of me," I said very quietly, "and just maybe I won't tear your nuts off and shove 'em down your throat."

Again, he must have thought I was bluffing. He kept his hand on my arm, actually tightened his hold, and said, "I'm writing you up, and you're going to regret your lack of cooperation."

Regret? Yeah, right. The only thing I regretted was ever talking to the pervert in the first place. I looked down at his hand, and something in me just snapped right in two. "I'm going to hurt you, and you're going to regret you ever met me." Then I kicked him in the groin. Hard. He doubled over and threw up.

Leaning down, I said, "Go ahead and write me up, Mr. Maloney. I've got a good friend in the FBI who would be happy to look into your portfolio. Wonder what the suits at the IRS will think about your Marvel Energy holdings?" He was spluttering and coughing, but I honestly had zero compassion. It was like Ronnie Maloney represented everything about the system that was unfair, that screwed over the good guys and rewarded the crooks. "If you ever come near me again, I'll get a restraining order and sue you for harassment. I've got nothing to lose and the rest of my life to lose it. You get my meaning, Mr. IRS Agent?"

He nodded and threw up some more.

I walked out of the conference room, went to my cubicle and called security. "There's a molester in our conference room. Please come up and get him out of here. And ask janitorial to come up and clean the floor. I had to kick him to get him off of me, and he lost his breakfast."

I went to Mom's office and briefly explained what happened. She looked like somebody died and I said, "I'm okay, Mom."

"Oh, Pink! How could you kick an IRS agent? Every client we have will get audited after this!"

Whatever was in me that snapped earlier must have grown back in a hurry because it snapped again. I lost it, right there in my mom's office, and didn't care who heard me. "Was I supposed to let the son of a bitch slobber all over my tits, screw me out of legitimate deductions and manhandle me, just so he won't audit your clients? What is *wrong* with you? What is wrong with the whole f'ing country? Jesus H. Christ! This isn't freaking Communist China! This is America, where the truth is supposed to mean something, where honest people who do the right thing shouldn't be crucified!" I turned around to leave and nearly ran into Gert, who was glaring at me like I was Satan. "You know what, Gertie?"

"What?" she answered in a smug tone.

"Get a friggin' life and *get out of my face!*" Moving around her, I headed for the door.

"Pink! Wait!" Mom hollered. "Where are you going?"

I stopped, but didn't turn around. "I'm going to call Senator Santorelli and tell him to get the IRS off my back."

"Pink...I'm sorry."

"Yeah, okay." It was way too late for an apology. Sometimes, my mother is just a little too hard-edged, too concerned about the bottom line, too unemotional. I think in that moment, I hated her. Hell, I think I hated everyone. It was a very, very low point in my life, and I'd never felt so alone.

I had the senator's office number, but expected to go through fourteen people and maybe somebody with the CIA running a background check before I could even speak to his assistant. I nearly wet my pants when a low, serious voice answered after the third ring. "Good morning, this is Steven Santorelli."

"Good morning, Senator. This is Whitney Pearl."

"Yes, hello," he said, sounding much less formal. "How are things down there in oil country?"

I didn't even want to guess how he knew I was in Midland. "Actually, not so good."

"I'm sorry to hear that, Whitney. How can I help?"

The urge to really rip into him was strong, but I didn't think that would help my case in the slightest. I opted for Miss Manners. Briefly, leaving out the part about calling Maloney a low-life bastard and kicking him in the gonads, I explained what happened. "I understand the IRS's need to perform audits, and I have no problem with my return's selection, but this agent stepped over the line."

"Yes, I see. Tell you what. Let me look into this and call you back. Give me your number."

I gave him the office number.

"Is that your office?"

"Yes, sir."

"Whitney, we're not in front of the committee. No need to call me sir."

"Oh, well, I beg your pardon."

"In fact, you can call me Steve."

That was pretty cool, I thought, being on a first name basis with a senator. "All right…Steve."

"Let me have your home phone, as well, in case I need to catch you after hours."

I gave it to him, then said, "Thank you very much for your help. Lately, I've been wondering if I did the right thing because this has messed things up for me in a lot of ways I never anticipated."

"Well, Whitney, I'll tell you what my father told me. There's got to be somebody who points out that the emperor is naked."

I waited for the rest. He didn't say anything else. Man, his father was pretty lame in the homily department. Poor guy. I hoped Steve had a good speech writer. "Yes, of course," I said graciously, "that's very…inspiring."

"Not really. My dad generally makes things up as he goes along, to fit the circumstance."

"Just curious, Steve. What circumstance brought on the line about the emperor?"

He laughed. "Actually, he said that about two weeks ago, when I was debating whether to vote for the president's energy bill."

"I take it you thought the bill was no good?"

"Worse than no good, but I was the one who instigated the idea, so it wasn't very kosher of me to stand up and say it sucked."

I smiled because I thought Steve was an okay kinda guy. "So did you?"

"I did, and now I'm not very popular at the White House, but that's okay, because I did the right thing. And so did you, Whitney. If you have any more trouble, please let me know and I'll take care of it."

I said I would, said goodbye, and hung up, thinking the senator sure was a lot nicer when he wasn't sitting in front of me with eight of his senator buddies next to him.

Because I was afraid he'd take me off the project, I didn't tell Sam about my late-night stakeout of the Shankses' yard, or what the Dog Doo Stalker said about somebody not liking me looking into the pipe sales. I was keenly interested to know more, and no way I could find out if I told Sam. He'd take me off the project and say he knew all along I couldn't hack it because I'm a girl.

And since I couldn't tell him, I couldn't grill him about Ed's ties to the Shankses. That was a bummer.

When Sam stopped by my cube, later in the day, he checked my progress, seemed pleased with my elaborate spreadsheets and told me to carry on. Before he left, he mentioned that Ollie and Bert were out of town and not expected back until late the following day. Being a little more suspicious than most, I wondered why he'd told me. I hadn't had any interaction with either of them, and didn't intend to. Sam knew that, so why had he told me? Did he know about the fiasco of the night before? Was that his way of telling me?

I decided not to worry about it. If he knew, if he wanted me to lay off, he'd say so. Sam was the most direct man I'd ever known.

As unproductive as the night before had been, I still thought it was a good plan, and if it could work on the front end, there was no reason why it wouldn't work just as well on the back end. It came to me as I was at the drive-through window at Taco Casa during lunch, picking up a burrito and some nachos. If the new pipe was gone now, it had to be replaced with the crappy pipe. Instead of going at this from the new pipe guy's standpoint, I'd go at it from the crappy pipe guy's. If I knew who he was, I could find out for certain he was selling lousy pipe to Bert.

While I ate lunch at my desk, I made plans to be at the yard again that night, just in case Bert had the crap pipe unloaded. About the time I finished off the nachos, I remembered what Sam had said, and a lightbulb illuminated above my head.

He *did* know, and he'd already figured out the next logical step. By telling me Bert and Ollie were out of town, he was telling me it would be pointless to hang out at the yard because no one would be there.

I sat back in my chair and smiled to myself. Sam really was as smart as Mom thought he was.

Since I didn't have to be anywhere that night, I decided I'd go home right at five, take a hot bath, get some reading in and hit the sack early.

Unfortunately, like everyone who makes those sort of plans, I had to abandon them. I'm convinced the hot bath, reading, early-bed evening can only be had under entirely spontaneous conditions. Plan it, and your hosed.

My stumbling block was August Fifteenth.

Every year, on the night of summer tax deadline day, Mom throws a big party at her house for the staff, a pat on the head for their dedication to late nights and new tax laws. In light of the fact I was not one of the tax staff, I didn't intend to go, but that was before Mom called me into her office and asked me very nicely if I would come. Maybe I could have begged off, but she was so contrite about what had happened earlier in the day, so anxious for me to be at the party, I didn't have the heart to say no. Or to continue being mad at her.

Mom could win Travel Agent of the Year when it comes to guilt trips. How she does it, I have no clue. I was the wounded party, but in the end, I was the one who felt guilty. The woman is amazing.

So I went to the party and made small talk with the other staff, most of whom still looked halfway scared of me. Not that I blamed them. I attracted things like dog poop and smoke bombs and guys in ski masks.

I'd had one too many margaritas when Ed showed up. He walked into Mom's kitchen and my temperature went up several degrees, but it wasn't due to tequila or sexy thoughts. I was mad at him and feeling sharp stings to my feminine pride. The night before, he'd given me a lecture, warned me away from another guy and kissed me, all of which meant he had certain responsibilities as a male. Responsibilities he'd failed miserably to fulfill.

All day long, I'd expected him to call, but as of three margaritas past eight, he still hadn't called.

So I was pretty cool to him, and when he asked if I was okay, the margaritas made me say, "I've decided to fire you, because you aren't adequately representing me."

"You care to elaborate?"

"I was railroaded by the IRS and you shoulda been there."

"I heard about that. In fact, everyone in town's heard about it. You're gaining in the polls, by the way."

Ignoring his teasing, I stared up at his wonderful face. "Where were you? I needed you to be there while the little toad was running me through the rack line."

"No, you didn't. You handled it just fine. Besides, how could I have been there if I didn't know about it? This attorney-client thing works both ways."

"So does the man-woman thing, but you kinda dropped the ball."

"I'm on the ball."

"Couldn't prove it by me. What is it, Ed? An ethical thing, or do you just think I'm too dangerous to be around?"

"Neither."

"Then why didn't you call me?"

"After last night, I figured you'd blow me off."

"That's a load of bullshit, Ed. Why don't you just be a man and say you don't have it nearly so bad for me as I've got it for you?"

Somehow, we were alone. We started out in Mom's kitchen, next to the margaritas and the queso, but then we were in the laundry room, all alone, except for the washer and dryer and some kind of weird clothes rack made out of wood, with a few lacy, black bras hanging from colored clothespins.

Ed came close and crowded me against the wall and laid a kiss on me that I swear to God curled my hair. He tasted like beer and chips and jalapenos. He smelled like aftershave and male stuff and soap. He was just the right height for me, so I could bend my neck a bit, and we fit together like puzzle pieces. Or a man and a woman who really should get naked. When he drew back a little, I blinked and said in somebody else's voice, "Hot damn, Ed, where'd you learn to kiss like that?"

"My ex-wife was pretty good at it. Wasn't too good at anything else though."

"You were married?" It occurred to me, I didn't really know much of anything about Ed. It also occurred to me, I didn't really care. At least, not right then. I was love-starved and lonely and half-drunk and Ed looked about as good as anything ever had in my whole life.

"For a while," was all he said. Then he kissed me again.

I have no idea how long we stood next to Mom's racy, sexy bras playing tonsil hockey, but after a time, I wanted to play something else entirely. From the hard bulge pressing against my belly, I thought Ed did, too.

"Are you staying here tonight?" he asked against my mouth.

"No, why?"

"Because you're too tipsy to drive."

"Why don't you take me home?"

"Okay."

I said goodbye to Mom and the rest of the standoffish staff, and Ed and I left. On the way to my apartment, I thought about telling him what the Dog Doo Stalker said about the pipe sales, but I changed my mind when I remembered how pissed he was that I was on the project in the first place. If I told him, he was bound to tell Sam, or Mom, and I'd be stuck in the tax department with Gert.

When he turned into the parking lot, he shot me a sexy look. "Guess I better walk you to your door."

"Guess so."

We almost ran the last few yards to the stairs.

As soon as we got through the door, we went to the bedroom and fell on the bed, and it was nothing like any romantic interlude they show in the movies. We jerked each other's clothes off in record time and rolled around on the squeaking bed, still kissing. Ed's large, tan hands were everywhere and I remembered things I thought I'd forgotten. Like how good it feels to have a man's hands on my breasts, how awesome it is to be desired, how incredible a man's naked body can be. Ed was magnificent, all muscle and hair and hard penis.

He reached for his jeans and took a condom out of his pocket.

"Aren't you the good Boy Scout?" I asked. "Did you have this in mind all along?"

He laughed. "I've had it in mind since the first night I met you."

"Aw, come on, Ed. You're just saying that so you'll get lucky."

Losing his smile, his dark eyes moved up and down my body and he said seriously, "If there's any question about my luck right now, you'd better say so."

"Hey, I was only kidding."

Ed kissed me then and all the playfulness was gone. It was so intense, I could hardly breathe. I've never been that turned on in my whole life. He was all over me, his lips, his hands, his body. It was like he wanted to touch every inch of my skin, wanted to claim me and make me forget everything else in the world.

He did a good job. I was out of my mind. I shook and moaned and begged him to take me. Finally, he handed me the condom and I shakily unrolled it, dying to feel him inside of me, wanting to look up into his incredible face while he stroked me to what would surely be a mind-blowing orgasm.

He was there, above me, his erection nudging me, when I heard the door open.

"Whitney Ann!"

I thought Ed would cry, he looked so disappointed. I wasn't anywhere close to crying. What I was close to was murder.

Rolling off the bed, I slid into a robe, went out of the bedroom and closed the door. "Mom, what are you doing here?"

"I brought your car home. Gert followed me over to take me back to the house." She glanced toward the bedroom door. "Is Ed in there?"

"Is that any of your business?"

"No, but just remember, it's not professional to sleep with your attorney, Pink."

"Professional for who? Me, or him?"

"Both. I suggest you wait until after your next appearance before the finance committee to start a relationship with Ed. If anyone found out, it could look bad. You don't want to lose your credibility."

"Mom, you live in the Dark Ages. Who on earth would care if Ed and I sleep together?"

"Senator Santorelli. He's got the hots for you, and if you're hooked up with Ed, he might not be so understanding about Marvel."

I stared at her, wondering if aliens had invaded her body and eaten her brain. "Mom, have you been smoking funny cigarettes?"

"I'm serious. You've never been able to tell when a man finds you attractive, and I'm telling you right now, the senator is attracted. During that hearing, he looked ready to murder Barbara Clemmons when she tried to railroad you. His attraction was so obvious, the political pundits are saying he'll probably manage to get you immunity, even if you don't come up with the disk. Didn't you notice how he kept smiling at you? And don't you know that he's usually a major hard-ass? He treated you like a foreign dignitary, with kid gloves."

I admit, I was shocked. Maybe she was right and I'm not so great at picking up sexual signals, but the notion that Steve Santorelli had the hots for me was way off the page. She had to be wrong, because the idea was too weird to be true. But I knew this was an argument I'd never win, so I nodded and lied through my teeth. "Okay, Mom, you're right. I'll send Ed home and we'll just hold hands at the malt shop until I go back to D.C."

Mom left then, and I went back to my bedroom, all ready to tell Ed about Mom's goofy idea about the senator. But the story died on my lips when I saw Ed, fully dressed, stuffing his wallet into his back pocket. "Ed! What are you doing?"

"Going home. She's right, Pink. This isn't such a good idea."

"Dammit! Who the hell will know?" I glanced at the messed-up bed and wanted to tear my hair out and throw a fit. "Ed, don't go."

"I have to."

"Okay, how about we do it just this once? Then we won't do it again until after D.C."

He came close, but didn't touch me. "We can't do it just once, and you know it. This is one of the reasons I didn't call today. You're too hot, Pink, and I'm not that nice of a guy. It's best if we stay away from each other, except when we need to talk about the hearing."

I watched him leave and wondered if my life would ever be good again, or if I was doomed to celibate misery in hell.

That night, I slept without interruption, courtesy of the off button on my cell phone and the snail-like speed of the phone company to get my phone turned on. When I woke up the next morning, I felt pretty good, in spite of the dry taste in my mouth from all the tequila.

Before I went to the office, I decided to get some better equipment for the field, like an air compressor to air up a flat, a can of tire fix-it stuff, a stash of flashlight batteries and maybe a pair of steel-toed boots. No way the rattlers could bite me through a layer of steel.

Most of the stuff I found at Wal-Mart, but the steel-toed boots I had to get at Buster's Boots, over on Florida Street. Buster's is a great big barn of a place where all the boots are out, stacked in boxes. After finding the boots I wanted, which were a cross between army boots and Ropers, I started looking for my size. Not easy since these were men's boots.

Fairly frustrated, I saw the smallest size they had at the top of the stack, just out of reach. I snagged a stool and pulled it close, then climbed up and reached for the box.

Before I could get it, a pair of hands slid around my waist and I let out a little yell, then fell backward, right smack into a man's arms. I caught a whiff of some serious B.O. and tears sprang to my eyes.

Scrambling away, I got my footing and turned around fast, glaring at Mr. Stinky. "What's the idea, buddy?"

"Whitney Pearl!" he exclaimed with a lopsided smile.

He didn't look remotely familiar.

"Don'tcha know me?" he asked, still grinning. "It's me! Lucky Barnes!"

Oh man, that was criminal, and a sad testament to the lousy hand fate deals some people. Lucky didn't live up to his name. Gone was the hot kid from sixth grade who rode a cool bike and listened to Def Leppard. In his place was a thirty-year-old man who looked forty, with thinning hair, dirty oil-field clothes and a running start on a beer belly. I summoned up a smile. "Lucky, what a surprise."

"Sure is! Been a month a Sundays since I seen you. Howya been?"

"Great, just great. How you been, Lucky?"

"Purty good. Thought about joinin' the Marines and dropped outta school before we graduated, but that didn't work out."

"Oh? Why is that?"

"They won't take nobody don't have a diploma. Didn't matter much anyway, 'cause me and Darla got pregnant."

"Darla?"

"Curry. You 'member her, don'tcha?"

"Yeah, I remember her. How is Darla?"

Instantly, his smile faded and he sobered. "Well, after she had li'l Bernice, she took off and we ain't heard from her since. Other than that time I got some divorce papers. Reckon Darla just didn't take to bein' a mama."

I felt sorry for him then. Okay, so I'd felt sorry for him all along. But hearing he and his baby were abandoned was too sad. "Tough breaks, Lucky. How old is little Bernice now?"

"'Bout three."

Confused, I added and subtracted in my head. "How old is the baby Darla got pregnant with in high school?"

"You mean Lucky Junior?"

"Uh, yeah, that's the one."

"Fourteen. And there's three in between Lucky Junior and li'l Bernice."

"So you have five children?" Hadn't he and Darla ever heard of birth control?

"Yep. I cain't raise 'em though, what with workin' all the time, so my mama's got 'em at her place, over in Snyder."

Lucky Barnes could be the poster child for Oil-field Trash, but I still felt sorry for him, even if he did impregnate a woman as ignorant as Darla Curry not once, but *five* times. "So, Lucky, where do you work?"

"I work part-time here at Buster's, and I get some other work once in a while. Mostly roustabout stuff, but sometimes I work as a relief pumper. Wish I could get on regular like, and get me a truck, but things is real tight right now and nobody's hirin'." He glanced down, at my boobs, I suppose, then refocused on my face. "How 'bout you, Whitney? You married?"

"I was until about a year and a half ago."

He moved maybe an inch closer. "So you're single? Not datin' nobody?"

"Not really." I didn't think I was dating Ed. I wasn't sure what I was doing with Ed.

"Reckon you'd like to go out sometime? There's a tractor pull over at the coliseum in Odessa this weekend."

Be still my heart. A tractor pull with a guy who has five kids. "Thanks, Lucky, but I guess I better pass. I'm going to be working this weekend."

"Aw, too bad, but maybe later, huh?"

"Yeah, maybe so." I smiled and stepped sideways. I'd have to come back for steel-toed boots later. "Hey, Lucky, it was real great to see you, but I gotta run." I turned and hurried out of Buster's, feeling a tad guilty, but mostly relieved.

Chapter 5

When I got back to the office, I had a message from Ed, asking me to lunch. I returned his call, but he was tied up in court. His assistant said he asked if I'd just meet him at Mr. Maynard's, so about ten minutes before noon, I drove to the north side of town.

Mr. Maynard's is in an old Chinese restaurant, but bears no resemblance to the Ding How of old, except for the ceiling tiles, which are fake wood with cavorting dragons. Having been to China, I know dragons don't cavort, but the guy who built Ding How didn't get the memo. And I guess Mr. Maynard fancied the cavorting dragons since he left them there. Or maybe he just ran long on his decorating budget and figured no one would notice the ceiling. Much.

Ed came in just after me. He had on a suit. Or most of one, including navy trousers, a white dress shirt and a red power tie, the knot loosened and the top button of his shirt undone.

Remembering what he looked like naked, I broke out in a sweat that had nothing to do with the August heat. "Hi, Ed."

His dark eyes moved from the top of my head to the toes of my shoes, then back to my face. "Hi, Pink."

The hostess came to seat us while I was wondering how a man could put so much sexual innuendo into a simple greeting. I also wondered how we'd last until after the hearing. I don't consider myself a sex fiend, or anything like that, but it was all I could do to keep my hands off of Ed.

Once we were seated, a big guy in a chef coat came to the table and slapped Ed on the back while he grinned at me. "Whitney Pearl. Haven't seen you since high school. You probably don't remember me since I was two years behind you." He stuck out his hand to shake mine. "I'm Maynard Ravenaldt."

This shocked me because everyone knows the Ravenaldts are a big giant family of seven kids, all of them rednecks and just barely one step up from white trash. The oldest was a guy named Cuss, who spent time in prison for knocking over a 7-Eleven while a cop was buying a cup of coffee. The Ravenaldts aren't too bright. In high school, I remembered Maynard as a chubby kid with a mullet who got picked on a lot. Now, he was big and husky, with a short haircut. And he was a chef. Too weird. "Sure, I remember you. Nice to see you, Maynard."

"I hope you enjoy your lunch," he said with another slap on Ed's back and an obvious wink before he turned and headed for the kitchen.

"What was that about?" I asked curiously.

"I'm part owner in Mr. Maynard's."

"You're joking."

"Nope. Me and Maynard go way back."

"How far back?"

Ed gave me that killer grin. "Birth. We're brothers."

"You're Ed *Ravenaldt?*" My voice sort of squeaked.

"You had no idea, did you?"

It's incredibly stupid, I know, but up until that moment, I didn't know Ed's last name. Mom introduced him as Ed, and I never caught his last name. Hard to believe I nearly had sex with a man whose last name I didn't know, but there it was. I opted to blame it on the margaritas. I also opted not to admit it. "Of course I knew."

He didn't believe me. "I was a year ahead of you at Lee High School. Remember?"

All I remembered was Eddie Ravenaldt, a tall, skinny guy with long hair, who smoked and skipped school and had an attitude. A bad one. "I remember. But I never really knew you," I finished lamely.

His smile slowly faded. "There are a lot of people you never really knew. Like Gert."

"Gert went to Lee?"

"She was in your class."

"So were six hundred other kids. No way I could know everyone." I narrowed my eyes. "Is that why Gert hates me, because she thinks I ignored her in high school?"

"She doesn't hate you, but if she's a little cold, that's probably part of it."

"You obviously think I ignored you, but you're not cold. You're not even lukewarm. In fact, I could have ironed my clothes with certain parts of your anatomy last night."

He laughed. "Hey, life is not high school. Things change and people change and even though my family's probably still as low-rent as ever, most of us didn't turn out so bad. Even Cuss took up welding and opened a shop down at Big Lake."

I still couldn't get over how different he was. Amazing what fourteen years could do to a person. "If I was rude in high school, I'm sorry."

"You weren't rude. You were just really full of yourself."

"Was not!"

"Yeah, you were." He leaned forward a little. "But I always thought you were hot, even with your nose up in the air."

A waiter came to the table just then and after he left, the conversation turned to how much Midland had changed since we were in high school. While we talked, a blond bombshell walked into the restaurant, alone, and took a table close to ours. As she turned to sit down, I saw her black leather bag and nearly exclaimed aloud with excitement. In pink leather, inset into the black, were the words, Birds in Flight.

"That's weird," Ed said, his eyes on the woman.

"What's weird?" Did he know something about Birds in Flight?

"From behind, that woman looks like you. Her hair's sort of the same color, same length, and she kinda walks like you."

I didn't see any resemblance, but all the same, I spent the whole rest of lunch shooting glances at the woman, wondering about her, and the bag, and Birds in Flight. I thought about going to the ladies' room so I could ask her about the bag on my way past her table. But she was sitting close enough for Ed to overhear, and something told me that wasn't wise. He wigged out so bad about me checking into the pipe deal, I wasn't up for another lecture about it.

After we polished off an excellent crème brûlée, I dawdled over coffee, trying to wait her out so I could follow her.

Ed got impatient, which was obvious by how many times he checked his watch. "Do you suppose you could get some more coffee at the office?" he asked. "I have to be back in court at one-thirty."

"Sure," I said, noticing the woman asked for her check. Perfect timing.

Ed walked me to my car. "Thanks for lunch," I mumbled, inhaling the smell of him. "About last night, don't you think we could—"

"No, Pink, we couldn't. Wait until you go back to Washington. I'll be with you and we'll get a room at the Watergate."

"Really?"

"Really." He looked like he might kiss me, but he didn't. Instead, he turned around and went back inside Mr. Maynard's. I felt like a bottle rocket, about to blast off, the result of stress and chronic sexual tension brought on by sharing air space with a guy named Ed who smelled like starch and sweat and aftershave. I either needed a martini or hot sex, and neither one was on the horizon.

In my car, I piddled around, plugging in the cell phone to charge, putting on lipstick in the rearview mirror, jotting down a list of things I needed for the apartment. About ten minutes passed when finally, the blonde came out and got into a black Lincoln SUV. I started the car and drove behind her, purposefully letting a couple of cars get in front of me so I wasn't obvious.

She drove about a mile away, to Tracy Steven's, a tony shop that sells megaexpensive clothes. I pulled up and got out of the car, noticing the parking lot looked like a Mercedes/Volvo/BMW dealership. Next door to Tracy Steven's is Beau Blue, a beauty salon that everyone who's anyone goes to. Very swanky. But I don't think it's popularity has anything to do with the services they offer. I think the haircuts are just as good at Mabel's. But at Mabel's, they treat people pretty much the same, no matter who you are or where you come from. At Beau Blue, they kiss ass if you're rich, suck up if you're on the way to being rich and treat you like shit if you look remotely close to ordinary. This makes them enormously popular with every rich girl, or rich girl wannabe in Midland. Me? If I had more money than God, I wouldn't darken the door of the place. Pretentious people really get on my nerves, and I dislike my ass being kissed. Just give me what I ask for and things are good.

Inside Tracy Steven's, the air conditioning felt great against my hot skin and I almost wept with joy at the delicious smells of bath stuff and perfume. Man, what a switch from Lucky Barnes and Buster's Boots. Thick, soft carpet the color of rain clouds cushioned my footsteps while clear, recessed lighting made the store more welcoming.

While I was looking through the sale rack, thoroughly ignored by the clerk, I surreptitiously watched her walk about with the blonde, pointing out this "darling" outfit and that "stunning" gown, and those "delicious" earrings. The Birds in Flight chick had hair the color of Frosted Mini-Wheats and I wondered if it was natural. Probably about as natural as her gi-normous boobs. I figured Ms. Mini-Wheats was a regular customer who didn't shop the sale racks, thus the clerk's rabid interest in her and cold shoulder to me.

I went back to shopping. After a while, my arm was groaning under the weight of the clothes I carried and I hoped my prey was close to trying something on, so I could corner her in the dressing room and ask about that bag.

Finally, they walked toward me, but the clerk, whom I'd mentally named Helga, breezed past me and opened a room for her pretty little blond customer. "Please let me know if you need another size, Jessica." She went to the corner dressing room, opened the door and mumbled, "There you go."

I went in with my stash and realized the room was half the size of the others. All those dressing rooms empty and Helga made me tromp all the way to the end so I would have a closet. I had to go outside the small space to look in the mirror, and got lucky when Jessica came out at the same time. She was friendly and chatted like we were old friends, commenting that she'd seen me at Mr. Maynard's and didn't I think the food was excellent? That led to a chat about restaurants, which led to talking about diets. I was trying to get the subject around to fashion, particularly handbags, when everything went south.

Merry Thornton came into the dressing room, Helga leading her along, gushing about their "marvelous" ball gowns.

"Whitney!" Merry spotted me and abandoned the clerk, rushing me, wrapping me in a tight hug. "Oh, my God! I heard you'd moved back to town, but I waited to call, to give you time to get settled in. How are you?"

"Great," I answered, wanting to cuss a lot when Jessica turned and went back into her dressing room. Damn!

I was way less enthusiastic to see Merry than she appeared to be to see me. Merry and I were great friends all through high school, shared clothes, confidences and a close group of friends. We were all tight, and did everything together. I loved all of them like sisters. Until my mom saw Merry kissing my longtime steady, Bobby Tom, in our living room. After that, I couldn't ever quite forgive her and our little group unwound.

I'm sure to her, it was all ancient history, and no biggie. To me, she betrayed me, and I never forget a betrayal. Bobby Tom swore she threw herself at him, that he was innocent, and I forgave him, because he was so sincere. We continued to be steadies until our junior year at University of Texas, when I met George and broke it off with Bobby Tom. Next thing I knew, he was getting married to Merry. I put a good face on it, came back to Midland for the wedding, and did my best to make nice. But I still didn't trust her as far as I could throw her.

I had to say something, even if I wasn't really interested, so I asked, "What are you up to these days?"

"Oh, goodness," she said, looking radiant, "I'm just doing the mom thing. Bobby Tom and I have three children now. B.T. Junior is seven, and the twins, Tyler and Taylor, are three."

Same age as li'l Bernice. Somehow, I didn't think li'l Bernice had anywhere close to the life li'l Tyler and Taylor had. "That's nice," I said.

"And Bobby Tom built us a house out in Saddle Club."

Saddle Club? Just the lots in Saddle Club start at two hundred grand. Most of the houses are in the half-million- to two-million-dollar range. "That's nice," I said.

"We spend most of the summer down at the lake, you know Horseshoe Bay at LBJ? But I had to come home and find a gown for the Silver Gala, which is in October, and you've simply got to come, because I'm chairing it this year."

"That would be nice."

Helga looked ready to explode while she waited on Merry to finish telling me how fab her life was. Jessica was still trying on clothes, and I kind of liked bugging Helga, so egged Merry on. "How's everyone doing?"

"Oh, let's see," she started, looking off into space, "Katy is living in Houston with that dreamy man she married, and Alex is out in L.A., working for NBC, and..."

She went on and on and I sort of listened, but mostly, I watched Helga fidget, waiting for her rich customer to wind it down and pay attention to all those "delicious" clothes she'd very nicely hung in Merry's dressing room, which incidentally was big enough to land a plane in.

When Merry was done, she blinked up at me. "I saw you on TV, and I have to say, you're as brave a person as I know."

Helga's eyes widened.

"Thank you, Merry."

"You know, I could be wrong, but I think that senator, the Italian-looking one, has a crush on you."

Helga perked up considerably.

"Oh, you mean Steve," I said, laughing inside, enjoying myself immensely. "He's a good man, a wonderful senator, but we're only friends."

"I don't know, Whitney," Merry said, "it looks to me like he has a real crush. You could be Mrs. Senator if you play your cards right."

"Gosh, Merry, I'll have to think about that." Not.

Jessica came out just then, and I tuned out Merry's silly chatter so I could hear the woman say to Helga, "Thanks for your help, but I didn't much care for anything today." She waltzed out of the dressing room and I wanted to gnash my teeth. Son of a bitch! She was getting away before I had a chance to ask about that purse, all because of stupid Merry. I thought about cutting her off and saying I had an appointment, but her next words stopped me.

"As for that whole oil company mess, it's just awful. Bobby Tom says they'll all get what's coming to them, and he says he's real proud of you for standing up and telling the truth about things, even if it was partly your fault."

Match. Set. Game over. "Be sure and tell Bobby Tom how much I appreciate that, Merry. And while you're at it, remind him how he blamed that sneaky kiss in my living room on you.

He said you jumped him, that he didn't kiss you back and none of it was his fault. And I believed him. How stupid of me."

Ignoring her shocked look, and Helga's wide eyes, I stepped around them and headed for the register. Helga came behind me and rang me out, looking very nervous. At one point, she looked me right in the eye, and whispered, "I'd be careful if I were you. Mrs. Thornton can be…difficult."

Deciding to forgive her for treating me like a second-class citizen, because after all, she had to put up with a lot of spoiled rich women, and she undoubtedly worked on commission, I nodded and said, "Thanks for the heads-up."

She handed me my shopping bag and I turned to leave, thinking I'd have to hunt down Jessica to find out about the freakin' purse. Then, it dawned on me that the clerk knew her, so before I walked away, I turned back and asked, "Do you know what Birds in Flight is?"

She blushed a bright shade of hot pink and whispered, "It's a very high-priced escort service. They fly all over the world." She moved a step closer and added, "Some of my best customers used to work for them, but you'd never know it now. Married to rich guys, they're in the Junior League, the PTA and the ladies' circle at church." She raised one brow. "Go figure."

Shocked in spite of the fairly wide world view I consider myself to have, I could only mumble, "Yeah. Go figure."

I drove away from Tracy Steven's, my question about Birds in Flight finally answered, but replaced with several more. Why was Bert paying for high-priced call girls out of the business account? Did Ollie know? Was Ollie's real purpose in hiring us so he could have third party documentation of how much cash Bert was shelling out for prostitutes? And I admit, maybe the most puzzling question to my female psyche—which of Midland's leading ladies were ex-call girls?

* * *

I was on my way out that night when Steve Santorelli called.

"Hello, Whitney," he said in his smooth-as-chocolate-icing voice. "How are things?"

"Much better. I'm working in a field I understand."

"Wonderful! You found another audit position?"

"Not exactly. Forensic accounting."

"Hmm, sounds fascinating. Just watch out for the other half of those divorces. Some people get very weird when it comes to divorce."

"Actually, right now I'm working on a cheating partner. Pipe sales and the like."

"Pipe sales? Better be careful, Whitney. I've heard stories about those pipe guys."

Was there a *Godfather*-like movie about pipe guys that I missed? "Yes, I'll be careful." Whatever that meant. Stay out of dark alleys with pipe guys? Don't take candy from pipe guys? Avoid pipe guys with violin cases?

"You're probably wondering why I'm calling you."

"On the contrary, I assume you're calling with news about Mr. Maloney."

He was quiet for a bit, then said, "No, I'm afraid not. I'm still waiting on some information about Mr. Maloney."

Okay, so why had he called? I waited for him to say something, determined not to fill up the awkward silence with nervous chatter.

Finally, he said, "Under the circumstances, it would be highly inappropriate for you and I to see one another socially, but after the next hearing, after you've finished with your testimony and handed over the evidence you have, I wonder if you'd be interested in having dinner with me."

Now I know Mom said he had the hots for me, and silly Merry thought he had a crush on me, but I thought they were both way off base. That's why I was completely floored. For a few heartbeats, I couldn't say a word. I just sort of swallowed and looked for Miss Manners to be my guide. How does one respond to a United States senator asking for a dinner date?

"You know, I haven't dated at all since Lauren died, and I gotta say, your silence is sort of unnerving."

I laughed and said quickly, "I'm so sorry. It's just that I…well, I don't know because you're a…and I'm a…and, well, exactly how would this work, Steve? Would you come here, would I come there, would we meet in the middle somewhere?"

"I hadn't thought about it, to tell the truth. I figured I'd get the hard part over and worry about details later."

I thought of Ed and how much I wanted him. Definitely I was ga-ga over Ed. But I couldn't very well tell the senator no because I was crazy over a wild child like Ed Ravenaldt. Mom's lecture was heavy on my mind.

And I confess, Steve's humble explanation, his obvious nervousness was terribly endearing. I was flattered. A lot. I needed to say no, really wanted to say no, but I couldn't. Later, when it didn't matter so much, I'd explain about Ed. In the meantime, I figured I'd have to play along. "Well, sure, Steve, we could do that. After the hearing."

"Good idea! You'll already be in Washington, so we can go out here."

He sounded well pleased with the idea, but all I could think about was Ed. *We'll get a room at the Watergate.* "I don't know if that would be a good idea," I said, "with the hearing just over. There's bound to be a ton of media there, and you know how that goes."

"Yeah, I know all too well. They'll have me playing favorites and crawling into bed with you…oh, shit, I can't believe I just said that. I meant it figuratively." He coughed. "Honest."

"It's okay. I know what you meant."

"You do?"

"Sure. You mean they'll all put the spin on it like you went after Marvel and Lowell Jaworski and the firm because of your friendship with me. It will destroy my credibility."

He was quiet for a while. Then he laughed. "I really, really like you, Whitney."

"Well, thanks, Steve. You know, my friends all call me Pink."

"Clever. Like Pink Pearl erasers, I guess?"

"That's right."

"Okay, Pink, so you'll go out with me?"

"Yes, Steve, I'll go out with you. How about you call me about two weeks after the hearing and tell me the details." And I'll tell you I'm sleeping with another man. Yikes. This was so not gonna be easy.

"I'll do that. Thanks."

"Glad to oblige."

"Guess I'll go now. I've got some fascinating pending legislation to read over."

"Really? Is it the new tax bill?"

He sighed into the phone. "Yeah. I gotta tell you, Pink, this can be incredibly boring."

He was reading over tax legislation. It hit me then. "Steve, tell me you're not a CPA."

"Why? Do you have something against CPAs?"

"Absolutely. They're all boring and half of them are drunks and most of them are know-it-alls."

He laughed again. "Does that include a CPA named Pink?"

"No way. I'm very not boring, I rarely drink and I'm the first to admit, I don't know much of anything."

"Rest easy. I'm a lawyer. You don't have a thing for attorneys, do you?"

If he only knew. "Not like I do for CPAs."

Two hours later, dressed in a pink T-shirt, khaki shorts and a pair of cowboy boots I bought for roundup three years ago, I sat in the Mercedes, parked behind my mesquites, waiting for the crappy pipe to arrive, thinking about Steve Santorelli. I did that juvenile, immature thing we used to do in junior high and imagined my life if I was Mrs. Senator vs. Mrs. Wild Child.

As Mrs. Senator, I guessed I'd have teas in my elegant town house, go on the campaign trail and pretend that I was Miss Manners twenty-four/seven, like I never had sex with my husband. That made me wonder what sort of lover Steve would be. Something told me he would be nothing like Ed. He wouldn't just take what he wanted and make me want it, too. He'd ask nicely.

As Mrs. Wild Child, I'd probably be on my own a lot of the time, free to chase down pipe guys, or march on city hall or raise herbs in the backyard of our quaint fixer-upper over in the old part of Midland. And at night, Ed would blow my socks off. Shoot, he'd probably blow 'em off in the morning, too. Maybe meet me at the house every once in a while for a nooner.

Definitely, Ed won. I liked Steve, but no way he'd ever make me sweat like Ed did. Didn't matter, though. I was now a confirmed single girl. My six-year marriage to George taught me a lot of things I wished I didn't know, which kept me from going at the whole commitment thing with the same starry-eyed romantic ideals I once had. As it was, I was cynical and jaded.

I seriously wanted to have sex with Ed. And I liked him. But no way I would ever love him. That way led to disaster.

While I was sitting there imagining my name as Pink Santorelli and Pink Ravenaldt, headlights approached. I killed the CD player and Kenny Wayne Sheppard stopped singing. Rolling down the windows, I listened to the sounds of the night and the low hum of the Suburban's engine as it pulled into the yard. The soft scent of summer in the desert, like nothing else in the world, sailed through my open window and I inhaled deeply. Sage and mesquite and yucca, mixed with the barest hint of rain, which wasn't really rain but the moisture of the mesquite, finally able to breathe in the cool night air.

It wasn't long before another set of headlights appeared. The truck pulled into the yard and turned at the exact angle the other one had, so I couldn't see the license plate and could barely make out that there was some lettering on the truck door. I grabbed my binoculars and peered through them, trying to read what the letters said.

It looked like S. Dragon, but I wasn't sure. It was too dark over there. The lights from the Suburban shone on the back of the truck, where the pipe was, along with the forklift and the only man on the scene besides Bert.

The man was tall and thin, his legs sort of bowed out, like he'd been riding a horse since he was in the womb. From where I sat, he looked kinda skanky, but maybe that was just my imagination at work. After all, everyone seemed to think pipe guys were akin to mob guys, and this one seemed to fit the type. He worked steadily, operating the forklift, moving the pipe onto the empty pipe racks while Bert stood by and watched.

It took a while but finally, the man was done. He drove the forklift behind the pipe racks where it had been before, then came over to Bert. I heard their voices, but couldn't make out the conversation. It looked as though Bert was severely aggravated and the skanky pipe guy was holding his ground. Maybe they were arguing over the price.

Slowly, I gathered up my legs and squatted in the front seat, then slung a foot out the window and climbed through, trying like everything not to make too much noise. I couldn't open the door without tripping the interior light, which might as well be a beacon announcing my presence. Creeping closer to the mesquite, I tried to see through the branches and multitude of tiny leaves, but it was no use. I skirted the clump and went to the east, ducking behind a tall yucca, then scooting behind another mesquite, this one close to the fence.

"I told you the price before I came out here, Shanks, now what's it gonna be? You gonna give me the money, or am I gonna tell Ollie what you been doin' out here?"

"You've added twenty-five cents a foot, you lowdown bastard! Now you're blackmailing me? I oughta—"

"You wanna turn me in? You gonna call the sheriff?"

"Maybe I will!"

"You do that, Bert, while I'm loadin' up my pipe."

"I don't have that much cash. Either you have to take a check, or take the cash I brought."

"I'll take the cash, plus a check for the difference."

Bert went back to the Suburban, I assume for his checkbook and I waited for him to come back to the skanky pipe guy. He didn't. The pipe guy went to Bert and they continued their conversation on the opposite side of the Suburban, where I couldn't hear.

Frustrated by my inability to hear them, I slipped between

the rusted metal fence rails and crept closer, staying in the shadows of first a pumpjack, then a heater treater.

"There's your check," Bert said angrily. "Don't do this to me again or I'll make sure you never sell another string."

"I didn't do nothin', you old coot. You're just gettin' hard of hearing. That's all."

There in the dark, I froze when I heard a sound, just next to me. A distinct rattle. Oh, shit. I had no idea what to do. If I ran, I'd blow my cover. If I stayed still, I'd be bitten by a poisonous snake. Granted, I had on my boots, but the majority of my legs was bare and in that moment, I granted all sorts of human qualities to the snake. He would know not to bite my boot and would jump up to bite my leg.

Get outed or die. Yeah, it wasn't really a contest. I turned and hauled ass, dove through the fence, then screamed when I heard a gunshot. For a split second, I thought maybe the shot was to kill the snake, but I knew I was wrong when another shot whizzed by, exploding the yucca I'd just darted in front of. Either Bert or the skanky pipe guy was shooting at me and I decided it was time to go.

I dove through the window and rolled across the front seat, then scrambled to get situated and start the car, seriously scared and pretty pissed that they were shooting at me, an unarmed woman, a CPA for God's sake. Never mind that it wasn't logical to think that since they couldn't know I was unarmed, or a CPA. I just do not like getting shot at before anyone bothers to ask a question. I turned on the headlights just as the pipe man raised his arm and I must have blinded him because his shot went wide, pinging against something metal.

Backing up, I turned the wheel and peeled out in the opposite direction, choosing to avoid the caliche road where I'd be an easy target. Jerking and jumping as the Mercedes rattled across whole mesquite bushes and rocks, rabbit holes and deadwood, I hoped it would make it to the highway. Lucky for me, it did, but not before I ran up on some oil-field equipment. It was un-freaking-believable, but that little Mercedes mowed down the equipment, a submersible pump, I think, like it was made out of tin foil. I glanced at the location sign and about had heart failure. The well was operated by Marvel Energy.

When I got to the highway, my inclination was to hook it for home. Bert and the skanky pipe guy might be out in the mesquites, looking for me. But if I left the area, I wouldn't figure out who was selling the crappy pipe to Bert. I wouldn't be able to get the proof I needed. I'd be a failure. Again.

So I didn't go home. Instead, I drove across the highway, with only the moon as light, and parked behind a clump of mesquites to wait for the pipe truck. I would follow it back to the pipe guy's yard and I'd know for sure who he was.

It wasn't long before I saw Bert drive past, then the pipe guy. Slowly driving out of the cover of the mesquite, I waited until his taillights were way off in the distance before I turned on my headlights. Following at a safe distance, I noticed when another set of taillights turned onto the highway and I sped up a little, afraid I'd lose the pipe truck. As I drove along, well pleased with how things were turning out, someone pulled onto the road behind me, blinding me with their headlights in my rearview mirror.

We were close to the city limits, passing a lot of other oil-field yards, when I heard my tire blow. No, that wasn't my tire. It was a gunshot! The son of a bitch had faked me out, pulled off the road, then pulled on again after I passed.

Really scared now, I sped up, but so did he. I heard another shot, then a loud pop, and suddenly, the Mercedes was flying sideways, into a roll.

Chapter 6

The instant the SUV hit the ground, the driver and passenger side airbags exploded, sending a god-awful smoke into the car. A cloud of powder stung my eyes and burned my throat. Gasping for air, I started praying and didn't stop until I'd rolled over again, the SUV landing on its top.

An awesome silence came then and I wondered if I was dead and didn't know it. Hanging upside down in my seat belt, I knew I wasn't dead when I heard a loud hiss, coming from the engine, like it was dying, taking its last breath. The Mercedes, I was afraid, was totaled. The last remnant of my life in Dallas was officially toast.

I tried to unfasten my seat belt and couldn't. The thing was jammed, or broken or maybe locked up because of the wreck. My eyes were still stinging from the airbag stuff, so I reached for the window control and was shocked when it rolled down. Or was it up? I sucked in the fresh air and felt a little better.

Except for the blood pooling in my head. A headache was coming on fast.

While I said several prayers, thanking God I wasn't dead, I saw the pipe truck pull up next to me. Great. I was a sitting duck and about to be shot by a skanky pipe guy. Mom would never get over it. A pair of jeans-clad bow legs appeared next to the window and I heard a heavy Texas twang. "Who the hell are you?"

I had the sudden idea to play dead. If he thought I was dead, or at least unconscious, maybe he wouldn't shoot me. I closed my eyes and forced myself to be calm, to not breathe when I heard the rustle of his jeans as he bent over to look at me.

I heard him say, "Shit!" then the sound of rapidly retreating footsteps. The truck pulled away from the side of the road and I gathered in a huge breath.

What to do? I had my cell phone there, but who to call? I hesitated to call the highway patrol since the equipment I ran over belonged to Marvel. Who would believe it was an accident? And how bad would that look to the finance committee? I needed to concoct an explanation that looked better than the truth. I needed time. I needed to call somebody to help me.

Rationally, I thought I should call Ed. He was my attorney, after all. But I didn't want to call him because he'd had to save my butt the night before last and I was pretty sure I'd never hear the end of the lectures. Besides, he might tell Mom and she'd take me out of forensic accounting and stick me in perdition with Gert. No, Ed was definitely not the one to call.

That pretty much left Sam, so I dialed him up and when he answered, I said very calmly, "Sam, I've had an accident and I could sure use some help."

"Pink?"

"Yes, Sam, it's me."

I heard a woman's murmur, then heard Sam say, "Just a minute and I'll be right back."

Great. Sam had a date over at midnight. He was most likely working on getting laid and I wasn't going to help his chances, which meant he would be very unhappy with me.

He lowered his voice and asked, "What's going on?"

"It's a long story, but I've had an accident, I'm hanging upside down in my car, and I need you to help me."

"Call the highway patrol. That's what they're for." He hung up on me.

I called back, but he didn't pick up. So I left a message. "Sam, please, you gotta help me. I ran over some of Marvel's oil-field equipment and it's gonna look bad when I have to go back in front of the feds. I'm already up shit creek because I nailed that IRS guy in the nuts. It would really help if you'd be here when I call the highway patrol. You can explain why I was out here and they'll listen to you, but I'm afraid they'll haul me in when they find that equipment. Please, Sam, come and help me. I'm just outside the city limits, south of town on Rankin highway. Look for the Mercedes SUV on its top, just next to the east side of the road."

I ended the call and while I debated about calling Ed after all, the phone rang.

It was Sam. "You wanna tell me what the hell you're doing out on Rankin highway at midnight?"

"I was checking out Bert Shanks's pipe deal."

"And you had a wreck on the way back to town?"

"That's about the size of it."

"You shouldn't speed."

"I wasn't. My tire blew after the skanky pipe man shot it out and I rolled."

"Well, hell, Pink. I'll be there in a minute."

I guess he called from his cell phone because he was there within just a couple of minutes. He parked his car, a late-model Beemer, in front of mine and left his headlights on. I turned my head to keep the light from burning my retinas and saw him as he bent to get a look at me. He had on his usual Hawaiian shirt and jeans, but his hair was loose. "Hey, Sam."

"Hey, Pink. Can you unbuckle your seat belt?"

"No. I think it's jammed."

He reached into his jeans pocket and pulled out a pocket knife that unfolded into a wicked-looking blade any serial killer would be proud to own. As he reached for the belt, he said, "You're going to fall and it's going to hurt."

"I was afraid of that."

"Man, your face is red."

"I must be embarrassed."

"No, it's because—"

"Sam, I know why my face is red! Every drop of blood in my entire body is now concentrated behind my eyeballs and I'm about to have an aneurysm. Just cut the freakin' seat belt already!"

He did and I crumpled into a heap on the ceiling of my little SUV. I'd have some major bruises in the morning, but at least my head wouldn't explode. "Thanks."

"No problem." He reached in and grasped my arm, tugging me, helping me, guiding me through the window. Wrapping an arm around my shoulders, he walked me back to his car, opened the passenger door and gently pushed me inside. Then he got in and killed the lights.

"What are you doing?"

"Settling down to wait for Nolan Beeps and his wrecker.

He's going to haul your car to his shop and not call the cops. Start praying one doesn't drive by before Nolan gets here."

"How much is this gonna cost me?"

"Probably five hundred bucks."

"Ouch."

"Hey, illegal things cost extra."

"Why is this illegal? My wreck didn't involve anyone else."

"It involved a gunshot. If there's a bullet in your tire, Nolan is technically required to call the cops."

"Oh. Wonder if there's a chance the car can be repaired?"

"I don't think so. It looks totaled to me."

"Great. Now I'll be without a car."

"I've got a car you can borrow until you get a new one."

Turning to look at him, I asked, "Really?"

"Really. It's just an old Ford I keep for going out in the field, but you can use it for a few days."

"Thanks, Sam," I said, grimacing when a sharp pain zapped my head.

"Is your head hurting?"

"A little."

We sat in silence for a while. Then I said, "Sorry I screwed up your date."

"It's okay."

"Will she still be there when you get home?"

"I doubt it, but I don't much care. This sort of thing doesn't do much for the mood, if you see what I mean."

I didn't. Not really. But I'm a girl, so what do I know?

"Are you gonna tell me about Bert's pipe deal?"

"I'd rather save it for my report."

"That'll work." He reached over and brushed my hair out of my face. "Your boyfriend called me about you yesterday."

"What boyfriend?"

"Ed."

"He's not my boyfriend." I turned to look at him. "What did he want?"

"He wants me to only give you small divorce clients. Said I was a sorry so-and-so for giving you a cheating-partner client, especially one doing pipe deals."

My head began to pound again. "Tell me you told Ed to back off."

"Damn straight. Told him you work for me, that what I give you isn't any of his business, and if he wanted to make a big deal out of it, he could hire you himself."

"Yeah, like that would ever happen."

"He said he'd think about it."

"No way!"

"I'm just tellin' you what the man said." He stretched his arm across the seat, his fingers brushing the back of my head. "Suppose Ed offered you a job. Would you take it?"

"It would mean I wouldn't have to work for Mom, but it would also mean I had to work for a hardheaded chauvinist who lies to me."

This seemed to interest Sam a lot. He turned his body toward me and stared at me intently. "What does he lie about?"

"He says he's not doing anything with the Shankses and I know he is. He was really ticked at me about chasing a pipe truck, but it was more than just concern. He was worried I might get the goods on Bert, but when I confronted him, he insisted he's not working for either of them."

"Yeah, he lied like a dog on that one. Pretty sharp of you to figure that out."

"What's he doing for them?"

Sam shook his head. "I can't tell you."

"Why the hell not?"

"Because you like the guy and when I tell you, it'll make you hate his guts."

That was so out there, so totally unexpected, I sat there for a bit, wondering what on earth Ed could do that would make me hate his guts. And why Sam would care if I did. "Tell me."

"Are you sure? Because you're not gonna like it."

"I'm sure."

"You know how I told you so much of the oil is getting lost to the hole because of the bad pipe?"

"Yeah."

"Ed's been retained to represent a whole group of landowners who're about to sue the Shankses for losing oil, which is contaminating their land."

"Wouldn't proof that Bert is switching the pipe make his case? Why doesn't he want that proof?"

"Because the landowners are suing them both. If Ollie proves he had nothing to do with the switches, he can't be held liable."

"So? Bert can fork it over for what he's done."

"He could, if he had the dough. Bert has a bad habit that costs him a lot of money, and he has nothing left but debt. That's why he's pulling this pipe scam."

"So the landowners can win against Bert, but they won't get a dime."

"And if they win against Ollie, they'll get a lot of cash. Ed will get forty percent of whatever they're awarded in damages."

"That's why he doesn't want me to prove Bert is a dirty, rotten crook?"

"Right."

I looked at Sam in the dim light of the dash and asked a question, even though I already knew the answer. I was curious to see if he'd tell me. "What's Bert Shanks's bad habit?"

"He likes prostitutes. Very expensive ones. Has 'em flown in from Los Angeles and Miami Beach, puts them up at the Hilton, then keeps them for weeks at a time, sometimes four or five at once. At a grand every day, plus expenses, it adds up."

"Birds in Flight," I mumbled. "He wrote a lot of checks to them and I couldn't figure out what it was, until I ran into one of the, uh, girls this afternoon. I'm wondering why Bert's been writing the checks out of the business account."

"I think Ollie lets him because it'll give him more leverage when he lowers the boom on the pipe deals. He's accounting for all the checks as draws to Bert's capital, which is why Bert's busted and flat-ass broke."

It pleased me that Sam wasn't hiding anything, that he trusted me. "And I thought the pipe guy was skanky."

"Undoubtedly, he is. It's probably the prostitute connection that got them together in the first place."

I thought about that, trying not to think too much about Ed and his willingness to ignore the truth and ruin a good man for the sake of some money. "Sam, why do men like prostitutes?"

"That's a pretty weird question, Pink."

"So? Are you too embarrassed to answer? Do you hire prostitutes and that's why this is an uncomfortable subject?"

"No, I'm not embarrassed, and yes, I did hire one once, when I was in the Navy and hadn't been laid in about six months and had shore leave for one night, which isn't enough time to sweet-talk a woman into bed, and this isn't an uncomfortable subject. Just weird."

"Did she fake it?"

"Jesus, that was fifteen years ago. I don't remember."

"Well, it seems to me that most women can't get there without a lot of effort, so I figure most men wouldn't put forth the effort for a prostitute, but would expect her to go over the moon, so she must fake it."

He shrugged. "Makes sense."

"You never answered my question. Why do men hire prostitutes?"

"They're horny, I guess."

"What about men like Bert, who are married?"

"Just because a man's married doesn't mean he's getting regular sex."

"Sam, you're deliberately misunderstanding. If a man's getting steady sex, why would he go hire a prostitute?"

Sam looked at me and said evenly, "Because even though the sex is steady, it's not what he wants. Maybe he wants a woman who screams a lot, or does it standing on her head, or who's very submissive, or who dresses up like Vampira."

"Oh." I returned my gaze to the windshield.

"Hey," he said in a deep, soft voice, his big hand touching my chin, making me look at him, "it's really got nothing to do with his steady."

"If he's out screwing a prostitute, it's got everything to do with his steady." I tried very hard not to think about George, but I couldn't help it. Remembering made me sad and mad all over again.

"Some men cheat and some hire prostitutes, but most men are happy to hang out with one woman. You just have to pick the right one."

"How? Come out and ask, 'Hey, do you plan to cheat, or hire prostitutes?'"

"I'd say, if a man deals with his business on the up-and-up, if he treats other people fairly, if he has integrity in all parts of his life, it'd be a pretty safe bet he'll be faithful."

I turned my face away from him and looked down at my hands, folded primly in my lap. "That makes Ed a bad choice."

"Guess so." He stroked my hair and said softly, "I'm real sorry, Pink."

"Yeah," I said, feeling tired down to my bones, "me, too."

By the time I got home, it was past two in the morning. I took off my shorts and my stupid-looking cowboy boots, crawled under the covers and went to sleep before I had time to think any more about Ed.

In the middle of a really great sex dream where my lover switched from Ed to Steve to Sam, I was jerked awake by the sound of a loud bang. I sat up, groggy and confused. What woke me up? Glancing at the clock, I was shocked to see it was exactly one hour since I'd climbed into bed. Three-ten.

I heard the bang again and realized, someone was at my door. It had to be the cops. Nolan Beeps had ratted me out. Moving toward the door, I peeked through the peephole, fully intending not to answer it. But there was no uniform on the other side. It was Ed, looking extremely mad.

"Go away," I mumbled as I opened the door.

He came in, closed the door behind him, grabbed my shoulders and squeezed. Hard. I truly dislike being manhandled, and decided to kick the crap out of Ed, just as soon as I was awake.

"What the hell were you doing at the Shankses' yard tonight?"

"Watching Bert take a load of pipe from a scumbag pipe guy who ended up shooting my tire out, and made me roll the Mercedes."

"I told you to stay out of it, Pink!"

"Since when do I take orders from you?"

"Then you called Sam, when I specifically asked you not to."

"Couldn't call you, because you'd tell Mom and she'd make me work for Gert in the tax department."

"I should tell your mom. You should be working for Gert."

Looking down at his wonderful hands, still gripping my shoulders, I said, "Get your hands off me. Now."

He did, and stepped back. "What's wrong with you?"

"I've had exactly one hour of sleep, my whole body is a big bruise, I totaled my car and I don't like you."

"Is that it?"

"That just about covers it. You can leave now."

"I will after you tell me why you don't like me."

"Remember how I told you I'd find out about you and the Shankses, and you'd feel like a heel because you didn't tell me yourself?"

"And I told you, I never feel like a heel."

Scowling at him, I turned away. "You should. You're going to cheat on me. Go away."

"Pink, what the devil are you talking about?"

"I'm talking about you taking Ollie Shanks to the cleaners, when none of this is his doing, and how that makes you a man with no integrity, which means you're going to cheat on me. Did you know, I divorced my husband because he cheated on me?"

"No."

"Well, he did, and even worse, he didn't go pick him a nice girl home-wrecker. George picked a prostitute named Luscious. I asked him if that was her real name, and would you believe, the idiot said it was? Have you ever, in your whole life, known a woman with a name like Luscious? What parent would actually name a baby girl Luscious?"

"I'm assuming that's a rhetorical question."

I took a deep breath and walked toward my bedroom. I got into my bed and turned off the lamp. "Goodbye, Ed. Lock the door on the way out."

The bed squeaked as he sat down.

"Get off my bed and get out. I hate you."

"Don't I get a chance to explain my side of things?"

"Maybe. But not right now. I'm tired. Just go away."

"Answer me one question first."

I rolled over so my back was to him and mumbled an affirmative.

"While you were there tonight, did you see anybody but Bert and the pipe guy?"

"No."

"Did you notice anything out of the ordinary?"

"It was midnight, a man off-loaded a whole lot of pipe all by himself, and then he shot at me. I'm a CPA, Ed. For me, this is out of the ordinary."

"Was there anything that didn't jive with the pipe deal?"

My curiosity at full alert, I rolled over again and sat up to face him in the half-light from the parking lot. "Why?"

"I just need to know."

"Tell me why and I'll tell you."

He sighed and shifted his weight, setting the bed to squeaking obnoxiously. "This bed sucks."

I made no comment.

"You're not gonna like this."

"That happens a lot lately. Can't get much worse."

"Pink, a woman was killed tonight, a woman connected to Bert Shanks."

Oh, man. Murder? My skin just about crawled all the way off my bones. "Was she one of his prostitutes?"

"Yes, and...wait a minute. How do you know about Bert's prostitutes?"

"Sam told me."

"What's with that guy? He shouldn't be telling you things

like that. It's...he's not...you're not..." He stopped and gave up.

"Because we're not intimate and a man shouldn't talk to a woman like me about things like prostitutes?"

"Exactly!"

"Ed, get a clue. I'm a big girl and I know all about prostitutes. I shared my husband with one."

"I'm sorry about that, Pink. And by the way, I'd never cheat on you."

"Says you. How could I trust a guy who's willing to sell an innocent man like Ollie Shanks down the river?"

"He's not that innocent."

"Would you care to expound on that?"

"No, I wouldn't."

"Even if it would make me like you again?"

"Even then. Some things, you don't want to know."

"I hope you know you're pissing me off. A lot."

"Later, I'll tell you, but for now, there's too much riding on it."

"Meaning you've got some dirt on Ollie you can blast him with in court?"

"Something like that." He shifted again and waited for the bed to quiet down before he spoke again. "So answer the question. Did you notice anything tonight that didn't have to do with Bert's pipe deal?"

"No." I was all tied up, torn between wanting to ask him to stay with me and telling him I never wanted to see him again. Maybe I had PMS. I'm not usually so indecisive. I knew he was a low-down rat, but some instinct, whether in my head, my heart or my hootus, I didn't know, told me there was more to the story than what Sam told me. Sam and Ed obviously had a thing and I was just one more sticker in a whole field of them. Truth be told, I probably shouldn't have believed what either of them said about the other.

"Listen, Pink, if anybody asks, you were here, all night long. You were never out at that yard."

"How will I explain the car being wrecked?"

"Did Beeps come and get it?"

"Yeah."

"Then don't worry about it. Tell anyone who asks that it's in the shop for repairs."

"Ed, it's totaled. Won't it be kinda obvious when I don't drive it anymore?"

"Tell everyone you traded it in, that you couldn't afford the payments after you lost your job."

"Why does it matter so much? It's not like I'm a suspect."

"No, but you were out there tonight and the police will want to question you, and that won't look good to the finance committee. No matter what, you've got to keep your nose clean."

"Was she found out there?" The thought made me want hurl.

"Close by. Her body was dumped next to a Marvel Energy location where she might not have been found for a long time except that somebody, I guess whoever dumped her, ran over some equipment and it triggered an alarm. The pumper went out and while he was trying to make repairs, he saw the body."

Well, shit. The night just got worse and worse. "Um, Ed? Suppose I know who ran over that equipment?"

For a long time, he didn't answer. It was so quiet, I could hear the tinkling of the little waterfall in the duckless duck pond outside.

Finally, he said, "Pink, you didn't run over that equipment because you were never there. Understand?"

"I understand."

He got up and I heard his footsteps all the way to the door. Then I heard the door open, the door close and, a few minutes later, a car engine turning over. Ed drove off and I figured I'd be awake all night, freaking out about what all he'd told me. But I went right to sleep and dreamed about having sex with him. Less than thirty minutes later, just as Ed and I were getting to the good part, my phone rang. Miss Manners was still asleep. *"What?"* I yelled into the receiver.

There was some heavy breathing, then an icky man's voice. "Do you know what happens to bad girls, Pinkie? They get their pus—"

I hung up.

He called back.

"Look, bucko, tell you what. I'll think about it. Really. Just lemme get some sleep, willya?"

"Not until you say you won't hand over the disk."

"Okay. I won't. Now lay off, or I'll change my mind."

"I don't believe you. You're just saying that so I'll leave you alone."

I sucked in a deep breath and let it out very slowly. "Okay, you got me, but the truth is, I don't really think you intend to hurt me. You're just trying to scare me, and I'm not scared. I'm just really, *really* tired."

"You're not scared? Even a little?"

Uh-oh. I'd hurt his male pride, and that was very not smart. I laid back on the pillow and stared up at the ceiling. "Yeah, I guess I'm a little scared." Only not.

"What would it take to scare you a lot?"

He could threaten Mom, or Aunt Fred and Uncle Alvin, even Lurch. He could sabotage my car, if it wasn't already headed for the junkyard. He could even show up and rough me up a little. But I wasn't about to give the guy any ideas.

He was harmless as he was, and I wanted him to stay that way. "Look, I've lost everything I worked for, I'm humbled and pathetic and a total loser. Isn't that enough? I mean, it's not like this whole thing is benefiting me. I am not the bad guy, unless you're one of the Marvel execs, or Lowell Jaworski."

"Oh, you're the bad guy, all right. If you go back to Washington and give those people the disk, you're definitely the bad guy. And you'll regret it."

"Well, buddy, all I can say is, somebody's got to point out that the emperor is naked."

He was quiet for a moment, then said, "That's it?"

"Yeah, that's it."

"What a dumb thing to say. It makes no sense. Why does someone have to point out that he's naked? Maybe he wants to be naked. Maybe nobody cares if he's naked. Maybe—"

"It's lame, but gimme a break. It's almost four in the morning. Call during the day and I'll have better homilies."

"I can't call during the day."

"Look, I gotta go. I'm unplugging the phone, so don't bother calling back. You should get some rest." I hung up and unplugged the phone and curled up under the covers, trying to put a name to the voice. He spoke with a little gravel in it, like he'd gargled with Drano, but I was sure he did that on purpose so I wouldn't recognize him. Spoke like that. Not gargled with Drano. The guy was a sicko, and pretty twisted, but no way anyone would gargle with Drano.

Finally, I fell asleep again, but I didn't have the good sex dream again. Instead, I dreamed I'd gargled with Drano, and couldn't talk at the hearing. I just sat there and pointed and opened my mouth and nothing came out.

Chapter 7

Incredibly, I woke up at seven and didn't feel too bad. I was sore, and still pretty bummed about Ed's bad news, but I wasn't tired anymore. In Sam's old Ford, I stopped at Donut King and bought three dozen donuts for the office. When I got to work, Tiffany took one look at the donuts and said, "Did you get some with cinnamon sugar?"

"Just one."

She looked relieved. "Your mom's looking for you. She's in the conference room." Tiffany started to turn back to her computer, then stopped and said, "I almost forgot. You got a call yesterday afternoon from a man named Lucky. Said to tell you he got front-row seats at the tractor pull." This she relayed without even a crack of a smile.

"Was I supposed to call him back?"

"I asked, but he said no, because he don't…doesn't have a phone."

"Thanks, Tiffany."

Terrific. Now I had something to do on Saturday night besides watch reruns and eat Chee•tos. Gee, if only Lucky had a phone, I could call and say I'd be there, wearing a spandex skirt and my cowboy boots. Yee-haw.

Remembering how donuts magically disappear when out of sight, I carried them with me to the conference room. "Good morning," I said to Mom, then stopped in midstride when I saw Mrs. Colder sitting at the conference table. I set the boxes on the table. "Hello, Mrs. Colder. How are you?"

"Been better," she hollered. "Didn't know you were *Jane Pearl's* daughter. Small world."

Mom said, "Mrs. Colder was my very first client."

Yes, it was a very small world. I nodded and smiled at the old lady.

Mom looked happy when she said, "Pink, I've got great news. Mrs. Colder wants to hire you and Sam to do a little investigative work for her."

"Got a nephew tryin' to *steal me blind.*"

"Her nephew is Bert Shanks." Mom gave me the hairy eyeball, which meant, don't mention you're already checking him out.

Too weird. I mean, what were the odds? The world got even smaller, narrowing down to *Twilight Zone* coincidence. "How is he trying to steal you blind, Mrs. Colder?"

"First, he talked my boy into locking me up over at that *hole in the wall* they call a retirement village. Humph! Just another name for a big, *stinky place* with bad food. And they've got people so old, they're *startin' to rot,* sitting right there in plain sight."

I didn't think it was P.C. to mention that she was ninety-three, and most considered that on par with the age of dirt.

"Then Bertram told my babies they should take over my assets, on account of I'm *too old* to take care of 'em myself."

"And did they?"

"Like hell!" she yelled, slapping her hand against the table. "The little snots took me to court, but Frank Jolly knows better than to mess with me, especially since it was *my money* got him elected as county judge, so he told 'em to leave off and let me be."

Mom patted Mrs. Colder's shoulder. "I'm sure your children only have your best interests at heart."

"'Course they do. It's that *sneaky skunk* Bertram's got 'em all hot and bothered." She looked across at me, her blue eyes flashing sparklers of fury. "I know what he's doing. He's trying to get me out of the driver's seat, so he can *con my babies out of the money.* As soon as they have control, he'll be sellin' 'em bad oil deals and *shady investments,* and talking them into selling off the *ranch.*"

Her eyes suddenly clouded with tears and I felt my heart turn over. Until her children forced her to move to town, she'd been running that ranch most of the past century, according to Ed. No doubt it meant everything to her. "Okay, Mrs. Colder, tell me what I can do for you."

"I want you to get the goods on Bert. Prove he's a *snake* so my kids'll understand why I don't want him *anywhere near* my money, or my land."

"Do you have something in mind?"

Her tears dried up and the anger was back. She hauled her Big Mama black bag up and set it on the table, then rifled around in it for a bit. She pulled out some check stubs and laid them next to the bag. "These are royalties I get every month from a whole bunch of different producers. Jane knows all about that since she does my *income taxes.*"

Watching her page through the check stubs, it occurred to me that she wasn't wearing glasses. How could a ninety-three-year old woman read without glasses? Peculiar. Very peculiar.

"I'm old as Methuselah, so I get confused sometimes, and I forget who's paid me and who hasn't. Started *writin' 'em down* about nine months ago, and figured out I'm missing some. Called the producers and they said I cashed the checks. Now I'm old and *slippin'*, but I know what I write down is right because I'm faithful about it. Every day when the mailman comes. I asked real nice and one of the producers sent me a *copy of the back* of one of my cleared checks." She dove into the bag again and came out with a piece of copy paper. "Here 'tis. If you look at the endorsement, it's *not how I sign my name,* and it's going into an account that *isn't* one of mine."

"So you think Bert is taking your checks and depositing them into his own account?"

"*Got to be.* I want you to figure out whose account it is, and then I want you to look over these check stubs, look at my interests and *compare 'em* to the division orders I signed." She dug around in the bag again and withdrew a green pressboard file. "Right *here's* my division orders."

"You think Bert had the producers change your interests?"

"Darn tootin'! My checks got a lot smaller, and that makes *no sense* with crude prices bein' what they are."

That was a lot worse than ripping off her checks. That was enough to send Bert to prison for a long time. I wondered if Ed knew any of this. The whole thing was like a dog chasing its tail, everything connected. And not in a good way. "Any chance Bert has sold any of these interests he took from you?"

"Could be." She looked confused all of a sudden. "If he sold them, does that mean I can't get them back?"

"No. He doesn't have clear title to the royalties, and whomever bought them from him is out of luck because they didn't do a title search." I watched her gather up her bag and get to her feet. "Mrs. Colder, how far do you want to take this?"

"What do *you mean?*"

"If I can prove Bert transferred those interests, he could be charged with embezzlement and fraud and a few other crimes."

Gripping her walker, she looked across the table at me with a hard, determined expression on her wrinkled face. "I want you to fry the *son of a bitch.* He's my nephew by marriage to my second husband, and the *whole family* is a bunch of bums. Do him good to cool his heels in jail." Her old gaze fell to the boxes of donuts. "Can I *have* those? Be nice for my *poker game.*"

Poker? Sweet Mary, she was a piece of work. What could I say except, "Be my guest"?

An hour later, I was looking over Mrs. Colder's division orders, getting familiar with everything, when Sam came by my cube. "Need to see you, Pink."

I followed him to his office and wondered why he closed the door.

"Have a seat," he invited.

I did, then watched curiously when he didn't go around his desk and sit in his chair, but propped a hip on the edge, his knee close to my arm. "What's up?"

"Ed came to see me last night. In fact, he was waiting on me when I got back from following you home."

"I wondered how he knew where I'd been."

"It wasn't until later that it came up. He came over to tell me that one of Bert's prostitutes was murdered last night."

"He came and told me, too." I looked up at him. "Now that I think about it, how did he know so soon after it happened?"

"One of his brothers is a cop."

"Which one?"

"Hank, the one just behind Ed."

"Why did he come over in the middle of the night to tell you, Sam?"

He broke eye contact and looked down at my legs. "He insisted I take you off the Shankses' account, and I agreed."

"What?" I stood and glared at him. "Are you serious?"

"Pink, there's a real problem now. Namely a dead body, and with you having to look good for the finance committee, you can't afford to be involved."

Sinking back into the chair, I had to fight to keep from screaming in frustration. "How about if I promise not to go out there again? I have a really great idea to find out who the pipe man is, and it's not the least bit dangerous."

"What?"

"I can ask my ex who he is."

"How would your ex know him? I thought he was in the car repair business."

"Not my ex-husband. My ex-boyfriend, Bobby Tom Thornton. He works for his daddy at Thorn Pipe. He'd know about a skanky pipe guy." I could tell Sam didn't believe me. "At least let me see if he can give me a name."

Sam crossed his arms over his chest and thought about it for a while. "If I say yes, you have to promise you won't go looking for the guy. Come and tell me and I'll go talk to him."

"No problem," I said, neatly avoiding the promise part of the equation. I left his office and the building, just in case he changed his mind. I was determined to prove I could handle this client, that I wasn't dead weight.

Deciding to wait until after lunch to go see Bobby Tom, I spent the rest of the morning with Nolan Beeps, discussing possible ways to fix the Mercedes. He said it was impossible. I said it wasn't. We finally came to a meeting of the minds and he offered to buy it off me for less than half its value.

Leaving his garage with a check in my purse, I felt very despondent. Like the loft, that car had meant something. It meant I was good at something, that I wasn't just wifey material like Lurch always seemed to think. Not that I cared anymore what he thought. I didn't aim for success to please him, because I knew it was pointless. Lurch is so mired down in negativity and arrogance, I could run for president and win, and he'd ask how much they paid me, then criticize it and tell me how much he made before he retired as a vice president of an oil company.

No, I aspire to be successful because it's all I have. I'm not ugly, but I'm not pretty. I'm not boring, but I'm not witty. I'm not a nobody, but I'm not a somebody. I'm just plain old Whitney Ann Pearl, with an ego that needs something to make me be okay with that. The CPA thing always did it for me.

Until now. Leaving the beat-all-to-hell Mercedes with Beeps was just the worst bummer.

I grabbed a meatball sandwich from Gino's for lunch, then ran home and changed into an electric-blue suit before I drove to Bobby Tom's office. He and his dad work together, their business located in a nice, one-story building next to their pipe yard on the east side of Midland, close to downtown.

After I parked Sam's old Ford, I checked my lipstick then got out and walked to the front door, more nervous than I'd expected. I stepped inside, out of the one-hundred-ten degree outside, and felt a blast of arctic air in my face. I made an mmm sound and the receptionist smiled.

"Nice, isn't it?"

"Like heaven," I agreed. "I'm an old high school friend of Bobby Tom's and thought I'd stop by to say hello. Is he in?"

"Sure is," she replied, picking up the phone. She punched a few buttons and said, "B.T., there's an old friend of yours out here. Says she wants to say hello." She nodded and hung up, then stood and walked away down the hall. "I'll show you where it is," she said, waving me to follow her.

Down the hall, we turned and went down another hall, and walked all the way to the end. After she offered me something to drink and I declined, she left me there in the doorway to Bobby Tom's office. I admit I was a bit nervous. Okay, not a bit. More like a lot. I swallowed and stepped inside.

His office was huge, furnished with rustic furniture and Texas paraphernalia, the two outside walls made of limestone and the flagstone floor covered with various animal pelts. He had lots of deer heads hanging on the walls and I got the creeps with all those eyes staring at me. Including Bobby Tom's.

"Well, well, look who it is," he said, his gaze taking inventory.

I didn't blame him because I was checking him out, too. Bobby Tom was my first, and only, until George, and I'd always thought he was one fine-looking guy. The years had been nice to him. He was still trim and handsome, his hair still coal-black and his eyes the color of cornflowers. I sort of expected to feel something. Remorse for throwing him over when I met George? Remorse for not marrying him when he would have been such a better husband than George? Remorse for never really getting the sex thing until after we were no longer together?

But I didn't feel any of those things. What I felt was a wee bit of nostalgia and maybe even a little happiness to see him. "How are you?"

"I was fine until Merry came home yesterday bawling her eyes out. Now I'm getting the silent treatment. Just curious,

Whit, do you create disasters everywhere you go? Because I think you could qualify for help from the Red Cross."

All warm fuzzy feelings dissipated and I frowned. "I was glad to see her until she said you think I'm to blame for the Marvel fiasco."

"Well, aren't you?"

"About as much as you were to blame for Merry jumping you in my living room."

"I was to blame."

I blinked. "You said it was all her."

"You were always too naive."

Stepping closer to his desk, I felt a little short of breath. "You *cheated* on me, then lied about it and made me think Merry was a sleaze-puppy?"

"That's about the size of it."

"She was my best friend! I hated her for that, and for no reason! You lousy, scum-sucking—"

"Whitney, please. That's been over fourteen years ago. Get over it."

I choked back the serious cussing-out he deserved, remembering my purpose for the visit. "You're right. No sense digging up old dirt."

"Besides, what I did with Merry couldn't hold a candle to what you did with George. You were over there at his apartment screwing his brains out while I was studying for midterms."

"That's bullshit and you know it. I didn't even go out with George until after we broke up."

"You have selective memory. I remember finishing studying and going to get you for a beer, and I found you at George's, naked, doin' the nasty."

That truly blew my mind. No way I would have done that. "We'd already broken up, and you were in denial."

He stood and walked around the desk. "I'm outta here. You know the way out."

"Why are you leaving?"

He turned at the doorway and gave me a look that put Gert's go-to-hell looks to shame. "Because you make me sick."

Then he was gone and I was left standing there, staring at the empty doorway like a fool.

I'm not sure how long I stood in his office, feeling mad and sad and vengeful, but after a time, Bobby Tom's daddy passed by and saw me. He did a double take, backed up and came in, wrapping me in a big bear hug. "Whitney! What a nice surprise! What brings you to our neck of the woods?"

Bobby Tom's daddy is huge, at least six and a half feet tall and maybe two-fifty. Handsome in an old salty sea dog sort of way, he's a real man's man who hunts and fishes and loves to bird-dog women. Not that he ever cheated on Bobby Tom's mama, a genteel southern lady who's maybe the nicest woman on earth, but he does love to look—and flirt. No matter the age, from little girls to old ladies and everything in between, there isn't a female alive who can resist him. His name is Jeb, but everyone calls him Thorn. He's such a great guy, even men can't resist him. He sells lots and lots of pipe.

I grinned up at him, terribly glad he didn't hold it against me that I broke it off with Bobby Tom. "Would you believe, I'm back in Midland, working for my mom?"

He pulled me to a chair and sat me down, then took the opposite chair. "How is your mama?"

"Great. Just busy."

"Always admired your mother for puttin' up with that daddy of yours. He's a real tough old boot."

Amazing how he could insult someone and make it sound good. I explained what I was doing for Mom, and how I was working for a client who'd had a bad pipe sale and I needed to know some names of some pipe men who weren't exactly on the up-and-up.

Thorn laughed and said, "Sugarplum, don't you know there isn't a pipe man alive who's on the up-and-up?"

"I've been told they're kind of a different breed, but I don't see it. I mean look at you. You're as honest as the road is long."

"It's not about honesty, baby girl. It's kinda like poker. The guy with the best hand doesn't always win. The guy who bluffs best is the guy who wins. That's why most pipe guys make great poker players."

I still didn't really get it, but I nodded and smiled like I did. Then I asked him for some names.

"I gotta tell you, sweetheart, I'm mostly up here for looks these days. I come in and look official and play golf and take customers on hunting and fishing trips, but the business is all run by Bobby Tom. I'm outta the loop, if you see what I mean. You need to ask him for some names."

Maybe my disappointment showed in my face. Thorn chucked me on the chin and growled like a bear, which was Thorn-speak for "Buck up, little lady."

"He's always been too proud for his own good, you know. Just between you and me, I think he never got over you, and all that about you cheatin' on him with that boy you married, well he knows he's wrong. It just makes him feel better. Tell you what. He's probably gone to the barbershop to get his shoes shined. Then he'll stop by a customer's office for a while, and he'll end up at The Bar around five." Thorn shook his head. "The boy drinks too much, but I reckon I would too if I was in his shoes."

A tiny little alarm began to go off in my head. "Uh, why is that, Thorn?"

His usual jolly mood took a hike and he became dead serious. "Don't take this like I know you'll want to, bein' a woman and all, but I think he married her out of spite. He was mighty ticked off at you, and he thought marryin' her would get you back for breaking off the engagement."

The alarm grew louder. "Are you saying Bobby Tom's marriage is in trouble?" I remembered Merry's happy glow from the day before and had my doubts.

Thorn leaned over. "He's about to file for divorce."

Why was he telling me this?

"She's cheatin' on him. I told him he'd regret marryin' her because she showed her true colors when she went after him, bein' your favorite friend and all. Bad stuff, that."

"Bobby Tom told you about that?"

"Sure did. Came home and asked me what he should do about it. Didn't want you thinking he was a cheater. Told him to be honest about it, and that's what he did. When he came home from Austin and told me he was broke up with you and planned to marry what's her name, I knew it was a bad mistake."

Thorn had always been happy and funny. Never serious. To say I was uncomfortable would be like saying it was a little warm outside. Casting about for something to say, I blurted out the first thing that popped into my head. "Who's she cheating on him with?"

Thorn stared into my eyes and said in a low, quiet voice, "A good friend of mine." He grimaced. "At least, he used to be. Little younger than me, but old enough to be her daddy. Makes me sick, I can tell you, sugar."

"What's his name?"

Thorn took a deep breath, let it out real slow and said, "Ollie Shanks."

Chapter 8

Bobby Tom was already gone from the barbershop by the time I got there, so I went to his customer's office and hung around outside the building until he left. He saw me, looked way pissed and turned the other direction. I ran to catch up to him, wishing I had on tennis shoes instead of my high-heeled mules. "I'm just going to keep following you until you tell me what I want to know."

"I'm going to call the police and tell them you're stalking me," he said, pulling a cell phone from his pocket.

I watched him dial 9-1-1, listened to him tell them a crazy woman was stalking him, give them my name, description and location, then hang up. He took off walking again and I turned around and walked the other way. I wasn't sure if he really called, or faked me out, but I wasn't taking any chances. Amazing how I'd never even had a parking ticket before I blew the whistle on Marvel, but ever since, I was constantly walking the edge of the law.

Still, I wasn't going to give up on Bobby Tom. I was determined to get a name and I was certain he had one. At five, I walked into The Bar, took a booth toward the front, ordered a Corona, and scoped out the place.

The Bar is an institution in Midland. Oil deals, golf dates, marriages, divorces and drunk people are all made there. They also make a pretty tasty green chile cheeseburger. On the western edge of downtown, a stone's throw from First Presbyterian Church, the building that is The Bar is long and narrow and the interior is a mishmash of paneling and wooden floors and neon beer signs and all sorts of oil-field stuff, like old well signs and long defunct oil company signs, like the Stanolind dinosaur and the Mobil flying horse. The actual bar, where people sit on barstools and heckle the bartenders, takes up the middle third of the east wall, and a tall bench hugs the opposite wall, fronted by tables and more barstools. The front third has regular booths and tables, and the back third has tables and the restrooms and the bear.

I've never gotten the actual story behind the bear, but as long as I can remember, a stuffed bear, reared up on his hind legs, has occupied the northwest corner of The Bar, right there in the back. He's usually got a cigarette between his claws because there's always some clown who thinks it'll be real clever to give the bear a cigarette, not realizing thousands before him had the same idea. Sometimes, more often than anyone would think, somebody gets way past drunk and into idiot territory and starts buying drinks for the bear. I once saw a guy order ten shots of peppermint schnapps for the bear. They say the guy drove the porcelain truck all night long, but the bear just did his usual and stood tall and still, never the worse for being a drunk smoker.

I'd been there about half a beer when Bobby Tom came in. He spotted me right away and went to the back, but happy hour was in full swing and the place was packed with people having a quickie before they headed home to dinner, or to take the kids to soccer practice or mow the lawn. He eventually made his way back to the front, resigned himself to the inevitable and sat across from me in my booth.

"Whit, why are you doing this? I really don't like seeing you."

"I just have one question, and then I'll leave you alone."

He ordered a double martini, then looked across the table at me. "Okay, shoot."

"If you wanted to do an under-the-table sort of deal, who would you call?"

"In the pipe business, you mean?"

"Yeah."

"Do I want to know why you're asking me this?"

"No, I'm pretty sure you don't." Especially since I needed the information to help my client, who just happened to be the man bagging his wife. Oh, man.

"Skeeter Dawson."

"Is he a tall, skinny guy with bow legs?"

"Looks like he's been ridin' a horse since he was in the womb. If you want a deal that won't pass the smell test, he's your man."

The waitress brought his martini and I ordered a green chile cheeseburger. "You want one?" I asked Bobby Tom.

"You buyin'?"

"I'm buyin'."

"Then, yeah, I'll take one." He looked up at the waitress. "And some fries."

We drank in silence for a while, then he said the weirdest thing. "We *are* happy."

Telling him what Thorn said to me didn't seem like a good idea, so I just smiled and nodded and said, "I'm happy for you."

He took another drink. "You never had kids."

"I don't think I can."

"Really?" That seemed to perk him up and I thought that was extra weird.

"Really."

"So you tried, but couldn't?"

"I tried, once, and didn't. Then I decided I didn't want one with George."

"Why's that?"

"Because George would have made a terrible father."

"Was he abusive? Did he smack you around?"

"No. Would it make you happy if he did?"

He smiled then, reminding me of old times. "Nah, not really. Don't get me wrong, because I do hate your guts, but I don't like it when men do that." Taking another drink of his martini, he lowered the glass, picked up the toothpick and popped the olive into his mouth. "If he didn't slap you around, why did you think he'd be a bad father?"

Some masochistic dysfunction in my psyche made me say, "He slept with prostitutes."

Slowly setting the toothpick beside his glass, Bobby Tom lost his smile and looked at me with the saddest look on his face. "Aw, Whit, I'm real sorry. I wondered why you got a divorce."

I couldn't believe it then, and can't believe it now, but I started to cry. Big, huge, fat tears popped out of my eyes way too fast to catch them and I thought I'd die of embarrassment. I'd had friends who offered to castrate George, my mom and cousins offered to put a contract out on him, and even Lurch said George shoulda been horsewhipped. But no one's support and sympathy hit me the way Bobby Tom's did. I guess because deep inside, I felt guilty about breaking up with him back in college, and knew I'd made a huge mistake, and knew how bad I'd hurt him. And there he was, handing me sympathy.

It was definitely a humbling moment.

"You gonna be okay?" he asked.

"Fine," I said, scouting for a tissue in my purse.

"How'd you find out?"

"George has a shop up in Oklahoma City. He used to go up there for several days at a time, every month. I thought I'd go up and surprise him, but it was me who got the surprise. He told me he'd never do it again, but after something like that, no way you believe it. So I sort of obsessed about it and started following him around. Turned out, he had a regular routine, with regular girls. So I left him and filed for divorce and that was that."

"And then you became a whistle-blower."

"Well, yeah."

"Remember how you always wanted to have a garden and get into politics and work just until you started having kids?"

Those tears would not stop and he wasn't helping. "I remember."

"You sure came a long way from that, didn't you?"

I nodded and kept wiping away the tears. "You always wanted to work with your dad and have a house at the lake and coach your son's Little League team, and that's just what you got. I'm happy for you, Bobby Tom. I really am."

He was quiet, staring into his glass. I half expected him to tell me about Merry and her affair, but suddenly, he looked up, smiled and said, "Yep, life is good, Whit. Things worked out for the best, I reckon."

The waitress came with our burgers and when she was gone, he said, "After this, don't come around anymore. With everything in the past, it's best."

"Okay," I said, sniffling, rubbing away the last of the tears, "but if you ever need a—"

"I won't. I can promise you, I won't."

He'd shown too much vulnerability and now he was back to being hard and cold and determined to prove to me he was happily married. I didn't make an issue of it. I just ate my green chile cheeseburger and watched the steady stream of people moving in and out of The Bar.

Suddenly, Bobby Tom set his burger down and his face turned red. "Are you okay?" I asked, concerned he was choking.

"Never better," he said in a voice that indicated anything but. His blue gaze was fixed on the table three over from our booth, on a medium-built man with salt-and-pepper hair and a face that could be on a magazine, it was so handsome. If George Hamilton and Harrison Ford had a baby, it would be that man.

Not that I thought he was attractive. I didn't. He looked like he'd worry too much about messing up his hair, or wrinkling his perfectly pressed pinstriped dress shirt that looked handmade and probably cost three hundred dollars.

Bobby Tom looked ready for battle, the veins in his neck sticking out, his eyes hard and his hands clenched into fists.

Glancing at Mr. Beautiful, I asked, "Who is that guy?"

I shoulda known, but I have to blame it on the beer and the tears that I was so clueless.

In a voice like his dad's, with a low growl behind the syllables, he bit out, "Oliver Shanks."

"Oh." I cleared my throat and made a big fuss over laying out some bills to pay for the drinks and the burgers.

He turned, slapped his hand on the money and shoved it toward me. "Keep your money. I'm paying."

"But I offered to—"

"I said, I'm payin'! Put your money away."

Waving the waitress over, he ordered another round, in spite of my protests that I needed to get home.

I drank that second one pretty fast and thanked God I'd never met Ollie Shanks. I kept thinking how horrible it would be if he came over and said hello to me, all chummylike, after I'd finally sort of buried the hatchet with Bobby Tom.

Things got a lot more weird after my third beer. For one thing, I remembered that I'd decided not to drink any more because I was thirty-one and didn't need to be goofy, or hungover. Age makes 'em hurt worse. A lot. For another, I remembered I was supposed to be at Mom's at seven for chicken spaghetti with Aunt Fred and Uncle Alvin and it was six forty-five. Then Bobby Tom said something about Ollie Shanks being a worse skank than Skeeter Dawson. I was about to ask him why when Merry came in.

Now I know I should have gotten up, said goodbye and hit the road. Anything else was bound to be a disaster, and hadn't he said earlier, I could qualify for Red Cross relief?

But of course I didn't. It was like watching a train wreck. Impossible to look away. All the time, I was thinking Merry would stomp over and be righteously offended about me having cocktails with her husband, especially since I was the first girl he ever had sex with.

Imagine my beer-induced fuzzy confusion when she waltzed over to Ollie's table and sat down, with that radiant look she'd had in Tracy Steven's. Oh, man. There was another man at the table, an older guy who faded into the woodwork next to Ollie's looks. He shook Merry's hand, then winked at her as he nodded his head toward Ollie. Sort of one of those "Hey, you're doin' him and I know it and aren't you a babe?" nods.

I'd had enough Coronas to be very brave. I said to Bobby Tom, "I know."

Without looking at me, without tearing his gaze away from his wife's open flirting with not one, but two men, he said in a very quiet voice, "I know you know."

"You wanna go home with me?"

"And do what? Sleep together for revenge?"

"No, I was thinking maybe we'd just hang out and talk."

He turned to look at me then. "I liked the sleeping together idea a lot better."

"Only because you're so mad at her. You'd feel rotten about it later."

"No, I wouldn't. Look at her. Do you think she gives a flying fuck about me? About our kids? They're at home right now with a babysitter, while she's up here in front of God and everybody, proving what a ho she is."

"Really, Bobby Tom," I said, noticing the looks we were getting, "let's get outta here. If it'll make you happy, we can walk out and make her think we're going home to sleep together. Then you can go with me to Mom's and have chicken spaghetti."

"I just ate."

"She made coconut meringue pie for dessert."

"Really?"

"No lie."

He said yes, then asked if I was serious about faking out Merry.

"If you'll swear that whole kiss in my living room thing really was all her fault."

He smiled at me then, a little lopsided. "It was totally her fault. I swear."

Narrowing my eyes, I turned my head and looked at her. Did the woman have no shame? And to think, I let her keep my favorite Stevie Ray Vaughn tape. Bitch. "Okay, Bobber-uski, let's go."

We stood up, he threw some money on the table and reached for me. It really was like old times. With one arm looped around my neck, his hand lightly brushing across my breast, we walked toward the exit. I kept my arm around him and looked up at him like I was totally mooning over him. I can admit it now, I kinda was. I guess you never really get over your first love.

I never looked at Merry. Neither did Bobby Tom. I seriously think we forgot about her, about the plan, about why we were tighter than panty hose on a fat lady. We made it out the front door and down the sidewalk to the parking lot, then he pulled me behind the building and kissed me. Somewhere in my brain, I knew it was wrong. I knew I'd regret it later. I knew he'd regret it later. But, oh, was it nice, being there, kissing Bobby Tom like I was sixteen years old and vibrating with sexual excitement and the very real possibility we'd get caught with his hand up my shirt, or down my jeans. But we weren't sixteen. We were thirty, and getting caught with his hand inside my suit jacket, caressing my breast through the flimsy lace of my Vicky's bra would have a lot greater consequences now than it would when we were sixteen.

Still, I let him, shameless hussy that I am. And I wished like everything I had no principles so I could take him home and make that awful bed squeak a symphony.

I finally pulled away, and it scared the hell out of me how hard it was to do.

"I'm sorry," he said, because that's who he is.

"Don't be," I said, because that's who I am. "Are you ready to go to Mom's?"

"I'm going to pass," he said, "because I need to get home to the kids." He reached up and pushed my hair behind my ear. "You still have the most beautiful hair, Whit."

I stared up at him and felt a great bittersweet sadness.

"I'm filing for divorce. When it's over, I'll have three kids to raise by myself because no way she's getting them." He looked so sad, it broke my heart. "They shoulda been your kids. We should be going home right now to your garden and a Little League game and great sex."

My breath caught in my throat.

Grasping my shoulders, he leaned down and kissed me again, sort of soft and sweet. "I was just never enough for you, was I?"

"What do you mean?"

"You were always fascinated with badass guys who live life on the edge. I was always steady and safe and boring."

"You were never boring."

"Tell me you're sorry."

"That I married George?"

"That you blew me off."

Looking up at his gorgeous blue eyes, his dear face, his firm lips, still wet from kissing me, I had to give him an honest answer. "I'll regret it until I die."

That made him happy. I could tell. "Goodbye, Whitney."

Watching him walk away, I leaned against the sunwarmed bricks of the building and wished I could turn back time, to that summer, nine years ago, when I decided I was too boring, that I needed something wicked and wild and exciting to make me complete. How could I have known then, nothing outside of myself would ever make me wicked and wild? I was doomed to be a CPA, an anal-retentive neat nut who'd really rather stay home and read a good book than go out to a martini bar, or ride on the back of a Harley, or have sex on an elevator. I like sex in a bed just fine. Better, actually.

I was still holding up the wall when an old, beat up 4-Runner pulled into the alley and stopped right in front of me.

"Hi, Ed."

"Who was that guy?"

"What guy?"

"The one you were making out with in plain sight?"

I glanced up and noticed sixteen stories of windows, all looking down on the alley behind The Bar. Ed's building. Then I looked at Ed, who looked very unhappy with me. Then I burst into tears.

Yeah, definitely I had PMS.

Ed took me to Mom's and gave me a lecture all the way over, about the committee and my respectability and stuff like that. When we pulled up at Mom's, I looked over at him and said, "You are so full of it, Edward."

"What's that supposed to mean?"

"You're mad as hell I kissed my old boyfriend."

"Maybe I am." He killed the engine but made no move to get out. "Why'd you do it, Pink? He's married now, you know."

"Not for long. He's getting a divorce because Merry's boinking Ollie Shanks."

"You planning on marrying him when he's free?"

Bobby Tom would be a peach of a client for him. So would Merry. But Ed didn't look the slightest bit interested from a business standpoint and that's how I knew this bugged him even more than he was letting on.

Geez, since when was I such a femme fatale? Going around

wounding men with my seductive wiles. Yeah right. "Ed, I think I have PMS."

"Thanks for sharing. Answer the question."

"No, Ed. I don't ever want to get married again."

He looked out the windshield at a couple of mockingbirds, splashing in a puddle made by the sprinklers. "Not all men are like George."

"That's not why I don't want to get married."

"Why then?"

The beer made me say, "Because I don't think I have it in me to love someone like I'm supposed to."

"Maybe that's because you've never met the right man."

"Maybe. I guess I'll reserve the decision until later."

Out of the blue, he said, "Sleep with me, Pink."

"Now? But Mom's got chicken spaghetti in there, and coconut meringue pie."

"Okay, we'll eat spaghetti and pie, then we're going back to my house and get naked."

"What about that waiting thing?"

Grabbing my arm, he tugged me closer to him, until we were nose to nose. "Pink, I wanted to kill the son of a bitch, and that scared the shit out of me. I don't do this. I don't care this much. Do you understand?"

"Sure, Ed. You think if we sleep together, we'll be more committed, and I won't go kissing other men in alleys."

"Are you making light of this?"

"No way. I've wanted to do it since five minutes after I met you, and it's got nothing to do with being love-starved and lonely, or that you're maybe the very best-looking man I know, or that you kiss better than any male on the planet."

"Then what does it have to do with?" he whispered, his gaze traveling across my face.

"I like you, Ed."

"I like you, too."

"But I'm having second thoughts about you because of that lawsuit."

"Do you still think Ollie Shanks is an innocent man, about to be crucified by me and all those greedy landowners?"

"I think he's a bounder, fooling around with another man's wife like that, but that doesn't make him fair game for a lawsuit over something that's not his fault."

"Suppose I told you it is his fault, that hiring Sam to prove Bert is switching the pipe is a smoke screen to cover up something even worse?"

"Hmm, I don't think so. I'd need details."

"Is this a test to see how bad I want to have sex with you?"

"No. I know how bad you want it. I just really want to like you like I did before, and I don't think that's gonna happen until you tell me how you can justify what you're doing."

"You're a very difficult woman, Pink."

"So you'll tell me?"

"I'll tell you, but if you spread it around, I'll have to cut out your tongue and shove it up that tight little—"

"Ed!"

He laughed as he let me go and got out of the car. We went inside Mom's and I introduced him to my aunt and uncle. "This is Mom's sister, Frederica, but everyone calls her Fred."

Five feet tall, with a blond curly cap of hair, twinkling blue eyes, a round face and a rounder body, Aunt Fred is a real character. She and Mom are almost complete opposites, but get along famously. Fred winked at me and smiled at Ed. "So, Ed, whatdya think of our Pink?"

He looked confused. Like he had no idea how was he supposed to answer that. Finally, he said, "Your Pink is a nice girl."

Fred frowned and made a negative game-show buzzer noise. "Wrong answer, Ed. So sorry. You have to leave now, but we have some lovely parting gifts."

Mom laughed. "Fred, behave. Ed, ignore her." She pointed at Alvin, who looked like he always did, gnomelike, with prematurely white, snowy hair, and a face full of character, lined with years in the sun on construction jobs from as far away as China and Argentina, to as close to home as Dallas and Houston. "This is my brother-in-law, Alvin," Mom said.

He and Ed shook hands, and as he always did, Alvin said just the right thing and made Ed feel like he'd been in the family since the beginning of time. I really love that about Alvin. Shoot, I love everything about Alvin. Fred, too. I sometimes hope I'll be just like her when I'm her age. That's only eighteen years from now, so I suppose I should get started pretty soon.

We went in to eat and I wished like everything I hadn't eaten that burger because I love chicken spaghetti and I could hardly eat any at all. Mom noticed. "Pink, I thought you liked chicken spaghetti."

"I do. I'm just a little queasy."

Wrong thing to say. Fred said, "Let me get you some of my herbal stuff. I've got just what you need."

"Don't take it," Alvin warned. "You'll blow up like the Hindenberg. What you need is old-fashioned Pepto-Bismol."

"The best thing for a queasy stomach is Alka-Seltzer," Mom announced, scooting her chair back, on her way to fetch a couple of fizzing tablets I needed as much as a hog needs a sidesaddle.

"I think the best thing for an upset stomach is plenty of bed rest," Ed said, twirling his spaghetti around his fork.

Fred announced, "*Ding! Ding!* You are correct, Ed! You can step up for sudden death now."

He grinned at her and polished off his food.

Mom came back with the Alka-Seltzer and I took it to the kitchen, dropped the tablets in a glass of water, then poured it down the drain. When I went back in the dining room, she asked, "Better?"

"Lots."

"Good. Maybe you'll feel better for pie in a while."

"Yeah, Mom, I'm sure I will."

Ed laid his fork down and looked at Fred. "You must be the aunt who nabbed Mister Bob."

"That'd be me, yes." Fred slanted a look at me. "The lady who bought it is a teacher."

"You're kidding."

"Not at all."

"How old is she?"

"In her sixties, I imagine. Said she wanted Mister Bob for the human body unit."

"Which human body unit?" Alvin asked. "Hers?"

Ed laughed, and I guess we all did, because hey, it was a funny thought. Then Ed asked, "When will she be home?"

"Next week."

"Does she have any idea that the whole nation wonders where Mister Bob is?"

"None. Where she's at, they don't get CNN."

"Do you think we'll have any problem getting the disk from her?"

"Heavens, no," Fred said. "She'll open the box, hand over the disk and there'll be an end to it."

Mom looked over at me, her expression worried. "Are you still getting doggie doo and phone calls?"

"He mailed me some dog poo yesterday and now the postman hates me. Last night, he called and I told him somebody has to point out that the emperor is naked."

They all stared at me. When I didn't say anything else, Ed said, "That's it?"

"That's it."

"What a dumb thing to say."

"Funny, that's just what he said."

I helped Mom clear the table while Fred and Alvin ran Ed through the third degree. Then we had pie. Then Ed and I left.

In the car, he said, "I like your aunt and uncle."

"They liked you, too."

"Is all of your family like that?"

"Not hardly. Mom had nine brothers and sisters, and it's split down the middle, with half of them normal, fun, ordinary people, and the other half mean, nasty and kinda insane." I glanced at him. "The jury's still out about which side Mom fits on."

He laughed. "You don't mean that."

"She has her moments, but yeah, Mom's great."

Ed drove me back to The Bar to get Sam's car, then followed me home so I could leave it parked in the lot. Thinking I'd like to get a toothbrush and a sleepshirt, just in case I stayed all night at Ed's, I told him I needed to go upstairs for a minute and he said to hurry.

When I went inside, I knew something was wrong. The bedroom light was on, and I knew I hadn't left it on when I left that morning. The refrigerator door was wide open and I knew for certain I hadn't left it like that, because there was hardly anything in there worth opening it for. Besides, I'm very energy conscious. Partly because I'm a closet environmentalist, and partly because Lurch worked in the energy business and lectured a lot about wasting energy. The television was on, another no-no, tuned to a Hispanic station, the volume low.

Deciding I didn't want to go and see who, or what was in my bedroom, I turned around and went back out to Ed's car. "You better come check this out."

"What's wrong?"

"Somebody's been in my apartment and they may still be there."

He opened his door and got out, then turned and bent over. When he raised up, he had a gun in his hand. A big, cool-looking gun, one of those square, black ones like the good guys carry in blow-'em-up and save the world movies. "Ed, what a big gun you have."

"Baby, I love it when you talk dirty."

I followed him to the doorway, but hung back like a big chicken while he went inside. Within forty seconds—I know because I counted—Ed yelled, "Call 9-1-1!"

"Why?"

"There's a dead guy in your bathtub."

My whole body began to shake. "Who is it?"

He came around the corner, his gun now tucked in the waistband of his jeans. "Larry Sparks."

"Sparky's dead in my bathtub? Are you sure?"

"Yeah, Pink, I'm sure."

The CFO of Marvel, offed in my apartment. Holy shit. I was going down. Way down.

He went to the phone since I hadn't yet and dialed emergency. When he was done, he hung up and came close. "Your stalker did it, I'm sure."

"How can you be sure?"

He sighed and wrapped me up in his arms. “There’s a pile of dog shit in there with him.”

So much for thinking maybe Sparky was the Dog Doo Stalker. I remembered the phone call. *What would it take to scare you a lot?* How about a dead guy in your bathtub?

Ding! Ding! You’re correct Mr. Psycho Dog Doo Stalker. You can step up for sudden death now.

Chapter 9

The police estimated Sparky's time of death at somewhere between five and six o'clock, when I was at The Bar with Bobby Tom, so I was off the hook as a suspect, thank God. They were much more interested in the Dog Doo Stalker than they'd been after he tried to haul me out of Mabel's, so I told them everything, including the guy's warning that I should back off the pipe sales. I had to explain about how I was checking into Bert's shady dealings, which interested them because of Jessica's murder.

I asked if Bert was a suspect in her murder, and the detective said, "I can't discuss an ongoing investigation, but I will say we have a very good lead on a suspect."

Ed frowned at me, I suppose because he was afraid I'd mention that I was out in the oil field the night she was found. I frowned back because I hate it when people assume I'm an idiot. Like I'd mention that night to the detective?

"Why would your stalker kill Mr. Sparks?" the detective asked.

"I'm sorry, I don't know. Maybe Sparky knew something and he killed him to shut him up."

Ed said, "Maybe the stalker was here, waiting for you to get home, and Sparky showed up. They might have argued. Or maybe Sparky surprised him and he killed him accidentally."

"If that's the case," the detective said, "why would he bother with the dog shit?" He shook his head as he looked at me. "I think he killed Mr. Sparks and left him in your bathtub to scare you into giving up that last disk you're supposed to hand over to the feds."

I held on to my shaking nerves, just barely. "He did a bang-up job of scaring me, but I'm still going to hand over the disk."

"We need to put a recorder and a trace on your phone."

"That's fine, but I don't think he'll call again. He's too smart. Besides, I'm going to go stay at my mother's for a while. Things around here are a little too dicey." Maybe living with Mom hadn't been appealing a few days ago, but at that moment, I wanted nothing more than to hole up in her house, with the security alarm on.

Ed and I didn't have sex that night. By the time the cops hauled Sparky away and finished asking me a bajillion questions, it was midnight and I was so tired, I couldn't say my name. Much less manage any *oh, babys,* or *faster, Eds,* or *yes, yes, yeses.* So Ed took me to Mom's and went on home.

Mom was supersweet, helping me get ready for bed because I was in a zombie sort of a trance. She made me some herb tea and put me to bed and tucked me in, like she did when I was little. Then she sat on the edge of my bed and talked to me. "You going to be able to sleep?"

"Probably," I said around a yawn. "I know you slipped a mickey in the tea."

She petted my hair. "I love you, baby."

"I love you, too, Mom." I could see the worry in her eyes and she looked older than I ever remembered. "It'll be okay. In just a week, I'll have the disk, Ed and I will go to Washington and it'll all be over."

The phone rang and we both started, then looked at it like we'd look at a two-headed monster holding babies in its mouths. She slowly reached for it and answered on the fourth ring. Her eyes widened and I just knew it was the Dog Doo Stalker.

"No, that's not possible." She hung up and patted me.

"Was it him?"

"Somebody with Larry King. They want you to be on the show tomorrow night."

The phone rang again and she answered it on the first ring. After a bit, she said, "No, not now, not tomorrow, not ever. It's late. Give it a rest and don't call again."

No sooner had she hung up and said, "That was CNN," then it rang again. She jerked the phone up and barked, "What?" Then she rolled her eyes and mouthed "Lurch." "She's fine. You want to talk to her?"

I shook my head so hard, I loosened my brain, I'm sure.

"She's asleep, but I'll tell her you called." She listened some more, then said a little irritably, "For God's sake, Jim, she didn't ask for this guy to stalk her, or knock off a guy and leave him in her bathtub." Again she was quiet. Then she said, "Would you have had her keep her mouth shut and let those people cheat millions of investors?" She stood up, indicating he was really pissing her off. "You are a moron. Her firm is considered the very best in the world, and it was a very big deal that they hired her. It was an even bigger deal when she got promoted to senior manager, and...what? Jesus, you are a real bastard to say something like that. Can't you just give her a little credit? Would it hurt you so much to let her have her due? She worked her ass off to get as far as she did, then gave it all up to do the right thing. But all you can think about is the money, you stingy skinflint. I didn't see her picking at you when you let Nelda burn up half your retirement. So how 'bout you lay off and shut the hell up?" She slammed down the phone and looked at me and smiled. "That was your father."

"Really? I had no idea."

Mom smoothed the sheets, cut off the light, left on the one in the closet without me asking and went to the door. "You holler if you need anything, okay?"

"Okay. Thanks, Mom."

"Now get some sleep, baby."

I closed my eyes and slipped into a dreamless, drug-induced sleep.

At seven the next morning, Mom woke me up with a fresh cup of coffee and a buttery croissant with blackberry jam she said Fred brought for me. I ate slowly, my brain finally assimilating what happened the day before.

"Pink, you need to be awake here in just a bit. Senator Santorelli called and said he'd call back at seven-thirty to talk to you."

Oh, man. A dead guy in my bathtub looked real bad, but when the dead guy was the CFO of Marvel, it looked especially gloomy. Would the committee stick with the immunity? Or would they throw it out, claiming I was just too neck-deep in controversy?

Steve called at seven-twenty-five. "Hey," he said in a warm, friendly voice, "how are you?"

"Let's just say I won't be taking any baths at my apartment for a while."

"Why didn't you tell me someone's stalking you?"

"I know it sounds stupid, but I really didn't think he was a serious threat. He always leaves the same note, and the same package, and his wee-hour death threat phone calls have gotten downright chatty."

"Pink, he threatened to skewer your, uh, well, he threatened bodily harm. Didn't that concern you?"

"At first, it did, but the Dallas police weren't terribly interested in hunting down a dog doo stalker and bringing him to justice. I finally just bought a pooper-scooper and went on with things."

"I really wish you would have told me. I could have gotten some results."

"I'm sorry I didn't. If I had, maybe Sparky would still be alive. Even though he was a crook, he didn't deserve to be shot and laid out with dog poop."

"Don't blame yourself, Pink. You've got enough to carry around without this."

I didn't say anything because I was pretty sure I would start crying. Damn PMS.

"Maybe it will make you feel better to know I've tracked down the Maloney problem."

I did perk up a bit at that. "Really?"

"Turns out, he set up the whole thing, sent the notice, came to your office, conducted a bogus audit, for the sole purpose of scaring you into losing the disk. He's nothing but a rogue agent. I thought he might have been put up to it by someone at Marvel, but he appears to have acted on his own."

I wasn't surprised. Mom told me how an audit should work, and no way Mr. Maloney was even close. "Thank you, Steve. What will happen to Maloney?"

"He'll be taken out and shot at dawn."

"Gosh, Steve, that's kinda harsh."

"I guess so, especially when he's still singing soprano after somebody landed a swift kick to his family jewels."

I blushed, sitting right there in bed, talking to a U.S. senator. "They told you about that?"

He laughed. "Oh, yeah. They also told me Mr. Maloney was verbally abused, his parentage slandered and generally told off in no uncertain terms."

"Some people just have no class. I'd certainly never do anything like that. My mama raised a lady."

"You know what?"

"What?"

"I'm really looking forward to getting to know you better."

Guilt washed over me because I was leading him on, and I didn't like it. I wanted to be open and honest and say, "You know, Steve, I think you're a real nice guy, and not half-bad in the looks department, and if I hadn't met Ed, you'd be right up there at the top of the list of men I'd love to hang out with. But I did meet Ed and I don't know what it is about him that makes me a little crazy. I only know I like it. And I like Ed."

Of course I said nothing of the kind. I swallowed and said, "Me, too," and asked God to forgive me for lying to cover my own backside.

Me and Mom managed to get out of the driveway later that morning without running over an eager-beaver reporter who was determined to get a couple of sound bites. I asked her to stop by Donut King and while she waited in the car, I went inside to buy a few boxes for the office. I guess I was still in buying friends mode. After a dead guy showed up in my bathtub, no one would want to be around me. I didn't really think donuts would help, but it was all I could think of.

In the store, I ran into Roy again. Talk about awkward. Sparky had been his boss. I said hello and sort of held my breath, waiting to see how Roy reacted to seeing me.

He gave me a sad smile. "You okay, Pink?"

Feeling a certain amount of relief that he didn't go off on me, I let out the breath and replied, "I'm okay. Scared, but okay." I glanced at the boxes in his beefy hands. "So you're still in Midland?"

"I was set to go back to Dallas yesterday, but after Sparky…uh, well, I need to be here a while longer. Also, I need to hire a few contract guys for some fieldwork we need done before we start selling off production."

Immediately, a picture of Lucky popped into my head. "I know a guy who'd be great, Roy. He's a hard worker, and needs the job."

"Great. Write down his name and number and I'll give him a call."

Scrounging for a slip of paper in my purse, I said, "He doesn't have a phone, but try Buster's. He works there part-time. His name is Lucky Barnes."

"Thanks, Pink." Roy moved a bit closer and patted my shoulder. "And really, take care of yourself."

I said I would, then watched him leave before I turned to order my donuts.

When me and Mom got to the office, there were no reporters, and Mom said that's because they didn't know where I worked. All of the staff, except for Gert, who stayed in her office, went nuts asking questions and Mom let them, I guess because she knew no one would get any work done if they were gossiping about it all day.

After I told them about Sparky, they all drifted back to their desks and I went to work on Mrs. Colder's division orders, looking to see if any of them varied from the producer payment interests. Mrs. Colder might be a nutty old lady with a pistol, but she was dead on the money with her suspicions. Every single one of her interests had been cut in half.

Sam was out of the office again and I debated what to do about Skeeter Dawson. I had no car, having left it at the apartments when Ed drove me to Mom's, so going to see Skeeter wasn't an option. Not at the moment.

Mom came to my cube at eleven-thirty. She was definitely hovering, checking to see if I was okay, obviously worried because a stranger who killed people was after her baby. I felt sorry for her and tried to allay her fears, but she was not to be deterred. She insisted I go to lunch with her and took me to El Corazon, my other favorite Mexican food restaurant.

After lunch, I had her drop me at the apartment to get the car. I hadn't told her about wrecking mine yet, so I had to wait for her to leave before I went to get Sam's. She made me promise not to go upstairs by myself, and after she drove away, I was tempted to do it anyway, but I didn't because I was kinda freaked out, and after all, a promise is a promise. I also saw a couple of people hanging around my side of the complex and I was sure they were reporters. No way I wanted to be interviewed. My fifteen minutes of fame was stretching out way too long.

Back at the office, I spent several hours working on Mrs. Colder's division orders, the legal documents that direct an oil company how to disbursc royalty income off of the wells it operates. I admit, I had a hard time concentrating, the temptation to go see Skeeter nagging at me. In light of all that had happened, I really needed something to do that would make me feel like I was in control, like I had some kind of choice in my destiny. Close to four, I gave in to temptation and looked up Skeeter's number. There it was, in bold, black letters: Dawson Pipe—Skeeter Dawson, Owner/Manager. I ran my finger across to the phone number, wrote it on the back of one of my business cards, then jotted down the address. Skeeter's yard was way the hell out of town, on Cotton Flat Road.

In the car, the air conditioner wouldn't blow anything but hot air, so I shut it off and rolled down the windows. Out on Loop 250, headed toward the southwest side of Midland at sixty miles an hour, my hair kept blowing in my face, but rolling up the windows was out of the question. Hell has nothing on Midland in August.

Skeeter's yard looked exactly as I thought it would. Where most pipe yards are neatly organized, like Bobby Tom and Thorn's, with the racks in rows, the pipe tagged and inventoried by diameter, the ground free of clutter and weeds, Skeeter's yard looked like Vietnam in '68. The pipe, what there was of it, was scattered about on the ground, some of it half-buried in the west Texas sand. A couple of racks stood lonely and useless toward the back of the yard, which was only fenced on three sides because the fourth side had fallen down. Gigantic weeds grew everywhere, the kind that die, come loose in the sixty-mile-an-hour spring dust storms, and become tumbleweeds, rolling across the road in front of motorists.

I parked the Ford and got out, went to the small trailer house that I assumed was Skeeter's office and knocked on the door. No one answered. I tried the knob and it was locked.

Walking around, I climbed up onto an old galvanized steel trash can and peered in a window, cupping my hands around my eyes to cut the glare. The trailer was a continuation of the yard, a disaster area of boxes and trash and an old, rusty bicycle. This was no one's office.

Back in the car, I wondered where Skeeter officed. Did he work out of his house? I dialed the number I'd gotten out of the phone book and got an answering machine. I declined to leave a message.

I drove north on Cotton Flat, past the Interstate, then stopped at a convenience store to check the phone book. I got Skeeter's home address and phone, then took off for the far north side of Midland.

Green Tree Country Club sits a couple of miles north of town, out on Midland Drive. The original eighteen holes are surrounded by large homes, most built in the early eighties when Midland was booming, when dentists became oil men and Rolls Royce opened a dealership and a tiny, one-bedroom apartment rented for the same as a tiny, one-bedroom in New York City. The newer, north nine is surrounded by homes built in the mid- to late nineties when the oil business stabilized a little and those who made it through the bust gained back some of the wealth that built Midland.

Skeeter lived on the original eighteen, across the street from the houses that backed up to the golf course. His house backed up to an open field of mesquite and cactus and tumbleweeds. I parked in his driveway, noting his lawn and house were in a lot better shape than his pipe yard. A middle-aged woman in tight, knit purple pants, dirty pink slippers and a T-shirt that said, "Do It Wild at The Wild West Club" answered the door.

"Mrs. Dawson?"

She grinned, revealing a gold tooth. "Naw, I ain't Miz Dawson. I'm the cleanin' lady. Maxine's down to the beauty shop. You can catch her there at the Blue place."

"Actually, I'm looking for Mr. Dawson. Is he home?"

The woman jerked her head to the left. "He's up at the club, playin' golf, or cards, or somethin'. Go ask at the desk and they'll tell ya. Skeeter's there all the time."

I thanked her and turned to leave, but stopped when she said, "You ain't from the gov'ment, are ya?"

"No."

Her gaze traveled from my head to my toes and back again. "Take some advice, and stay away from Skeeter. He's a nasty old pervert and you look like a real nice girl."

"To tell the truth, I just want to ask him a simple question. Won't take more than a few minutes."

"Yer not lookin' to buy some pipe?"

"No."

Her eyes narrowed. "You with the IRS?"

"Not hardly. I'm lookin' to find out who he sold some pipe to a few days ago."

"Skeeter don't like people askin' questions. Been runnin' from the IRS forever, and he figgers anybody askin' questions is bound to be a spy, out for the goods on 'im."

Good grief. What a scumbag. Skeeter, that is. Not the cleaning lady. "What's your name?" I asked her.

"Caroline."

Man, talk about a name not fitting somebody. I tried not to look surprised. "I'm Pink."

"Nice to meet ya, Pink." She looked over at the Ford. "No offense, but you got one butt-ugly car."

Stupidly offended anyway, I said, "It gets me where I need to go."

"Sure 'nuff. Well, you take care, and don't let that ol' side-winder scare you, hear?"

I agreed and headed off for the country club. The front desk lady sent me to the golf shop, and the guy in the golf shop sent me to the grill room, to wait for Skeeter to finish his round of golf, which would be thirty minutes or so. I watched a soap with the bartender, but after three glasses of tea, I had to go pee. In the hallway, I ran into Roy Kipper.

"What brings you out here, Pink? Have you taken up golf?"

"Oh, no, just a bit of business."

"Thanks for giving me your friend's name," Roy said. "I called and visited with him and he's all set to start to work."

"That's great, Roy. Thanks a lot."

"Well, I guess I'll see you round," he said with a nod and a smile. "I'll be in Midland another couple of weeks."

I said goodbye and started back toward the grill room. I was halfway there when I saw Skeeter come in from the golf course. The instant he spotted me, his face paled and he rushed for the door. I gave chase, but he was in his car and out of the parking lot before I could get to Sam's Ford.

Figuring he went home, I drove over and got to his house as he was pulling out of the drive, Caroline in the front seat with him. I decided he was taking her home, and followed him all the way to a neat little house on the west side. When he pulled up to let her out, I drove around and blocked his car so he couldn't leave.

He slammed out of his car and stalked toward me. "I shoulda finished you off when I had the chance! What the hell do you want?"

While I got out of the Ford, Caroline hovered close by, looking worried. "It's got nothing to do with you," I replied. "It's all about Bert."

"I don't gotta tell you nothin'."

Yeah, he did. And I knew just how to get him to tell me everything. "I happen to have a personal relationship with a guy named Ronnie Maloney, who works for the IRS. He'd be real interested in your midnight cash transactions, Skeeter. First off, I'd say it's a no-brainer you won't be picking up that cash on your tax return. And second, I'd bet you don't have a bill of lading for that crappy pipe. You probably stole it outta somebody's yard."

He drew himself up and clenched his fists at his side. "That's a load of bullshit! I paid for that pipe, fair and square, and I got the cleared checks to prove it."

"Who'd you buy it from? Somebody else who stole it? Hot pipe is hot pipe, bucko."

"I bought it from Marvel Energy."

Whoa! I hadn't expected that. "I know most of the people at Marvel, so tell me who sold it to you and maybe I'll start to believe you."

"Guy named Neil Dollar, right here in the Midland office."

I'd heard the name, although I didn't know the man. I hadn't ever actually met any of the Midland office personnel at Marvel. "If what you say is true, I want you to sign a letter saying you sold Bert Shanks a load of crappy pipe that's nowhere near casing quality."

Skeeter looked like he was gonna be sick. "Why do you want to know all this? What's it to you?"

"I want to hang Bert Shanks up by his balls."

"Did he do you wrong, or somethin'?"

"Let's just say, he screwed a friend of mine, and I intend to make him pay."

Skeeter took a step back. "Suppose I don't give you what you want?"

"Then the IRS will be all over you like syrup on pancakes."

"How do I know *you're* not lying? Maybe there is no Ronnie Maloney."

"Tell you what, why don't you call the IRS and ask 'em. Or better yet, I'll get Ronnie to come see you in person and he can show you his ID. Would that make you a believer?"

Skeeter gave up. "All right, dammit! Come out to the house in the morning and I'll get you what you want."

"No, Skeeter, that won't work. I want the letter now, on Dawson Pipe letterhead. We'll go to your office, which I assume is at your house because it's sure not at your yard, and you can write the letter there."

He darted a look at Caroline. "You go with us and type the letter, and if you say one word about this to Maxine, your ass is grass. Understand?"

Caroline made a face, but nodded.

An hour later, I had my letter, duly signed and officially stating that Skeeter sold crappy, used pipe to Bert Shanks. I offered to drive Caroline home and she looked grateful. In the car, she said she'd been married four times, and was thirty-four, which blew my original guess that she was middle-aged. She was only three years older than me. But what blew my mind the most was when she said she was about to be a grandmother. She had a son named Cary when she was fifteen, and he was now nineteen and married, living down at Big Lake, his wife about to have a baby.

"Is Cary your only child?" I asked.

"Yep. After I had him, they had to take everythin' out, on account of I had those cyst things real bad." She eyed my middle. "You don't have no kids, do you?"

"No." I looked down at my belly. "Can you tell?"

"Sure. You still got skinny hips. Anybody has a baby, them hips'll spread like butter in a hot skillet."

Looking at Caroline, I'd say she had pretty big hips. But she had really big boobs, too, so it sort of evened out.

"How 'bout you?" she asked. "You ever been married?"

"Once, but it didn't work out. He cheated on me."

"Only had one husband didn't cheat. The other three was way too pecker happy, if you know what I mean."

"Uh, yeah, I know what you mean."

"Finally figgered it out. If a man don't got no problem screwin' people outta money, he won't have no problem screwin' other women. If he cheats at cards, he'll cheat on his wife."

Remembering what Sam had said about Ed, I felt queasy.

After I dropped Caroline at her small, neat house, I used the cell phone and called the detective who was looking into Sparky's murder to tell him about Skeeter's pipe purchases. I explained that Marvel always sells their used pipe and equipment through a broker and it was very weird for someone in the company to be selling it directly. He seemed pretty bored with the whole conversation, which ticked me off. "The stalker told me to back off the pipe sales," I reminded him.

"So you think whoever's selling that pipe is the stalker?"

"It could be."

"Marvel is having hard times, so they probably started selling it without a broker, to save the fee."

"It's possible, but doesn't it make sense to check it out?"

He grew impatient, his voice becoming sharper. "We've already questioned and ruled out everyone in Marvel's Midland office as a suspect. The stalker wants you to back off of anything connected to Marvel, so maybe you should take his advice and leave those people alone."

"You're not going to ask about the pipe sales?"

"I don't think the pipe sales have anything to do with Mr. Sparks's murder, but I'll ask." He hung up then, and I knew he wasn't going to ask, wasn't going to follow up on the pipe sales at all. Clearly, the man thought I was a nut. Unfortunately, he wasn't alone in his opinion.

Chapter 10

Okay, so the detective blew me off. I'd go check out the pipe sales at Marvel on my own. At least I'd know for sure if they were on the up-and-up.

In the meantime, I'd managed to prove Bert was indeed cheating Ollie, and that was a major accomplishment. No way would I let the negative detective ruin the feeling of success zipping through me. I turned on the radio and sang along to the Goo Goo Dolls on the way home. It wasn't until I got to the apartments that I remembered I wasn't supposed to go there.

That put a damper on my little happy place, but not completely. I decided I'd go up, get some clothes, then head to Mom's and all would be well. She thought I was out to dinner, and it was only eight o'clock, so I was still good on time.

I parked the Ford and got out, checked for lurking reporters and didn't see a soul in sight, except for a guy in a Kid Rock sort of hat, sitting out by the duck pond, smoking a cigar.

I'd seen him out there before and figured the missus kicked him out to smoke. Breathing a sigh of relief that the coast was clear, I headed toward the building. It wasn't until I got to the breezeway where my stairs are located that I saw a figure in the shadows. My heart skipped a beat and I sucked in a quick, startled breath.

He moved out of the shadows behind the stairs and into the yellow light cast by the bug bulbs. "Hey, Whitney, hope you don't mind me stoppin' by, but I wanted to thank you proper for gettin' me that job."

Before I knew what he was about, Lucky Barnes hauled me next to him and granted the wish I'd held so fondly when I was in the sixth grade. Trouble was, he was about eighteen years too late. And Ed was way right about his kissing ability. Not great. Kinda wet. He shocked me so much it was a couple of seconds before my brain issued the command to my hands to push him away. A blinding light flashed around my head and I blinked, turning toward the sound of a voice yelling my name. The light flashed again and I realized it was a camera.

Mother of God. A reporter had snapped a picture of me kissing Lucky Barnes, who had just taken a job with Marvel. It wasn't gonna look good, or do anything at all to bolster my credibility. I knew how things like that went. An innocent nothing would be turned into a gigantic something. The Marvel legal team would make it look like I was spying, or milking information out of Lucky. Never mind that the poor man was practically illiterate and wouldn't know a stock option if it bit him on the ass.

What was left of my little happy place burst into flames and sank into the swamp of despair. Man, oh, man. I was so toast.

* * *

Ed lives in Old Midland, the original residential section of the city built in the forties, fifties and early sixties. The homes range from small to mansion, the trees are mature, and it's generally very nice. When I was little, we lived at the edge of Old Midland in a three-bedroom sixties ranch. Ed lives on an older edge, in a three-bedroom with a library and a very pointy roof. His house is a fixer-upper with a lot of potential, with hardwood floors and neat stuff like redwood paneling in the den. I hadn't been there since Ed moved in, but a friend lived there when I was in high school, so I was up with the layout.

He answered the door in his boxer shorts. "Hey, Pink."

I stepped inside and said, "Ed, I'm in trouble."

Grabbing my hand, he led me toward the back of the house, down a hall to the den. Ed's den is decorated in early-seventies disco bachelor cowboy. An interesting variety of orange leatherette, dark Mediterranean, faded barnwood and a light fixture that looks like a wagon wheel. "You should have my couch. It'd go great with your light."

"Have a seat." He tossed aside some files laying on the formal tuxedo sofa, upholstered in what was once cream but was now coffee. And tea. And maybe some spaghetti sauce.

"Nice sofa."

"It was my sister's from before she had kids."

"Before?" I checked out the stain closest to me.

"And a little while after." He sat next to me and wrapped an arm around my shoulders, drawing me close. "Come here and tell me your problem."

As briefly as possible, I did. Ed didn't say anything for a long time. He just sat there with his long, tan, hairy legs stretched out, crossed at the ankle, resting on the coffee table, and his hand rubbing little circles on my arm. Finally, he said, "I knew you wouldn't lay off the Shankses' deal."

"It all worked beautifully, Ed. If Lucky hadn't shown up, and that stupid jerk hadn't taken my picture, everything would be great."

"But Lucky did show up, and that guy did take your picture, which even now is being forwarded to every news service in the country and will be on the front cover of a lot of newspapers. You were already fairly interesting, but after Sparky gettin' offed and laid out in your bathtub, you're downright fascinating."

Turning my face into his neck, I sighed heavily. "Ed, what am I gonna do?"

"I can't see that you can do anything. And why would you? The whole world may see you as a sneaky woman, but all you care about is the finance committee, and making sure they leave your immunity in place. They aren't going to withdraw it because you kissed a Midland hick who works contract for Marvel."

"What about Santorelli? The whole reason we aren't having sex is because of him. Don't you think he might change his opinion?"

"I've been thinking about that, and I'm not so sure your Mom's got it right."

"Why?"

"If he had the hots for you, he'd call and ask you out."

Eh-oh. "Um, Ed, actually, he did."

Reaching for my chin, he lifted my face and looked at me with a serious lawyerlike expression. "Why didn't you tell me?"

"I just didn't think it was important."

"Pink, he's a United States senator, one who chairs the committee that holds your future in their hands. Don't you see how inappropriate it is for him to ask you out, and the impact this has on your situation? I'm not just the guy who has it bad for you, I'm your attorney. Would you try to remember that?"

"It wasn't like that. I called him about the IRS agent, and he said he'd get back to me, and when he called back, he asked if I'd have dinner with him sometime after the hearing's over."

Ed stared down at me, and I swear, I could see a little pulse in his temple.

"Are you mad?"

"Insanely jealous would be more like it."

"Really?" That made me very happy, sick woman that I am.

"Are you interested in him?"

"I would be, if I hadn't met you," I answered honestly. "He's actually a nice guy, and kinda funny."

"What did you tell him?"

"I said yes, because I didn't want to make him mad, but I figured I could weasel out when the hearing's over and the committee's done with me."

Ed stared at me for a long time and then, all of a sudden, he kissed me. I mean, he *kissed* me. Maybe it was stress, or PMS, but that was absolutely, bar none, the best kiss I'd ever had in my whole thirty-one years on earth. Man, is Ed good at kissing. It's the way he holds me, so close, but not too tight, and his hands always seem to be in just the right places, and he has really great lips, and I know this sounds weird, but he has this smell, that's just Ed, that makes me crazy.

He stopped kissing me, much to my disappointment, and gathered me up next to him again. "So what's on the agenda tomorrow?"

"I'm going to see Neil Dollar at Marvel and find out who's selling off pipe."

"I think you need to leave it alone, Pink. Let the police check into it."

"You know they won't. That detective as much as said so."

He was quiet for a while, then finally said with a heavy sigh, "Just be careful."

"Ed, what should I do about the picture?"

"Damage control. Call the senator in the morning and tell him the whole story, just like you told me. Otherwise, it's not going to look good. I really don't like that the guy asked you out, but there's not a lot I can do about it right now that won't screw the deal for you."

"You mean, asking me out is unethical of him?"

"Kind of, but mostly, I just don't want any competition."

We kissed again, and stayed there on the couch and watched the end of the Rangers game. Toward ten-thirty or so, I said I had to get home. Ed pulled on some jeans and walked me outside.

"Good night, Ed." In the moonlight, I could see his dark gaze travel across my face.

He crowded me against the Ford and I felt his erection pressing against me, but he didn't kiss me, because who knew where reporters and their cameras lurked? "I love that wide-eyed innocent thing you do."

"I'm not innocent."

"I know. That's the point."

Not really understanding what he meant, but very turned on, I got into the Ford and took off, before I made a fool of myself and started begging.

When I got back to Mom's, she was sitting in her bed, reading *Journal of Accountancy.* I went into her room and sat next to her. "Mom, we gotta talk."

She laid the magazine aside and gave me her full attention.

"It's a long story and you have to promise not to get upset, or mad at Sam, or me, or anybody else."

"Yeah, yeah, I promise."

So I told her, and she broke her promise, just like I knew she would. "Pink, you're a CPA. You're not with the FBI and you've got no business running around after skanky pipe guys. Don't you understand the seriousness of your situation? If you screw up, you could be indicted and tried for fraud. I can't let you trash your life this way. Starting tomorrow, you can just stay at the office and I'll give you some bookkeeping to do. Ashley's on vacation and you can fill in while she's gone."

Bookkeeping? Fill in for Ashley? "Mom, please don't make me do that. I swear I'll stay out of trouble, but don't make me do bookkeeping for Ashley. I hate bookkeeping."

"I oughtta kill Sam for sending you off like that."

"Mom, it's not Sam's fault. He didn't tell me to go hang out at the Shankses' pipe yard. He took me off the case."

"Then why were you off chasing Skeeter Dawson?"

I sighed and bent over to rest my elbows against my knees. "Mom, I've never felt so helpless and useless in my whole life. Everything I've done lately is a disaster. I just wanted to prove I could do something, that I could help."

"That's understandable, but how much help do you think you'll be if you're in prison?"

"Come on, Mom, you know they're not going to throw me in prison. Not if they can use the disk. When it comes right down to it, I've done nothing wrong."

"In this country, perception is everything. Even if you did nothing wrong, even if they use the disk, there's a way they can pin some of the Marvel nightmare on you, and they will if they perceive you to be a person with no regard for the rules."

She was right, just like she was always right, but I didn't have to like it. "Mom, I swear I won't get into any more trouble. Just don't make me do Ashley's job."

Reaching for her magazine, she said quietly, "You've got one more chance. Screw up again, and you'll be balancing Mrs. Colder's checkbook."

At seven the next morning, I sat at Mom's kitchen table, staring at the front page of the *Dallas Morning News.* Me and Lucky stared back. It was the second picture, the one where I turned to look and the guy snapped the camera. I looked surprised and my hands were on Lucky's shoulders, as though I was holding on to him, instead of shoving him off. The accompanying article had some information about the current investigation, and then it had some quotes from Lucky, which I guess the reporter got after I hauled ass.

To hear Lucky tell it, we were on the verge of a hot romance, and he was real glad because li'l Bernice and the "other kiddos" needed a mama.

It was so much worse than I ever imagined. With serious dread curling in my belly, I picked up the phone and called Steve. When he answered and I said hello, he immediately started laughing. I mean, he laughed so hard, I thought he was crying.

This shocked me more than I can say. I'd expected him to get that serious senator tone and give me a lecture and sound horrified. I never expected him to laugh. Every so often, he'd say, "I'm sorry!" Then he'd go off again. Finally, he slowed down, but when he spoke, a vein of laughter still colored his speech. "So, Pink, do you suppose you'll be a good mama to li'l Bernice?" He started laughing again.

I waited for him to slow down and said, "The whole thing is a big misunderstanding."

"Please, make me understand." He wasn't laughing anymore, but I could tell he still wanted to.

"It's really not a good story. Just long."

"I've got an hour, and I want to know. Really."

So I told Steve and he reacted pretty much like Mom did. Well, except he didn't tell me I was trashing my life, or that I would go to prison. "Pink, you really shouldn't be chasing skanky pipe guys. As for the kiss, you're right, it doesn't look good. But I don't think there'll be any lasting damage, at least not with the committee."

"What you're saying is, maybe the committee won't hold it against me, but the rest of the world will. The guy waylaid me in the dark and now I'm all over America, looking like Mata Hari."

"So you're not interested in Mr. Barnes?"

"You are kidding, right? Please tell me you're kidding."

He died laughing again. Yeah, he was kidding.

"You know, a lesser woman would have her feelings hurt."

"No way!"

"Way. You're a senator, a man to be looked up to and respected, a serious man whose job is to serve and protect."

"No, that's the FBI guys who serve and protect. I just read boring tax legislation."

"And laugh at your constituent?"

"First of all, you know good and well I'm not laughing *at* you, and secondly, you're not my constituent. I'm from California."

"Details." I couldn't help smiling a little. "Lord, it really is an awful picture."

I could hear paper rattling and I knew he was looking at the picture. "Oh, I dunno, I think you look kinda cute. But I hope you don't look like that after I kiss you. I have a fragile male ego."

The thought of kissing Steve was a little too enticing for comfort, so I cleared my throat and said as lightly as possible, "Let's just hope there's not a nosy reporter hanging around. I'm not gonna lie, Steve, that was really awkward. I don't know how you do it, living in the spotlight all the time, having reports made about you that are either totally bogus, or grossly exaggerated."

When he spoke again, he was completely sober. "Believe it or not, I couldn't care less what they report. My life is my life, and I have no secrets. If they choose to put a spin on things, that's their problem. I know who I am, and what I believe, and what I do, and that's really all that matters. That's why you shouldn't let this whole thing get to you, Pink. You know what you were doing, and why, and as long as you're okay with it, what everyone else thinks is irrelevant."

"Steve, that was awesome. No wonder you're a senator."

"Well that, and because I'm loaded. That helps." He rattled the paper again. "Do you remember when my wife died?"

I stiffened, feeling something heavy coming. "Yes. I remember."

"They did a little exposé about her before she got sick, because she was an amazing woman. She did so much for so many, and went way above and beyond, and accomplished miracles. Lauren was incredible. But you know what they focused on in that exposé?"

Remembering it, I cringed a little and said quietly, "I know. I saw it."

"There must be thousands of people in this country who were married at a young age, realized their mistake and got divorced. Lauren moved on, and went on to do wonderful things, but all that son of a bitch news anchor could talk about was her ex-husband and how he went to prison for scamming

Medicare. Lauren laughed about it, because Lauren laughed about everything, and she told me what I just told you. After she died, that same anchor went on the air and made a big deal about what a sad day it was for America and I really wanted to go over and fit him with some cement boots, but I let it go, because I know who she was, and what she meant to me and a lot of other people."

My PMS kicked in and I had to swallow twice to get the lump out of my throat. "You still miss her."

"Well, yeah, of course I do. She was my best friend. Hard to believe she's been gone almost three years."

"And you haven't dated at all since then?"

"No. I gotta tell you, Pink, nobody looked at all interesting until you walked into the hearing room and sat down with that fossil of an attorney and went off about Mister Bob." He chuckled again.

"Don't get started."

He chuckled harder. "You tried so hard to be serious, to be dignified and professional, and you have no idea how incredible you were, with those big, blue eyes, and your pretty hair, and your Texas accent, telling the whole world about the bad deal at Marvel, and so not wanting to be a snitch, and then telling about Mister Bob. I'll remember that until I'm an old man."

"Thanks. I think."

"I mean it." He took a deep breath and let it out slowly, as though he needed a little extra oxygen for what he was about to say. I steeled myself. "I've been thinking though, about asking you out, and here's the thing—"

"I understand, Steve. Really I do."

"You understand what?"

"Why you're having second thoughts. I mean, after Mister Bob, and now this Lucky thing, I'm definitely a liability."

"I'm not having second thoughts."

"Oh. You sounded like you were about to break the date."

"No, I just wanted to say, I don't want you to do this because of who I am. I'm a little slow when it comes to the way women think, I admit. Lauren said it's even worse because I'm Italian. But I got to thinking about it, and I would really hate it if you said yes because you felt like you had to."

Now I know that I should have said, "Hey, Steve, you're right on the money, because even though I think you're an all-right guy, I just can't get over this infatuation with Ed, and until I do, I'll never be able to get serious with you, so accepting the date was a direct result of who you are." But I didn't say that. How could I? The guy had just spilled his guts about his dead wife, and how I was the first girl he'd met who vaguely interested him, and even though he didn't say it, he was laying his heart out there and saying he was lonely, and he liked me, and gee, did I wanna go steady. There was just *no way* I could say what I should have said.

So I said, "I said yes because I wanted to."

"Honest?"

I crossed my fingers and said, "Honest."

"All right, then. So we're on for a couple of weeks after the hearing, right?"

He sounded so relieved, I vowed to kick myself in the ass for three days straight. I was supposed to be Ms. Honesty. "Right."

"I guess I better get back to work before they fire me. Thanks for calling and explaining."

"Thanks for understanding...and not thinking I'm a disaster."

"Who said I don't think that? I may ask the president for disaster relief."

"You think you're pretty funny, don'tcha?"

He laughed again and I decided I really liked the way he laughed. "Goodbye, Pink, and try to stay out of trouble."

Later that morning, I went over everything with Sam. He was way pissed. "I gave you a direct order to back off of this client, and the first thing you do is go after a scumbag like Skeeter Dawson. If your mother doesn't fire me, it'll be a freaking miracle. If you were working for me at the FBI, I'd fire you right now, then take you out back and teach you a lesson."

"Sam, I had no idea you're the violent type."

"I'm not! But you sure as hell bring it out in me!" He stopped pacing and bent low, until we were nose to nose. "If you defy me *ever* again, I can promise you will be keeping books for every pain-in-the-ass client your mom's got. Do you understand?"

"I understand, but, Sam, you've got to give me some credit. I did get that letter from Skeeter. Now you can tell Ollie he's got his proof."

He reached out and snagged the paper from his desk, where I'd laid it out earlier. Waving it in front of me, he said with that low growl in his voice, "This is not worth the risks you took to get it."

"Maybe not to you," I said defensively, "but it was very important to me."

"Why? You don't even know these guys."

"Not for them. For me. Have you ever failed at anything?"

He raised up and turned to prop his hip on the edge of the desk. "Not at anything that mattered."

"Must be nice to be so perfect."

"Perfection has nothing to do with it. I just refuse to fail, and so I don't. If something doesn't work out how I intended, I change my expectations and reevaluate the goal."

"Well, that's just what I did yesterday, because I'm not used to losing. I have to do something that matters, and getting Skeeter Dawson to admit he sold shit pipe to Bert seemed to matter."

"Okay, so you needed an ego stroke. There're other ways of getting that, Pink." He peered at me through narrowed eyes for a while, then asked, "Do you have a gun?"

"Of course not. I'm a CPA."

"You need a gun. I'm going to get you a gun."

"I don't want one. I'm hot-tempered and I might pull it out like Mrs. Colder and shoot somebody's fax machine."

"Don't be ridiculous. If you're going to get yourself in jams, you need to be able to protect yourself. We're going tomorrow morning to get you a gun. In the meantime, contact Mrs. Colder's producers and get copies of the revised division orders Bert sent them. When we have those, I'm taking it all to the sheriff. They have people who can prove Bert forged the old lady's signature, and he'll get sent up for a long time. Then Ollie won't have to worry about getting cheated."

I got up to leave, but stopped when he called me back.

"Did Ed tell you the latest on the investigation of that prostitute's murder?"

"No. Are they going to arrest Bert?"

"Bert has an alibi and they're looking at a woman who threatened the dead girl as the prime suspect."

"A woman? You mean another of the prostitutes?"

"No, a local woman. She's been having an affair with Shanks and was jealous of the prostitute. The cops seem to think she may have done the girl."

I felt sick at my stomach and wished I had some of Uncle Alvin's Pepto-Bismol. "What woman in her right mind would have an affair with a creep like Bert Shanks?"

Sam said, "Not Bert. Ollie. He was shagging the whore at the same time he was doin' this woman and she didn't like it much."

"Oh, my God! Merry Thornton!"

"Yeah, that's the one."

Chapter 11

While I was contacting Mrs. Colder's producers, I thought about calling Bobby Tom. He had to be freaking out if Merry was a suspect in a murder case, especially one so scandalous. I felt really sorry for him, and wanted to lend my support, but something deep inside told me he wouldn't want my support, that it would only make it harder for him.

So I didn't call.

Turned out, I didn't need to. He came to the office right after lunch, holding a thin leather portfolio. Tiffany had called me to the front, saying I had a visitor, but I never expected to see Bobby Tom there. Dressed in khaki slacks and a butter-yellow golf shirt, he looked awesome. "Hi," I said, suddenly awkward.

"Hey," he said, looking awkward, too. "Can we talk?"

I led him to the conference room, closed the door, in spite of Gert's sour frown of censure from her office across the hall, and we sat down at the table. He looked at me seriously. "Merry's gone."

"Where did she go?"

"I have no idea. She must have come home last night sometime, because a lot of her stuff is gone. I was just at the bank and they told me she came in this morning and cleaned out the checking accounts and cashed in three certificates of deposit."

"How much money are we talking about?"

"About a million, give or a take a little. I think she's left the country because she thought the cops were about to arrest her."

"I'd heard something like that."

Bobby Tom looked tired and very depressed. "To tell the truth, as much as I hate her, I don't think she did it. I think Ollie set her up."

"You think he killed that girl?"

"And tried to pin it on Merry."

"Why would he kill her?"

"She knew something and he snuffed her out to keep her quiet. It just so happened that he killed Jessica not long after Merry told her off."

Jessica. The prostitute's name was Jessica. The woman I'd tailed to Tracy Steven's so I could ask about that Birds in Flight bag.

"Merry told her off? For real?"

He gave me a wry smile. "Ironic, isn't it? She's carrying on an affair, but gets pissed off when her lover cheats on her."

I thought about Jessica and remembered standing in the dressing room, checking out that cute little capri set in the three-way mirror when she came out to check the back of a skirt she was trying and was very chatty. "The day I ran into Merry at that shop, the prostitute was there. She said she'd just come in to some money and was trying to decide where to move."

"I bet Shanks paid her off because she knew something, then killed her to get the money back and make sure she kept quiet."

"What would she know about him that's bad enough he'd feel the need to kill her?"

"Hell if I know."

I remembered Ed was going to tell me something about Ollie Shanks, but he never got around to it because Sparky was dead in the bathtub. "Maybe I can find out."

"How?"

"A friend of mine is about to file a class-action suit against the Shankses, and he may know something."

With his chair turned sideways, his knees pressed against my thigh, Bobby Tom propped his elbow on the table and rested his head in his hand. "Let me know what you find out."

"I will."

"In the meantime, I want to hire you to trace assets and document whose money is whose because I'm sure Merry will come back and I'd just as soon have this all done, so we can get divorced quickly."

It was terribly self-absorbed of me to think so, but I was elated that Bobby Tom entrusted me to work on his divorce. He didn't think I was a crook, and he didn't hate me anymore. "I'll be glad to do it."

He pulled out a stack of papers and we went through them, one by one. Most of them were copies of bank statements, broker statements and financial statements for Thorn Pipe. Bobby Tom had done well. Real well. Toward the end of the pile, he came to a letter, which he handed to me. "This is from Merry's dad, the day after we got married. He gave her some stock in Marvel Energy, and that's the only asset she brought to the table. Everything else was mine. So other than that stock, and her share of community property income, she's not entitled to anything else."

"Right, but there's usually some disagreement about what's included in community property income. I'm going to need a lot of stuff, Bobby Tom."

"Come out to the shop and you can have anything you want. In fact, if you want to work out there, you can use an empty office. Might be easier than traipsing all that stuff back up here. But do whatever is best for you. I just want this done and over."

"I understand." I stacked up the paper and laid it aside. "Who's representing you?"

"Nobody, yet. Do you have any suggestions?"

His name was almost out of my mouth, but before I could say Ed Ravenaldt, I stopped. I still have no idea why. And I still don't want to analyze why. "Not really," I said instead of Ed's name. "I haven't lived here in such a long time, I'm not familiar with local attorneys."

An hour or so later, I tried tracking down Ed to ask him about Ollie Shanks, but his law clerk said he was in court and not expected to be through until late. I asked her to tell him to call me, then hung up and went back to work on Mrs. Colder's producers.

But by three o'clock that afternoon, my conscience was completely preoccupied with Skeeter's pipe purchases. I wanted to know who was selling off salvage pipe at Marvel. It had nothing to do with the Shankses or anyone else associated with Mom's firm. My curiosity was solely for myself, because I felt responsible somehow for the well-being of Marvel, and I was convinced that one of the sleazebag executives was selling that pipe and probably other equipment and pocketing the money. That he might also be the Dog Doo Stalker was another major incentive to find out who he was.

I checked out with Tiffany with a cock-and-bull story about going to look over a new client's books, and hit the road. On the way to Marvel's Midland office, I rehearsed what I would say. At the reception desk, I would introduce myself as Shelby Smith and ask to see Neil Dollar about tying in some gas production to one of their pipelines. That would get me in for sure, because anyone with a pipeline wants all the producers they can get. More gas through the line, more money for them. Once I was in, I'd tell Neil that Skeeter sold his crappy pipe to my client, and he planned to sue. Neil would freak out and point the finger at whomever told him to sell, to keep his own ass out of a sling.

I figured everyone in the Midland office would recognize me since I was on C-SPAN, so I drove over to the wig shop, next door to the cancer center, and bought a short, dark brunette wig. Then I went to the drugstore and bought some red lipstick and a pair of shades that weren't too dark to wear indoors, that looked like those prescription glasses that get dark outside and never get light enough inside. In the car, I got ready and checked myself out in the rearview mirror. Not bad, I thought.

I drove back downtown, to the building where Ed has his office, which is also the building where Marvel has its Midland division. I parked the Ford in the garage and took the elevator to the tenth floor. The door dinged open and I stepped out, confident as I walked to the receptionist. She looked up and smiled. "May I help you?"

"My name is Shelby Smith and I'd like to see Neil Dollar about some gas production in Lea County, New Mexico."

Without missing a beat, she stood and said warmly,

"Certainly. If you'll just have a seat, I'll go tell Mr. Dollar you're here."

"Thank you," I said as I took a leather wingback against the plaid wallpapered wall.

It was maybe ten minutes later and I was paging through the *Oil & Gas Journal,* learning all sorts of fascinating tidbits about packers and fishing tools and horizontal drilling, when the elevator door dinged and a cop stepped out. I looked back down at the boring magazine, then realized the cop was right in front of me. Startled, I looked up quickly.

"Whitney Pearl?"

All the blood drained out of my head, and I swear I heard the angels singing "What A Friend We Have In Jesus." "No. My name is Shelby Smith."

"May I see some ID?"

"Why? What's this about?"

He looked over his shoulder and I bent to look around him. A crowd of people stood clustered in the entrance to the office hallway, glaring at me. The cop turned back and said, "We got a call that someone was up here harassing the employees."

"Well, it's not me. My name is Shelby Smith and I'm here to see Neil Dollar about tying in some gas production."

The cop turned toward the crowd and said, "Are you sure this is Whitney Pearl?"

Instantly, the entire group began to make noise, some of them yelling very bad cusswords at me, some of them telling the cop to take me away in handcuffs, some of them demanding I perform sex acts on myself that would be anatomically implausible. The resulting sound was a dull roar of angry villagers who all wanted my head on a pike.

So much for my disguise.

The receptionist yelled, "You're nothing but a snitch! You

blew the whistle to save your own ass, and now, we're all going to lose our jobs!"

The cop turned again and said, "I need to see some ID."

I stood and said as quietly as I could, but loud enough for him to hear over the din, "Skip it. I'm who they say I am."

"I think maybe you better come with me," he said.

"Good idea."

He stepped to the elevator, with one hand around my arm, and as the door opened and we stepped inside, the crowd cheered and clapped. As soon as the door closed, the cop spun me around, shoved me against the wall of the elevator and said in a very nasty voice, "Spread your legs!"

"Why?" I asked, wondering if his idea of foreplay was along the same lines.

"I need to check for weapons, so either you can spread your legs, or I'll do it for you."

I spread my legs, and cringed as the guy ran his big, beefy hands up and down my thighs, under my skirt, then patted me down. When he was finished manhandling me, he pulled out a set of handcuffs and before I could say a word, had my hands behind my back, bound together like I was a criminal. He dumped my whole purse out, pawed through tampons and change and a squashed snowball, then jammed it all back in when he found nothing more threatening than a roll of Certs.

He did all that in the time it took the elevator to get to the first floor. When the door dinged, he stepped out, dragging me along with him. I seriously thought he'd get me to the garage, escort me to my car, then tell me not to come back. When he headed in the opposite direction, I balked. "Where are you taking me? My car's that way!"

"Ms. Pearl, I'm arresting you for harassment and loitering."

"Harassment? Loitering? I was reading a magazine!"

He glared at me. "Haven't you caused enough grief for those people? Do you have to come up and rub their face in it?"

Somehow, I knew the officer would not be interested in my pipe story, that the more I said, the more I dug the hole. So I went along with him and listened to him read me my rights, and got in the squad car, in the back, behind the metal screen.

And so off we went to the police station and I found out all about getting booked, having a mug shot and hanging out in a holding cell. If I hadn't been totally and completely freaked out, I might have found it kinda funny that they really did tell me I had one phone call. As it was, I wasn't sure when anything would be funny again.

Mom was gone for the night, visiting a client in Alpine, and I knew Ed was still in court, so I called the only other person who I knew would know just what to do. Holding the phone with both hands because I shook so violently I was afraid I'd drop it, I called the office and as soon as Tiffany answered, I said a little hysterically, "Get Sam!"

It was nine o'clock that night by the time Sam bailed me out. I'd had plenty of time to run through the whole gamut of emotions. I was afraid, sad, hurt and angry. All in turns, and sometimes all at once. But mostly, by the time Sam came to get me, I was so mad, I could have shot a fax machine without one iota of remorse.

In his big, silver BMW, I said to him, "If you say *one* word, I will rip off your head and spit down your neck."

"That's not really fair, Pink, because I haven't said anything yet."

"Well don't! The very idea, I go over there to help, and they had me frickin' arrested! And called me things I bet porn stars would be embarrassed to say out loud. And I was felt up, not once, not twice, but three times! I'm tellin' you, Sam, I felt bad about this whole deal, but no more! If the whole damned company goes down, I don't give a flyin' rat's ass."

He didn't say anything. Just drove in his ten-two position, defensively and safely at one mile an hour below the speed limit.

"Well?"

"Well, what?"

"Aren't you going to say anything?"

"You told me not to say anything."

"Why don't you just be difficult!"

I'm not sure, because it was dark, but I think he may have smiled. The only reason I didn't hurt him was because I couldn't be absolutely sure. If I'd been sure he actually smiled, like any part of that was funny, I might have whacked him, right there in the front seat of his Beemer, then reached down and unmanned him, I was that pissed.

I stared out the front window and bitched and griped all the way home. Except, when he stopped the car, we weren't at Mom's or my apartment. We were in front of a little bungalow-style house, with roses and marigolds in the flower beds. "Where are we?"

"My house," he said as he got out.

I reached for the handle, but he beat me to it, and opened the door. "Why are we at your house?"

"So I can look after you tonight. I have orders."

"Mom told you to bring me over here?"

"She didn't want you staying by yourself and she's right. There's somebody out there who hates you bad enough to murder Larry Sparks, and after today, he might go over the edge."

"Yeah, well, bring him on! I'd like to get my hands on the son of a bitch. The sick, disgusting bastard! The selfish, arrogant prick! Thc evil—"

"Okay, sweetheart, you need to just simmer down." He walked to the front door, keyed it open and waved me inside.

Walking in, I didn't notice any one thing in particular, I guess because I was so mad, the world was colored red. But it did register that Sam had a very nice house, a decorated house. "They're gonna catch the guy, Sam, and he'll never make it to trial because I'm gonna get to him first. I know good and damn well he's the one who swiped my disks, and paid George to rip off the one in the lockbox. He's terrorized me, murdered a man and sends me dog shit in the frickin' mail! What kind of twisted SOB does something like that? I'm gonna cut off his dick and shove it down his throat! I'll make him—"

"Pink!" Sam grabbed me, and shook me a little. "Get hold of yourself."

Staring into his deep, Pacific-blue eyes, I saw a lot of things there that I never expected. Anger, sympathy and something close to affection. "I hate him, Sam. I do."

"I know, but getting yourself all worked up is not doing you any good, and it's doing absolutely nothing to him."

My PMS acted up just then and I burst into tears. Sam pulled me close and patted my back while I cried all over him and wallowed in the misery that was my life. Then he walked me to the back of the house, to a small den, where he found a box of tissues and handed me one.

Didn't do much good, though, because I couldn't stop crying. He reached out and held me again, and said into my hair, "You're just one of those people who gets more than their share. It's okay, because no way you can't handle this."

"You don't have to be nice to me, Sam. I know you probably hate squalling women. And I've ruined your shirt."

"I don't hate squalling women, at least not ones named Pink, and to hell with the shirt. I've got thirty more just like it."

My crying was slowing down. "Why do you always wear Hawaiian shirts?"

"Because they remind me that my goal is to retire at fifty and move to Hawaii and open a surf shop."

I leaned back and looked at him. "You look like a surfer."

"Good thing, since I am one." He reached up and wiped away a tear with the pad of his thumb, and then he did the strangest thing. He came close and kissed the tip of my nose. "Your nose is really red."

"I don't cry pretty. That's why I don't do it, but lately, I'm like a big whiny crybaby."

"So? Most people would whine and cry if they were in your shoes. I know some men who would've given up a long time ago. I know some who would never have the balls to step up to the plate in the first place."

That made me smile. "Are you saying I'm more manly than some men you know?"

"Only a lot." He came close and I thought he was going to kiss my nose again, but he didn't. He kissed me on the lips, and it wasn't a friendly, brotherly sort of kiss. I think I kissed him back, but the whole thing is a little fuzzy. I do know he was almost as good a kisser as Ed.

When he stopped kissing me, he said, "I have no idea why I did that, but it was sure nice." Then he did it again.

After he stopped, he looked a little surprised. "Man, Pink, you've had a rotten time of it."

"So you kissed me to make it better?"

"Something like that."

"Thanks. When it rains, it pours. In Dallas, it was over a year ago that anybody tried to kiss me, and I didn't let him because he was a jerk. I come back to Midland, and within the last three days, I've been kissed by four different guys."

"Were any of them jerks?"

"No, but I'd have to say Lucky Barnes wasn't somebody I'd want to kiss."

"So that leaves me and Ed. Who's the fourth guy?"

"Bobby Tom Thornton."

"I thought he was married."

"He is, but not for long. In fact, he's retained us to trace his assets for the divorce."

"Is that why you kissed him?"

"No. I kissed him for the same reason I kissed you."

"And that is…?"

"He kissed me first."

"So you didn't want me to kiss you?"

"It wasn't something I was thinking about before you did it. But it was a very good one. I guess lately I've got a one-track mind."

Sam dropped his arms and moved away, toward the back door of the bungalow. He opened it and a calico cat slid inside, rubbing against his legs. Bending to pet the cat, he said, "I thought you'd decided to back off since Ed can't be trusted."

"I have, but he says he can explain things."

Raising up, Sam looked across the room at me. "And you'll believe him?"

"I want to believe him."

His gaze moved all over me and he shook his head. "Damn waste, if you ask me. Ed doesn't deserve you."

It was maybe the nicest thing anyone had ever said to me.

He went into the kitchen and switched on the light. I trailed after and watched him get out food for the cat. While he scooped it into a small, ceramic bowl that had a fish bone painted on it, he said, "Let's just forget about the kiss, okay,

Pink?" He bent to set the bowl on the floor and stroked the cat gently while it settled down and daintily ate its food.

"Okay, Sam. Thanks for bailing me out and bringing me home with you and kissing me. I thought you were a real hard-ass, and now I know there's a nice guy under that whole FBI thing you do."

Still caressing the kitty, he said quietly, "Just don't spread it around."

I was asleep by ten o'clock, cocooned in maybe the best bed in the universe. Not too soft, not too hard, with crisp, snowy white sheets and big, fat pillows. Sam was the man that night. As I drifted off, I thought I might ask him to adopt me.

Later, I started awake and sat up in bed, wondering why my hair was standing on end. Then I knew. Someone was in the room with me. I could hear a breath, in and out, in and out, and I sensed eyes on me. Oh, shit. I opened my mouth to scream, sucked in a deep breath to give it some wind, but never made a peep because my visitor lunged at me, knocked me back and fell on me, his big hand clamped over my mouth. I fought for as long as it took me to breathe in and catch Ed's scent. Instantly going still, I waited for him to move his hand. When he didn't, I stuck my tongue out and licked his palm.

"Don't do that. What I don't need right now is a hard-on." He moved his hand, but not his body. He was half on, half off.

"How did you get in, and what on earth are you doing here?"

"Sam keeps a key hidden outside. I know because I had to feed his cat once. And I came because I was worried about you. My brother called and said they booked you downtown today for harassment over at Marvel. And he said Sam bailed you out. When I couldn't find you anywhere, I figured he brought you home with him. The slime."

"Mom told him to bring me here because she's out of town for the night, and she doesn't want me back at the apartment until they catch the Dog Doo Stalker."

"He shoulda called me."

"Ed, I can't stay with you."

"What's the difference if you stay here, or with me?"

"I work for Sam." I reached up and smoothed back his silky, dark hair. "And I don't want to have sex with Sam."

"Good for Sam."

"Hey! What's that supposed to mean?"

"It means, if you did want to have sex with him, I'd have to kill him, and he'd probably rather be alive."

I knew he was joking, but it still made me feel good.

"So your plan to ask Dollar about the pipe didn't work?"

"Not hardly. I hadn't even been there ten minutes, and all I did was ask for him, then sit down and read a magazine. That cop showed up and hauled me off to jail with the angry mob yelling for the guillotine."

We lay there for a while, in the dark, quiet and still. Then he came close, his lips closed over mine and I slid my arms around him. I was tired, and fed up, and so ready for the whole damn Marvel thing to be over so Ed and I could start a real relationship, where we could go out to movies, and cook dinner together, and have sex whenever we wanted. And he could kiss me whenever he wanted to, whenever I wanted him to, instead of sneaking around like teenagers.

When he broke the kiss, I said, "Ed, tell me about Ollie."

He laid his head down again and whispered, "You know Shanks Resources buys all their pipe from Domino, but what you and everyone else doesn't know is that Ollie is part owner in Domino. He set it up as a subsidiary of a complicated maze of partnerships and corporations, to disguise the real owners.

I pulled some favors at the State Comptroller's office and found out who's at the top of the pyramid. To a man, except for Ollie, every one of the owners are executives at Marvel."

"So they own Domino and sell pipe to their own company."

"At inflated prices. Domino's only customers are Marvel and Shanks Resources. Which means, when Bert sells their new pipe on the sly, he's actually selling it back to Domino for three-fourths what it cost."

"So Ollie sells the same pipe, over and over?"

"Right. And Bert's doling out the cash for the crap pipe. It's like a shell game and Bert is the biggest sucker of all."

"Why did Ollie want us to prove Bert is buying crap pipe?"

"Because of the lawsuit. What he doesn't know is that I know he owns part of Domino, which blows him out of the water. He's known all along about Bert switching pipe, because he's been the one buying it back, through a trucking company down in Iraan. And that means he's known all along about the crap pipe that's leaking all over west Texas."

"Why didn't you tell Sam all of this?"

"I couldn't tell him until I knew for sure, and I got the information I needed just today."

Ed shifted a little, moving closer. "I'd never have thought to look at Domino, except for Bobby Tom. When I took this class-action suit, I went to ask questions about pipe and he told me he suspected Ollie and the Marvel execs were the owners. He and Ollie used to be friends and Thorn used to sell pipe to Marvel, but after Bobby Tom introduced Ollie to all the Big Dogs there, all of a sudden, Marvel's exclusively buying pipe from a dinky pipe company nobody ever heard of. Bobby Tom says he suspected Ollie was behind Domino, but he couldn't prove it. Then Ollie started an affair with Merry, and that was the end of their friendship."

"I saw Bobby Tom this afternoon and he said Merry cleaned out the accounts and took off, he thinks maybe out of the country to avoid getting arrested for the murder of Bert's prostitute. His theory is that Ollie killed the prostitute because she knew something about him, then tried to pin the murder on Merry."

"Ollie's not a nice guy, and about as crooked as a drunk cat in a windstorm, but he's no killer."

"So you think Merry killed her?" I was mad at Merry, and had no respect for her, but everything in me said she couldn't be a cold-blooded killer.

"I think the dog-shit guy killed her."

"But the stalker is somehow connected to Marvel. That girl had nothing to with Marvel."

He put his lips right next to my ear and whispered, "Maybe she didn't, but you do. I believe the stalker mistook her for you. Remember I thought she resembled you? He broke the woman's neck, which means he must have snuck up on her, and from behind, you look very similar. When he realized his mistake, he dumped her body out at that location to hide the murder."

I couldn't help a shiver, thinking how close I'd been to dying. There is honestly nothing so terrifying as the idea that someone wants to kill you. I lay there, with Ed holding me, kissing my hair, my face and telling me not to be afraid, but I was icy cold.

Too bad the stalker didn't call that night. I'd have been able to tell him he finally succeeded in scaring the tee-total shit outta me.

Chapter 12

The next day didn't start any better than the one before had ended. Ed fell asleep beside me, and when Sam came in to wake me up, he wasn't a happy camper. "Ravenaldt, you sneaky son of a bitch, how'd you get in my house?"

While I lay there, trapped beneath the covers because I was buck naked, I watched Ed get to his feet and start a stare-down contest with Sam. "You're a sneaky son of a bitch, bringing Pink here, puttin' the moves on her. And she just spent half a day in jail. You're an animal."

I sat up, clutching the covers to my breasts. "Why do you think he put the moves on me?"

Without looking away from Sam, Ed said, "I can smell his lousy aftershave on your neck."

This really ticked me off. If he thought Sam put the moves on me, he shoulda asked me, instead of standing there like a bull moose in rutting season, about to do battle with another moose. "Maybe that's because Sam's a nice guy and when I did the crybaby thing, he hugged me."

"You cried?"

"Well…yeah. I told you the other day why I'm a little emotional."

"Don't listen to her," Sam said. "You're right. I did put the moves on her."

"You sorry, no 'count bastard."

"Last time I looked, she's not attached to anybody."

"So is it open season?" I asked.

"Pink," Ed said, "stay out of this."

"Fine. Then how about both of you take it somewhere else? I need to get up."

"Who's stoppin' you?"

"Both of you. I don't have on any clothes."

They both turned to look at me. "Oh," they said simultaneously, just before they walked out.

I have no idea how the moose standoff turned out. By the time I got dressed, Ed was gone and Sam was ready to leave. He was quiet as we drove to my apartment, and he was quiet while I took a shower, trying my best not to think about Sparky being dead in there, and got dressed and packed some stuff to take to Mom's later. It was on the way to the parking garage where I'd left the Ford when he said, "Ed says he told you about Ollie."

"So?"

"I just wanted you to know, that night we talked and I told you about Ed, I didn't know then. It looked like Ed was going after Ollie for his money."

"Are you apologizing?"

"Look, Pink, it's obvious you got it bad for the guy, and while I don't understand it, I respect it. I'm just sayin', I was wrong about him. That's all."

"And even though you found out about Ollie yesterday, you didn't tell me because you thought I'd get over it with the Ed thing?"

"That's about the size of it."

I got out and went to the Ford and he hollered after me, "That is one butt-ugly car, lady. You need to get your old man to spring for some new wheels." Then he pulled to the exit to wait for me and I didn't get to tell him, I had no old man, and I damn sure didn't need one to buy me a new ride.

I followed Sam to our office garage and parked and we rode up together. When we walked in, Tiffany beamed at me and said proudly, "I brought donuts!"

"Cool! Where are they?"

"I put them in the break room."

I didn't tell her that was not a wise move because I hated to burst her bubble. So I just said thanks and wandered back to the break room where sure enough, an empty box sat lonely on the table, right next to a full basket of Mom's sawdust diet bars. Resigned to my fate, I took one and went to my cube to eat it. I'd been there only a couple of minutes when Tiffany buzzed me and said I had a visitor.

Thinking it was Bobby Tom, I dusted the crumbs off of my blouse and went to the front. But instead of Bobby Tom, it was my favorite IRS guy, Ronnie Maloney. I took one look at him, said, "Go away," turned and started to walk back to my cube.

But he hurried after me and said, "Ms. Pearl, let me tell you why I'm here."

I stopped and said, "You've got exactly one minute."

"I came to apologize for what happened last week."

He wasn't sincere. I could tell because the little snot was staring at my breasts. That was so unnerving. "Is this part of your punishment? To come and say you're sorry?"

"No, of course not. I just feel really bad about it."

I bent over and made eye contact. "I'm up here, bucko. Now how about you take your apology and your boob-staring eyes and get out of here before I call security?"

He looked severely panicked. "But, I really mean it when I say how sorry I am."

"No, you don't. What's up? Is someone going to call later and ask if you showed up for your dog and pony act?"

I could see by the look on his face that I was right. "Just go away." Turning around, I went back to my cube and started to work on Mrs. Colder again.

Thirty minutes later, Tiffany buzzed and said I had a call. I went into Mom's office to take it since she still wasn't back from Alpine. As soon as I said hello, Steve said, "I thought I told you to stay out of trouble, and what do you do but get yourself arrested. If I didn't know better, I'd swear you're trying to get your picture in the paper."

"My picture's in the paper? Again?" I said that last part with a squeak in my voice.

"Yes, and it's very provocative, with you in handcuffs."

"Oh, no." I sat down in Mom's chair and stared out the window. I didn't remember anyone taking my picture the day before. "Handcuffs?"

"You may as well know, Pink, I'm not that kinda guy."

I was quickly discovering, Steve Santorelli had a major sense of humor. It didn't quite fit the image of a senator, but then I thought about it, and realized, senators are just people, like everyone else. They make sexual innuendos and put their pants on one leg at a time and pay taxes and stick their foot in their mouth and have sex and pretty much do all things human. I smiled and replied, "Don't knock it till you try it. Me and the jail matron had us a time with those handcuffs and the weapons search."

"So are you gonna tell me what happened, or am I going to have to call the Midland PD to get the story?"

I told him and expected him to laugh, but he didn't. In fact, he got downright pissed off. Mostly at the Marvel employees, but also a little at me, I think. "If something happens to you over all this..." He stopped, then said, "Do not go over there again. Understand?"

"I understand."

"Now don't worry about the harassment and loitering charges. They've been dropped."

"How'd you do that?"

"I'm a powerful senator with an attitude. When I tell people to drop charges, they drop charges."

"Steve, I hope you're kidding."

"Of course I'm kidding. Well, mostly I'm kidding. I did call the manager of the Midland office and ask him for his version of the story. By the time he'd told it, I think he realized how stupid the whole thing was. But he really wondered why you came over."

"And I guess you do, too."

"Naturally."

"Can this be just two friends and not the whistle-blower and the chair of the finance committee?"

"It can."

"Somebody at Marvel is selling used pipe and I think it's one of the higher-ups. I intend to find out who."

"Isn't it normal in the oil business to sell used pipe?"

"Marvel never sells its own pipe. They hire a broker to handle it. And Skeeter Dawson is the one buying it, so that right there tells me the whole deal is funky."

"Why do you care who's selling it?"

"Because I feel responsible for the company sliding. And it would be one small thing I can do to help."

"Pink, that's very noble of you, but surely you can see that it's like spitting on a forest fire? Marvel will never make it after the SEC hands it over to the justice department and they get through with their investigation. Just the evidence you have is enough to finish it for them."

"It's so unfair. All those people, out of work, and all those investors, losing so much."

"No, it's not fair, and the people responsible will suffer the consequences. I think what you have to remember is that you didn't create the problem. It's nothing to do with you, and it's not up to you to try and save a sinking ship. Leave it alone, Pink. If someone's selling pipe and pocketing the money, it will all come out in the investigation."

I didn't respond and after a while, he said, "You want revenge, don't you?"

"No."

"Then you want validation. If you could catch even one of those guys doing something blatantly illegal, you could prove to the world that you're not the bad guy in this whole thing."

"To tell the truth, I haven't given much thought to why I want to catch him. But you're probably right. My whole life, I've done the stand-up thing. I made good grades, drove the speed limit, respected my elders, didn't sleep around, became a CPA, served my clients well and generally always enjoyed respect and even a certain amount of admiration from other people. Ever since I blew the whistle, I've been treated like I'm a criminal, like I've done something terribly wrong."

"I understand. I really do. But you're going to get yourself in deep water by going after this guy. He's desperate, Pink, or he wouldn't be doing this, and desperate people can be dangerous. Please, I'm asking you not to pursue it any further."

I didn't want to agree, but I had to concede the point. Besides, after what Ed told me the night before, I wasn't nearly so brave as I'd been. "All right. I'll leave it alone."

"Good. I have to go now, but call me if you catch any more flak over what happened yesterday."

"I will. Thanks."

"By the way, did Mr. Maloney pay you a visit?"

"He did, just a while ago."

"Did he apologize?"

"Yes."

"Did he mean it?"

"No."

"How could you tell? Did he not sound sincere?"

"He never made eye contact. The man has a breast fetish, I think."

"That's actually pretty common, you know."

"Is it?"

"Absolutely. But most men who suffer from it figure out how to look without getting caught."

"I don't think I want to know this."

Steve laughed. "If you see him again, would you poke him in the eye, courtesy of me?"

"Consider it done."

We hung up then and I went back to work, but barely ten minutes had passed when Tiffany buzzed and said I had a visitor. As I walked to the front, I hoped it wasn't Maloney again. I rounded the corner and spotted a tall, thin man dressed all in black, which went well with his somber expression. He woulda made a great old west undertaker. I went closer, stuck my hand out and smiled, "I'm Whitney Pearl. What can I do for you?"

The man looked like he'd just swallowed a bottle of lemon juice, straight and uncut. He ignored my outstretched hand. "I understand you were lookin' for me yesterday."

I dropped my hand. "You're Neil Dollar?"

He jerked his head and I took that as a yes. "Would you like some coffee?"

"I won't be here that long."

We went into the conference room and I closed the door, but not before I saw Gert give me a look that would curdle milk. Someday soon, I was going to have to duke it out with Gert. Watching Neil take a chair, I took the one two away and sat down. "I'm very sorry I upset everyone yesterday."

"What do you want?" he asked in a dark voice.

"I just wanted to know who told you to sell pipe."

Obviously, that wasn't anywhere close to what he expected. "You came up to ask who's selling pipe? Seriously?"

"That's it. Just tell me who gave the order to sell Marvel's used pipe to Skeeter Dawson."

Neil's eyes widened. "You been hangin' out with the likes of Skeeter Dawson? Don't you know, pipe guys like Skeeter are bad news?"

"I'd heard something along those lines."

"What's it to you who told me?"

Sitting back in the chair, I took a deep breath. "The pipe Skeeter bought is being sold to a client of mine. That's how I found out about it. And I know Marvel uses a broker for salvage sales, so it struck me odd when he said you're the one making the sales. If somebody up the ladder is selling the pipe and pocketing the cash, I'd like to see that person caught, and made to pay for screwing the company."

"What is it with you? Have you got some kind of revenge thing with Marvel?"

"No, Mr. Dollar, I just really hate crooks."

"How do you know I'm not selling the pipe on my own and keeping the cash?"

"Because you wouldn't sell it to Skeeter Dawson. Anybody who sells pipe to Skeeter is either an idiot, or doesn't care how much money they get. Drug lords in South America probably have more integrity than that guy. I know you're not an idiot, because you're running the Midland office, and if you were swiping the pipe and selling it for yourself, you'd find another buyer. One who'd give you a fair price."

Neil looked at me with something like grudging admiration. "If I tell you, what do you plan to do about it?"

"I'll tell the police, because I'm convinced the guy who's selling the pipe is the same guy who murdered Sparky and left him in my bathtub."

"What's the connection?"

I briefly told him, then said, "So you see, this guy isn't just about ripping off Marvel. He's a murderer and a stalker, and you may be the only person who knows who he is."

Neil looked down at the table, his expression a mix between fear and dejection. "Look, I'd tell you who it is, if I could. The problem is, I don't know who gave the order."

"You expect me to believe you sold that pipe without a direct order from one of the top brass?"

Neil was very uncomfortable. He shifted in his chair, looked anywhere but my eyes, cleared his throat a few times and finally said, "I got a letter, several of them, actually, giving me instructions about which pipe to sell and what to do with the money. There was no name, but it was on Marvel letterhead."

"And you, as the Midland manager, sold it without making a few calls to see if the deal was kosher?"

In a low, quiet voice, he said, "I'm an honest man, but I've made a few mistakes in my life, same as anybody else. The letters always say, if I don't follow the instructions, some of those mistakes will become public."

"The asshole is *blackmailing* you?"

"That's about the size of it. So I didn't make a fuss, or try to figure out who wrote the letters. I sold the pipe to Skeeter and sent the checks to a post office box in Dallas."

"So you can't tell me who gave the order, even if you wanted to."

"No." He stood, and so did I.

"I appreciate that you came by this morning."

Neil looked sheepish and said, "I'm sorry about yesterday. But I had a whole office of pissed-off people who were already in a pretty bad mood. Most of them will be leaving within the next two weeks."

"I understand."

"And I did drop the charges."

"Thank you for that. And just so we both stay out of trouble, we never had the conversation about the pipe."

For the first time, Neil Dollar smiled, and it changed his whole face. "What conversation?"

When Neil was gone, I headed back to my cubicle, anxious to wrap up Mrs. Colder. Already, I had five producers sending me the division order copies, and that only left three more to contact. I was halfway to the bull pen when Sam stopped me and said, "Come with me."

"Where are we going?"

"To buy you a gun. Get your driver's license."

"I don't want a gun, Sam. They scare me, and besides, I have bad hand-to-eye coordination. I'm terrible at tennis and golf, and I'm sure I'd be a lousy shot."

"You can learn. Now get your purse."

He dogged me to the bull pen, made sure I had my license, then led me out of the office. In his car, on the way to Thunder Billy's Guns 'N' Ammo, he asked about Mrs. Colder.

"I'm almost done."

"So you're gonna need something else to work on."

"I already have something. Bobby Tom wants me to trace his assets so he can divorce Merry as soon as she gets back."

He cut me a glance. "Where do you think she went?"

"I haven't got a clue, but she's sure not helping her case by skipping out on her kids."

"Maybe she didn't actually go anywhere. A lot of wives who disappear turn up in shallow graves."

Horrified, I stared at Sam. "You think she was murdered?"

"It's possible."

The thought sent cold chills all over me. "Ollie Shanks? Do you think Ollie killed her?"

"If anybody whacked her, it'd be Bobby Tom."

"No way!" I refused even to consider the possibility. Bobby Tom a murderer? It couldn't be. "She'll turn up."

Sam didn't say anything else, but I could tell, he thought Merry was dead. Looking out at the streets of Midland, I chose to avoid any such depressing thoughts. Instead, I thought about what Neil had told me, and about Skeeter Dawson. He'd have canceled checks he wrote to Marvel for the pipe, and whoever was selling it would have endorsed them, then deposited them into his own account. I fully intended to go see my old buddy Skeeter and ask nicely for those cleared checks. I just had to know who was selling that pipe, and the endorsement on those checks was the best clue I'd get.

Thunder Billy's is a radical anarchist's fantasy world. When we walked into the store, a rustic building all on its own, just outside the eastern city limits, I noticed two things right off. There were enough guns at Billy's to invade Iraq—again—and the customers looked like they'd stepped off the bus from the retirement village. "Sam," I whispered, looking at a man old enough to be Moses, "what's with the geriatric contingent?"

"It's Friday morning."

"Yeah, and I hate brussels sprouts. What's that go to do with all these old people?" I noticed a woman with hair even pinker than Mrs. Colder's, and wondered if she wanted a gun so she could shoot up the beauty shop.

"Thunder Billy offers discounts to seniors on Fridays. Come back tomorrow and the bird hunters will be here."

"Do they get discounts on Saturdays?"

"No, they go hunting on Saturdays during dove season, which opens tomorrow."

"Are you going dove hunting tomorrow?"

Sam cut me a disgusted glance. "I used to hunt serial killers and bank robbers before I settled down and switched to embezzlers. Little birdies just don't do it for me."

At the handgun counter, a tall, well-built man nodded to Sam, then looked at me. Dressed in a khaki shirt, with Ted embroidered above the pocket in green, he looked like he belonged on the cover of *Field and Stream.* "Buyin' some protection for the little lady?" he asked

Sam went into FBI mode. He rattled off a lot of numbers and requirements that went straight over my head, but seemed completely logical to Ted. When Sam was done, he said, "I think the best thing is a Beretta Bobcat. It's subcompact, will fit in her pocket or purse and it'll blow a big enough hole in a man to let him know she's serious."

Horrified, I looked at Ted and said, "But I don't want to blow a hole in anyone. Isn't there something I can shoot that'll just sort of wing 'em?"

They both looked at me like I was an ignorant female, which would have gotten my back up, except that I knew they were right. To me, the world of guns is right up there with the world of aliens, or internal combustion engines, or men who think breaking wind is funny. I mean, I just don't get it, and frankly, don't want to get it. "Okay, fine," I mumbled, really not liking the whole situation.

Ted went to the wall, opened a glass-fronted case and pulled out a gun. Walking back to us, he handed it to Sam, who looked it over, asked a few more manly questions, then jerked his head toward the back.

Before I knew it, me and Sam were outside, walking toward a wide-open pasture with targets lined up at varying distances. "Sam, I don't want to do this. Loud noises freak me out."

He slowed and said, "Pink, you surprise me. And here I thought you had balls of steel."

"Did you miss sex ed? I'm a girl, Sam. I don't have balls, steel or otherwise."

"Stop being a chicken and let me show you how this works." He raised the little gun, that was so small it looked like a toy, and demonstrated how to load the magazine. "This holds seven rounds." He slid the gun into his pocket, held the magazine in one hand and slid seven bullets in the magazine. Then he took the gun out, slid the magazine into the grip and said, "There. You release the safety, which you'll know is released because you can see the red dot, aim and pull the trigger." He put the safety back on, released the magazine, unloaded the bullets, then handed it to me. "You try."

From somewhere deep inside, maybe a hidden well of testosterone God gives girls so they can fire guns, I managed to load the magazine with bullets and get it into the gun without too many prompts from Sam. I looked up at him when I was done. He had a strange look on his face. "What?"

"Would you be deeply offended and want to sue me for sexual harassment if I said you look really hot holding that gun?"

"No. Just mildly offended and I can't very well sue you since you work for my Mom, but I might tell on you."

He laughed and waved me to follow him. At a low fence, really just a metal barrier to keep people from wandering out into the range, he stopped and said, "Take a shot, Pink."

I did and missed. In fact, I missed the target every time, for all seven rounds. Finally, after I loaded the magazine again, Sam stepped behind me, held my arms out straight, in between his, and said close to my ear, "Look at that target and think of it as the stalker, coming right at you, and if you don't hit him, he's going to break your neck, just like he did that prostitute."

"Scaring me isn't going to make me a better shot. And even if it did, I can't get too hot and bothered about a piece of paper with circles on it."

"Use your imagination."

Focusing on the target, I tried to pretend it was the stalker, out for my blood, but it was too far a stretch. Maybe because I had no face to imagine.

Sam said, "Pretend it's your ex-husband."

I fired and nailed the target, dead center. Okay, it was a lucky shot, but I was pretty fired up nonetheless.

"Atta girl. Now do it again."

I never hit the center again, but I did manage to at least hit the paper a few more times.

"This is a sweet little thing," Sam said when I handed it back to him. "Let's go in, get you registered and pay Ted."

By the time we were done paying Ted, or should I say, I was done paying Ted a lot of money for something I didn't want, it was lunchtime and Sam offered to take me out. Starving because all I'd had was the sawdust diet bar, I happily agreed. We went to Bettina's, and after I ordered the enchilada plate and Sam ordered the Plato Grande, he said, "Midland may be a backwater, but they do have great food."

I nodded agreement. "Have you been to Ed's brother's restaurant? I had no idea he was a chef."

"For bein' all hot and bothered about the guy, you sure don't know much about him. I hate his guts and know more about him than you do."

"Why do you hate his guts? I thought the two of you worked together on a lot of mutual clients."

"We do, but that's business. This is personal."

It always amazes me how guys can work together and accomplish great things, but despise one another. "So what started the feud?"

Sam ate a chip, slowly, looking off toward the door, and I thought he wouldn't answer. Then he focused on me and made a face. "I had an affair with his wife."

That shocked me. A lot. Sam just didn't seem like the type. My respect was packing up to leave when he added, "It was after their divorce, but it still pissed him off."

"Who is she?"

"Her name is Marina Kraus. Ever heard of her?"

I dropped the chip I'd just picked up. "Yes."

"She's about your age. Did you know her from school?"

Did I know her? Hell, yes, I knew her. Me and Marina competed for everything. From class president to Homecoming Queen to Bobby Tom. I only won one out of three, but definitely Bobby Tom was the best of all, so I always felt a little superior. And Marina hated me for it. I'd heard, long ago, she moved to Hollywood to be an actress, which bugged me on some deep level, because she would be creative and famous and I would be stuck wearing suits and bean counting. "I know her. But I thought she was in California."

"She moved back here to work at the community theatre."

"Is she still in Midland?"

"Sure. Saw her just a few days ago."

I wasn't sure what to do with this information. I couldn't believe that of all the men in the world to go goofy over, I picked Ed, a guy who used to be married to my arch rival. A small part of me, the one that diminished a little more every day, the part that's small and petty and immature, really hated that Marina would find out I was nutty for Ed and be able to lord it over me that she got there first. I watched Sam drink his iced tea and tried like hell not to ask, but I was compelled. "Why did Ed and Marina get divorced?"

He set the glass down. "In the beginning, I think she was like Ed, into her work, and living a simple sort of life. If you've been to Ed's house, you know he doesn't put much emphasis on material things. He drives that old 4-Runner when he could afford a better ride. Marina was just like him, but then she became good friends with some women she met through the theatre, rich ladies who fork over time and money to the local arts and charities, and before long, she got sucked into the soccer mom thing. Wanted a Suburban and a few kids and a membership to the country club. Ed wasn't interested, so she left him."

"Is that why you and Marina didn't work out?"

"Sort of. I have no interest in getting married, and I damn sure don't want any kids. She figured out pretty quick that I wasn't going to get her what she wanted."

"Why don't you want kids?"

"That's kinda personal, Pink."

"Oh. Sorry."

Our food arrived and I ate quietly, lost in wondering why Ed didn't want kids. I didn't think too much about why that bothered me. Sam not wanting kids didn't set off any alarms, because he was Sam, and even if I didn't know him very well, I could tell he was way too into Sam to want kids. Ed, on the other hand, was from a big, close family, and he seemed like the sort who'd want children, who'd be a great dad. And as much as I'd wanted to beat Marina, I didn't dislike her. Truth be told, she was a lot like me, and if I hadn't been dead set to show her up, we probably would have been great friends. She wasn't bad mother material. So what was with Ed?

"Is it bugging you?" Sam asked.

"Of course not." No way I'd tell Sam my thoughts, especially when they made no sense to myself. I was nowhere close to wanting kids yet, wasn't even sure I could have kids, but Ed not wanting any bugged me in a way I didn't understand. I decided I'd bring up Marina and maybe he'd tell me about it, and I'd get it.

Chapter 13

By midafternoon, I was almost done with Mrs. Colder's division orders. All I had left to do was get the transfer copies from the producers which would show who got the other half of her royalty interests. I was certain the name would be Bertram Shanks. It was Friday and I was exhausted, so I decided to go home and escape everything for the weekend.

I cleaned all the bathrooms at Mom's, less because they needed it than because I just wanted to do something mindless. I was in the front powder room when the door opened. Expecting Mom, I stepped out, smiling.

My smile froze when Harry walked in. Harry had a key? "Hi, Harry."

"Oh, hey, Pink. Didn't know anyone was home or I woulda knocked."

"What's up? Mom low on Freon again?"

"No. She asked me to come over and check out the disposal. Says she put potato peels down there and I told her, everybody knows not to put potato peels down a disposal."

He walked off, whistling, and I went back to cleaning the toilet. Was Mom fooling around with Harry? I shook my head. No way. Mom's something of a snob, I guess because she came from trash and worked so hard to rise above it. Not that Harry wasn't a nice guy. But he was at least fifteen years younger than Mom, and he was an air-conditioner guy. Mom often said she wished she could find an educated man, one who would understand things like art and literature. I'd noticed Harry had a bumper sticker on his truck that said, Women Want Me: Fish Fear Me. Not exactly college professor material.

Harry left within the hour and I stowed away the cleaning supplies. Mom came home later in the afternoon and we had a nice evening, cooking dinner, watching a movie, avoiding the reporters who called and knocked on the door. I told her Harry came by and watched her reaction, but I couldn't see anything out of the ordinary. Certainly, I didn't mention my suspicions. Even if Mom was hangin' out with Harry, no way she'd admit it.

On Saturday, after I checked my mail and got another Doggie-Doo post, I spent most of the day in the pool, floating around, reading a mystery novel. Sunday, Mom and I went to church and it was nice to see a lot of old friends, even if they did look at me a little oddly. I was quickly becoming a local celebrity of sorts. By Sunday night, my jail time was all but forgotten, but the reason for it was fresh in my mind. I still felt icky over all those people shouting at me. It was terribly unpleasant to know so many hated my guts. The unfairness of it all sat ill in my soul, making me wonder once again if I'd done the right thing. That old saying about killing the messenger sure held true.

On Monday, I was back at the office, working on Mrs. Colder. I admit, I dragged my feet and spent way too much time on a job that shouldn't have taken more than a day or two. I kept thinking about Skeeter Dawson and those cleared checks, and how I could find out who was selling pipe out of Marvel if I'd just go over and ask for the checks, but I was anxious and jumpy and half-afraid to stick my neck out again.

Mom left late that afternoon to take Mrs. Colder down to her ranch outside of McCamey, to see the foreman and go over some accounting discrepancies. She fretted over leaving me alone, but I told her not to worry, then spent the night jumping at every noise.

After lunch on Tuesday, Sam called me into his office and said, "I never figured you for a coward."

I started to argue, but what was the point? "Me, neither," I said, staring at a photograph of him, shaking hands with George W.

"How much longer do you suppose you're going to hang around the office and feel sorry for yourself?"

"Does it matter?"

"Well, I need to work on my budgets, so I was just curious how much Pink Feeling Sorry For Herself time I should build in."

I finally met his gaze. "Okay, I get the point."

"Wrap up the old lady's division orders, then go on out to Thornton's and get started."

"Okay, Sam," I said apathetically.

It took all of half an hour to finish Mrs. Colder. I grabbed up my bag and started out, deciding maybe first I would go over and see Skeeter. I had to know. And maybe more importantly, I had to prove to myself that I wasn't a wimp. I wasn't going to hide out and be a chicken. Not after all I'd already been through.

Gert called out to me as I passed her office and I had a strong urge to ignore her and keep walking, but knew I'd pay for it later, so I stopped at the doorway. "What can I do for you?"

She eyed me like I imagine Custer looked over the Sioux, before he knew his goose was cooked, when he still thought he was righteous. "You should be ashamed of yourself."

"I have a personal policy never to be ashamed. That's why I don't do things to be ashamed of."

"If you had any decency at all, you'd resign immediately."

With a strong odor of dread in the air, I moved into her office and closed the door. "Okay, Gert, lay it on me. What have I done that's so shameful?"

"You have to ask? Not only are you a ho, cavorting with Ed, making out with a married man in a public alley, and leading on a United States senator, you're getting your picture in the paper every day, making a spectacle of yourself."

"I've never cavorted in my life, and as for the paper, the newspeople tend to get a little excited over dead bodies in bathtubs." How the hell did she know about that kiss with Bobby Tom? Mentally critiquing her messy bun, plain vanilla face and lavender satin blouse that screamed hand-me-down, I wondered if Gert had ever been kissed. No way she'd ever had sex. The woman was about as sexual as plankton. Maybe that was her problem. Maybe Gert needed to get laid. In one of my rare moments of impulsiveness, I decided I would make it my mission to get Gert a man. Then she'd focus on him, instead of me.

"Your mother's lost one client already, and it's only a matter of time before she loses more."

"Mom lost a client? Who?" This was very upsetting to me and it had nothing to do with Gert. I could give a shit what Gert thought of me. But Mom losing clients was so not cool.

Gert gave me the once-over and pursed her lips with disapproval. "This is Midland, Texas, where decent people live. People who have manners and morals."

I took a step closer to Gert. "Skip the sermon and tell me which client Mom lost."

"Mr. Halliday. He told Jane he could no longer entrust this firm with his financial needs, not with a woman like you working here. She was upset. Mr. Halliday was an important client."

"Okay, I'll resign."

"You mean you'll do it, just like that?" She looked so hopeful, her dull gray eyes actually took on a bit of sparkle.

"Of course I will. If it means Mom won't lose any more clients." I confess, I mostly said it so Gert would get off my back. I knew, no matter what, Mom wouldn't accept my resignation. I mean, she's my mom. Maybe she wasn't too happy with the way things were going in my life right then, but when push came to shove, she was in my corner. Always. Gert needed to get a clue. And a man.

"Good," Gert said with what might have been a smile, but looked more like she had gas. "I accept your resignation effective immediately."

Geez, she really did hate my guts. If there was any doubt before, there certainly wasn't after that. "Tell you what, Gert. Since you didn't hire me, I can't resign to you. I'll turn in a letter to Mom."

Looking for all the world like the second runner-up in a beauty pageant, Gert's smile was more fake than the dusty plastic food they used to have out in front of Ding How.

"In the meantime, if you need me, I'll be out running down the guy who left the dead body in my bathtub." And looking for a lonely, nearsighted nerd who was as desperate for sex as Gert.

As I left the office and went to the parking garage, Gert faded from my mind and I switched gears, going over what I would say to Skeeter to convince him to give me his canceled checks.

Not exactly paying attention, I was caught completely off guard when Lowell Jaworski stepped from behind a concrete piling in the dimly lit garage. I stopped in my tracks and stared at him, wondering if he was only a figment of my imagination.

"Hello, Pink," he said, sticking out his hand to shake mine, smiling very nicely.

Yeah, definitely I was hallucinating. Amazing how real his warm hand felt against mine. "Hello, Lowell," I replied, waiting for him to disappear into thin air.

He didn't. "Do you have a minute?"

"Lowell, I've got the rest of my life," I said as I dropped his hand and took a step back.

Was that a hint of guilt I saw cross his features? Surely not. No way guilt was in Lowell's makeup. I noticed he hadn't changed one iota from the perfectly dressed, midforties *GQ* guy he'd always been, complete with a Brooks Brothers suit, a Gucci tie and Italian leather shoes. His hair, not quite blond and not quite brown, was perfect, not a hair out of place. Sort of like Barbie's boyfriend, Ken. We used to make fun of Lowell's hair, threatening to mess it up in his sleep sometime, because we were all certain he woke up with it exactly like he went to bed. He looked uncomfortable, as though he had no idea how to start. Ordinarily, I would have said something to help him out of the awkward moment, but I wasn't feeling very charitable toward my ex-boss. In fact, I'm pretty sure I hated his guts.

He finally said, "I came out to Midland to offer your job back to you."

Of all the things he might have said to me, that was the last.

Except maybe that he was madly in love with me and did I want to marry him. That would have been the very last thing. Offering to rehire me was second to last. "Why?"

"Because the firm needs you."

The past couple of months had taught me a lot about life and people and the way things work. I was a certifiable cynic, jaded and bitter and totally lacking any faith in humanity. Or maybe just Lowell Jaworski. "Lemme guess. The only condition to me coming back is if I lose the disk and skip the trip to Washington."

"That's not why I'm offering to hire you again."

"Jesus, you really think I'm this stupid?"

"Pink, we need you. Several people have left and we're running tight on scheduling."

"Several people? You mean the rats are abandoning the ship before it goes down?"

His hopeful expression began to dissipate. "Some of them were nervous, which is understandable."

"It's totally understandable, considering the whole firm will be dissolved if the injunction doesn't go through and the justice department gets their hands on that disk."

He frowned, looking almost confused. "Haven't you heard? The injunction failed."

Keeping a lid on my immediate elation over that bit of news, I said, "So that's why you rushed to Midland to offer me my old job. Thanks for the offer, Lowell, but if I lie down with dogs, I'll get up with fleas."

Lowell's hopeful expression was gone for good, replaced with a tint of red in his cheeks and a murderous look in his eyes. I took another step back. He took two steps closer. "Since when are you so damn righteous? Don't you realize what will happen to you after you go back to Washington?"

"I'll come back to Midland, to this mercy job."

"No way," he said with a growl in his voice. "When they have what they want, the bastards will throw the book at you. How can you be so naive? That mafia senator is romancing you for information, and you're ignorant enough to believe him."

Narrowing my eyes, I took a hard look at the man I'd considered a mentor and a friend. "On the contrary, Lowell, I'm just now starting to grow up and see things the way they really are. I respected you, looked up to you, wanted to be just like you. Now, I'd sooner be a maid down at the Holiday Inn."

I stepped away, planning to go to the car and leave before I did something like spit on him, or cuss him out, but he stopped me with a hand on my arm. "Don't walk away from me."

"Lowell, I suggest you let me go."

With a swift jerk, he had my arm behind my back and his other arm around my neck, pressing painfully against my windpipe. "I gave you a chance, Pink. Never say I didn't give you a chance."

Truth be told, I couldn't say anything. Stars danced in front of my eyes and I knew I was going to pass out. Struggling only made it worse and I wondered if that was it, if I would be strangled to death by my ex-boss and left in a heap on the garage floor of the Old First National Bank building.

"I worked my ass off to get where I'm at, and I'll be damned if you're going to take it all away. Someone's stalking you, Pink, and it's not me. When they find you here, they'll look for your stalker, and nothing can be tied back to me. Do you understand? I want you to understand that before you die. I'm going to get through this because there won't be any proof because you won't be here to hand it over. I'm going to win, and you're going to be dead, and your stalker will go to jail."

I'd never passed out before and the sensation was terrible.

I clawed at his arm, desperate for a breath, my mind taking me back to the deep end of the Midland Country Club swimming pool. I could hear Mom, yelling, "Jesus, God! Pink! Pink!" Randomly, I wondered why she sounded so upset. After all, didn't she push me in? Wasn't this all her idea? The darkness crept closer and I fought with all my might, but I knew it was over. I was dying, dammit, and instead of my life passing before my eyes, I could only focus on two things—dragging a sweet breath into my bursting lungs and wishing Lowell Jaworski would burn in hell.

Suddenly, I heard a loud explosion and Lowell's arm fell away. My knees buckled and I fell to the concrete floor, sucking in air, wondering what happened.

"Goddammit!" Lowell shouted above me, reaching down to grasp my arms and pull me up. Before I could kick him away, another explosion came and I watched in horrified fascination as his hair flew clean off of his head, leaving two patches on either side, just above his ears. He let go of me and clutched his bald pate, screaming like a little girl, "My hair! My hair!"

Lowell wore a rug? Incredible. I never knew.

"Who the hell are you?" he cried, still holding his head, staring at someone behind me.

I turned my head and blinked rapidly, trying to clear my eyes of tears and the lingering fog brought on by oxygen deprivation. Standing maybe twenty feet away was Mom, her face white as a ghost, and next to her, a smoking pistol in her hand, was Mrs. Colder. "I'm your *worst nightmare,* sonny!" the old lady shouted. She waved her pistol at him. "Now sit down before I *take off* your sideburns!"

They hauled Lowell away in a squad car, bawling his eyes out, still holding his hands across his shining head. I sat in another police car and told the officer what happened, in between taking drinks of cool water. My voice sounded weird, like I ate rocks for lunch and some of them stuck in my throat. Poor Mom. She hovered nearby, looking scared shitless, worrying her suit jacket buttons so much, a couple of them popped off, leaving long, dangling threads. Mrs. Colder sat in the back seat of the squad car, nodding off, her pistol lying in her lap, her walker at the ready just outside the car.

When the officer had all the information he needed, he went round and woke the old lady up, calling her by name. Mom came close and wrapped her arms around me. "I love you."

"Me, too," I said over her shoulder.

"I'll be so glad when this is all finished. Maybe you should go up to Lake City and stay with Lurch until you can get the disk."

"You wanna know something true?" I asked in a whisper. "I'd rather take my chances with the Dog Doo Stalker."

Mom hugged me tighter. "Oh, God, baby, I'll never get over it. Never. When we came around the corner and saw him there, with his arm…" She started crying and I patted her back.

"It's okay, Mom. I'm fine."

She got herself under control and let me go, searching her pocket for a tissue. While she dried her eyes, I turned to Mrs. Colder. "Thank you," I said, searching for something that didn't sound so inadequate and coming up empty. How did one thank someone for saving their life? Twice. "If you hadn't come along, I'd probably be dead now."

"Reckon so," she agreed, her sharp old eyes looking at my neck, then my feet. "Had a husband used to like to *rassle me* around. I learned real quick, he'd let go if I got him on the instep with a spur. You'd look like a *fool* wearing spurs, but mebbe you should get you some of *those shoes* with skinny heels. Nail a man's instep with those wimpy shoes you got and he'd never *feel it.*"

Glancing at my mules, I replayed what happened in my mind and had to agree with Mrs. Colder. If I'd had the right shoes, I could have jabbed Lowell's instep and he would have let me go long enough to get away from him. "I'll buy some," I promised.

"Don't get 'em at Tracy Steven's. Place is a rip-off. Go over to Missy's."

"The lingerie shop?"

"They got shoes in the back with heels so pointy, you could use 'em to castrate a bull. Tell them *I sent you* and they'll give you a discount."

"You do a lot of business there?"

Mrs. Colder snorted. "I don't do any business there because they don't have anything for old ladies."

"Then how—"

"I wasn't *always an old lady,* and the owner is a friend of mine," she said as she gripped her walker and shuffled away, toward the elevator.

Mom reached for my hand and started to walk after her, but I pulled away and she stopped. "What are you doing? Aren't you coming upstairs?"

"Uh, no, Mom. I've got to go somewhere." Mom looked like she might cry again and I hastened to assure her, "It's just a quick errand, then I'm going home."

"Please, baby, be careful."

"I will, Mom." Turning, I went to the ugly Ford, well aware she watched me every step of the way.

After I left, I drove around Midland for a while, with all the windows rolled down, sucking in deep breaths, having a very long God moment. Coming close to death was something of a spiritual experience. I noticed how many birds lived in Midland, how green the lawns were, how blue the sky was and how friendly people can be when waved at.

Before long, I thought of Ed, and had a strong desire to talk to him, to get his take on what happened. Ed has a way of grounding things and the more I thought of him, the more I wanted to talk to him. I grabbed the cell phone and punched in his number, then lost all my enthusiasm when his assistant said he was at the injunction hearing in Washington. I'd been so preoccupied, I'd actually forgotten he was scheduled to leave that morning. I declined to leave a message and tossed the phone back into my purse.

It was past four o'clock when I headed toward Green Tree and Skeeter's house. By the time I pulled up to the curb, it was almost five. When the doorbell brought no response, I figured Caroline had already gone home. Turning to leave, I decided to go see her. She would know Skeeter's whereabouts.

All the way over, I thought about Ed in Washington and wished I was with him. Man, oh, man, I was so ready to get that disk and get the whole thing over with. I was tired all the way down to my bones, and so ready to settle into something resembling a normal life. Maybe even rent a real place to live, with my own furniture, where I could hang pictures and buy potted plants and get a cat.

Caroline answered the door with a grin. "Pink! How the hell are ya?" she asked, opening the door wide, inviting me in.

"Been better," I said, briefly explaining what happened in the parking garage.

She waved me toward the kitchen table and went to the refrigerator. "Sounds like you could use a beer." She brought me one, then sat across from me and said seriously, "Been readin' about you in the paper. You got more trouble than a man on a wrong train, an' that's no lie."

"Everything will be fine just as soon as I get that disk and take it to Washington."

"What's Lucky Barnes think about all this?"

I frowned as I set the beer down. "How should I know? And more importantly, why should I care?"

"Seein' as how you're datin' him, looks to me like you oughtta care."

"I'm not dating him." I explained it to her, leaving out my personal feelings about Lucky. No point being tacky.

"So he thinks you got a thing goin', and he's wrong?"

"That's right."

"Then, if you ain't interested in Lucky, reckon it'd bother you any if I go for him?"

I blinked a couple of times. "Well, sure, that'd be fine by me. I didn't realize you and Lucky were acquainted."

"We weren't. Until yesterday. I saw him at the grocery store and recognized him from that picture in the paper. Introduced myself and tol' him you're a friend of mine. He's a smelly guy, and needs a woman to whip 'im into shape, but I reckon he'd clean up real nice."

I wanted to laugh. Real bad I wanted to laugh. Not at Caroline, or even Lucky, but at the totally bizarro way things turn out, and what an amazing lady fate can be. But of course I didn't. Caroline wouldn't get my cosmic thoughts. "You know he has five kids, don't you?"

"Shoot, that ain't no problem. I love kids, and he showed me a picture of li'l Bernice. She's a ring-tailed tooter, I tell ya."

The urge to laugh nearly overcame me, but I managed to hide it in a drink of beer. "Did Lucky ask you out?"

"No, but he will if I want him to. I thought you and him was together, so I didn't act too interested."

Immediately I sobered. "Thanks, Caroline. You're really something, you know that?"

She looked embarrassed and said, "You ain't so bad yerself, Pink." She nodded at the Budweiser. "Want another beer?"

"No, thanks. I gotta drive."

"What for did you drop by?"

"I'm looking for Skeeter again."

"He and Miz Dawson's in Ruidoso. Should be back late tonight." She looked at me curiously. "Is this about that pipe again?"

"Yes. I want to look at some canceled checks, to see who's selling it to him."

"Well, hell, if that's all you need, I can let you in."

"Really?" The prospect of getting the checks without even asking Skeeter sounded very good to me. "You know where he keeps his bank statements?"

"Do I know?" Caroline looked dumbfounded. "Hell, girl, I don't just clean over there, I take care of most of Skeeter's bizness. Miz Dawson fired his old bookkeeper on account of Skeeter was playin' patty fingers with her, and after that, he asked me to pay his bills and keep his books for him."

"I had no idea."

"Shoot, I'm about as good with that as the little tramp he had in there before. Two days a week, I do his pipe bizness, and three days a week, I clean."

Caroline was chock-full of surprises. "Where'd you learn bookkeeping?"

"I took some correspondence classes. Weren't all that hard, but I was mighty surprised when I found out I can make more money cleanin' than lookin' after books." She got up, took my can to the garbage, then said, "How's about we go on over to Skeeter's before he gets home?"

"You want me to drive?"

"Are you kiddin'?" She looked horrified.

"Or we could take your car."

Thirty minutes later, we were in Skeeter's home office, Caroline digging through a stack of bank statements while I walked around the room and looked at the framed photos of Skeeter with different men, standing in front of pipelines and other exciting backdrops, like a pumpjack and a tank farm.

"Suppose Skeeter comes home right now? Will he be pissed?"

"Maybe, but I'm not worried. He and Miz Dawson never get home from New Mexico before ten." She held up a check. "Here's one."

I took it from her and checked it out. "This is made out to Marvelous Energy."

"Somebody added the 'ous,' 'cause I don't never remember writing a check to a company with as silly a name as Marvelous."

I turned it over. "And it's endorsed to Marvelous Energy, deposited to a bank Marvel doesn't use." I felt an electric current of good karma all through my body. This was it. At last. A dead solid way to nail at least one of the Marvel execs. All I had to do was figure out who owned the bank account, doing business as Marvelous Energy. "Can I make a copy of this?"

"You could if the copy machine wasn't broke down."

"How do you make copies?"

"I have to go to the office supply."

"Wouldn't it be cheaper to just get the machine fixed?"

"Of course it would, but Skeeter's a moron. I'm tellin'

you, Pink, it don't do no good to be logical about Skeeter. The man's basically dumber'n dirt."

"How long have you worked for him?"

"Couple of years. I'll let you in on a little secret. The pants in this family get worn by Miz Dawson, but he's too stupid to know it."

"Do you like working here?"

"Of course I don't like it." She shrugged. "But it's a job and lately, jobs are hard to come by." Glancing at the check in my hand, she said, "Keep it and give it back later. He won't never know it's missing."

"Are you sure? I'd hate to get you into trouble."

"I'm sure." She put the bank statements back in a file drawer and stood. "Let's get outta here, Pink."

Stuffing the check into the pocket of my skirt, I followed her out of the office and down the hall to the back door.

When she opened it, Skeeter and his homely wife stood on the threshold and I knew then, my electric jolt of karma wasn't the good kind.

Chapter 14

Skeeter wouldn't have fired Caroline, but Mrs. Dawson did. I tried to take the heat, tried to explain that I put her up to it, but Skeeter's wife wasn't at all interested. All she could see was that her cleaning lady was in her home after hours with a "lying whore." That, of course, was me.

I didn't care what she called me, but I tried like hell to put up for Caroline. Didn't matter. We were told to leave, or she intended to call the police.

In the car, I started to tell Caroline I was sorry, but she held up her hand and stopped me. "What's done's done, and there ain't no use talkin' about it. Understand?"

"I just wanted to apologize."

"Save it, Pink, 'cause that ain't gonna get my job back."

I remembered what Bobby Tom told me about qualifying for Red Cross aid because I was such a disaster, and decided he was right on. In all I'd done, I'd never felt guilty the way

I did then. Caroline was a hardworking, honest woman, and I'd just gotten her fired.

She never said a word, all the way back to her house. When we got there, she parked beside the old Ford, waited for me to get out, then drove away before I could say goodbye.

I got in Sam's butt-ugly car and sat there for a long, long time, wondering how in the hell I was gonna fix this mess.

That night, I went back to my apartment. Something had changed in me, whether because of the close call with Lowell, or the disturbing meeting with Skeeter's wife and Caroline's loss of her job, I didn't know. All I knew was that I'd had enough of hiding and running. If the Dog Doo Stalker decided to show up and kill me, he'd have to face my little Bobcat first. If I missed and he killed me anyway, so be it.

Mom argued until she was out of breath, but I was adamant. I had two days left before I could get the disk back from Mrs. Bohannon, and I intended to spend those days finding the son of a bitch at Marvel who was selling salvage pipe and ripping off the company.

Certain the calls were from reporters, I ignored the phone and inspected Skeeter's canceled Marvel check, debating the best way to figure out who the account belonged to. I thought about going to Dallas, to the bank where the check was deposited, giving a story about being the company's CPA and how I needed the bank statements because my client lost all of them, but I knew that wouldn't work. Ten years ago, maybe it would have worked. These days, nobody will hand over anything without Power of Attorney, preferably signed in blood.

I thought about all sorts of angles, but by nine o'clock that night, I knew I had no choices that were exactly legal. The only way to figure out who opened an account for a fake company called Marvelous Energy was to hack into the bank's records.

Being severely techno-challenged when it comes to computers, I knew hacking was as out of my league as rocket science and I thought about people I knew who were computer geeks. It took a while, but I eventually remembered a friend from high school who was always into computers. Somebody had told me he'd started his own software company. Praying he was still in Midland, I looked him up in the phone book and nearly whooped with joy when I found him.

Just as I reached for the phone, someone knocked on the door. I went to look through the peephole, holding the little Bobcat in my hand, even though I was sure it was a reporter. Instead, it was Ed. As soon as I opened the door, he came in and asked in his unholy sexy voice, "Are you all right?"

"I'm fine."

Pulling me to him, he held me tight and mumbled against my hair, "I don't know what I'm going to do about you, Pink. It's like you have a death wish."

"What's that supposed to mean? It's not like I did anything risky today. All I did was try to leave the office, and out pops Lowell from behind a big concrete pole. I think he showed up because the injunction failed."

"So he told you." Ed sounded disappointed, as though he'd planned to tell me and it bugged him that Lowell beat him to it.

I hugged him tighter, my face smashed against his shoulder. "Thank you, Ed."

He mumbled something against my hair that I couldn't quite make out, then said, "I want you to come to my house and stay with me until we go get the disk day after tomorrow."

Stepping away from him, I frowned. "You sound like Mom, wanting to lock me up until it's time to go back to Washington."

His gaze went to my hand, the one still holding the Bobcat. "What in blazes are you doing with that?"

"Sam made me buy it."

"I'm gonna beat the shit outta him, first chance I get. You've got no business carryin' a gun, Pink."

"Easy for you to say. You don't have a maniac stalking you."

"More likely than not, if he came after you, he'd end up using that little gun to kill you, instead of the other way around. I bet you couldn't hit the side of a barn with it."

"Maybe not, but I could sure scare somebody."

"It's not enough. You need to go home with me."

"I can't, because I have things to do and I know you'll keep me from doing them."

"What things?"

"Ed, why would I tell you when I just said you'll try to keep me from doing them?"

"How about if I promise I won't get in your way?"

"I wouldn't believe you because you're the Loophole King, and you'd find some way to double-talk it."

He grinned at me as he said, "You cut me deep, Pink."

Turning toward the incredibly ugly, turquoise Formica table, I laid the Bobcat down and asked, "You want something to drink?"

"I'd love something to drink, but I'd bet you don't have any Jack Daniel's."

"You'd be right. I have water, with or without ice."

"Skip it." He followed me to the wagon-wheel couch and sat next to me. "How about we just make out for a while?"

Eyeing my watch, I shook my head. "I have to make a call before it gets too late. Gimme a rain check."

He moved away, turned his back to me, and before I could stop him, laid back, his head in my lap. There's something incredibly erotic about a good-looking guy's head in your lap, and I didn't shove him off like I should have. Instead, I dove my fingers into his silky, dark hair. "What's the latest on Bert and Ollie?"

"With that letter you coerced out of Skeeter Dawson as his hard evidence, Ollie filed suit on Bert for selling the primo pipe and replacing it with crap."

"The guy's got nerve, you gotta give him that."

"Yeah, I'll give him that, but he'll give my clients a whole lot more before it's all said and done."

"He has no idea you know all about Domino Pipe?"

"None." His dark eyes focused on my breasts. "Who are you calling?"

"An old high school buddy named Owl, and why are you staring at my boobs?"

"I'm working on my superhero X-ray vision, trying to see through your clothes."

"It's not like you haven't seen them before."

"True, but looking at breasts isn't like looking at a lot of other things. Take, for instance, a good movie. See it once and it's great. Twice, it's still good but predictable. Three times, it gets a little old. Any more after that and it'll put you to sleep. Breasts aren't like movies. They're always interesting and look good each and every time."

"Ed, you're so romantic."

"Does it bug you? Should I run out for roses and candy?"

"Don't bother. I'll take the superhero thing." I bent over and kissed him. "Now you've really got to get up so I can make my call."

"Is it Owl Nunez?"

"You know Owl?"

"Sure. Used to kick his ass after school because he was always swipin' my smokes." He frowned slightly. "The guy's a major computer geek. Are you calling him for help with your computer?"

"Yes." I gently nudged him until he sat up, then I stood and went to get the phone. "You have to go away now."

"What if I refuse?"

"Then I'll be way pissed off at you and I won't let you look at my boobs any more."

"Hmm, sounds dire, except I don't believe you."

"You're way too sure of yourself, Ed. I've got a good mind to tell you to go away and never come back."

"So why don't you?"

"Because you promised a room at the Watergate."

"And you've always wanted to stay at the Watergate?"

"Oh, I've stayed there. In fact, that's where I stayed last time I went to Washington."

Ed stood and advanced on me. "That can only mean one thing, Pink."

Holding the phone, I eyed him warily. "What?" Ed grinned at me and I nearly dropped the phone. The man is just way too good-looking, and the best part is, he's completely clueless. "You're as ready as I am to accrue benefits."

"Maybe," I said, unprotesting when he took the phone and laid it on the table, then drew me into his arms and laid one of those Ed Wonder-Kisses on me. I was enjoying myself hugely when the thought of his ex-wife popped into my head, unbidden and unwanted. Marina's face floated past, mocking me, ruining the kiss.

Ed raised his lips from mine. "You just went from sixty to zero in a nanosecond. What's wrong?"

Before I could stop myself, I blurted out, "Tell me about Marina."

Instantly he dropped his arms and moved away from me. "What's to tell? We got married, stayed that way for a few years, then got divorced."

"Why?"

He seemed inordinately interested in the old, faded drapes across the window. "Does it matter?"

"No, I'm just curious."

"She wanted things I didn't, so we got divorced and she went to find somebody who does want the same things."

"Sam says he went out with her for a while."

Turning, Ed had a seriously dangerous, pissed-off look on his face. "Did he mention that we were still married when he started sleeping with her?"

"As a matter of fact, he said you were divorced."

"We were separated, but not divorced."

"And you think he should have waited until the ink was dry on your divorce papers?"

"Damn straight."

"What about Marina? Shouldn't she take some of the blame for hanging out with Sam before the divorce was final?"

Ed walked around the dinky room, obviously uncomfortable with the conversation. "Of course she's to blame, but she did it to get back at me. Not for any great interest in Sam."

"Why would she want to get back at you?"

He stopped and turned to face me, his expression suddenly devoid of anger. For that matter, his expression was completely blank, as though he had no strong feelings about Marina, one way or the other. "She thought I was sleeping with my assistant."

A weird buzzing noise started in my head. "So were you?"

"Of course not! My assistant is happily married, and she was pregnant with her second kid at the time. Marina was competitive, but certain that every other woman had her beat. It was always my job to be her backup, and after a while, I got sick of being stuck in the cheerleading section."

I wanted to believe him, and pretty much did, but only because I remembered Marina and he'd hit the nail on the head. She was needy, and definitely the jealous type. Still, I guess because of what I went through with George, even the hint of cheating on Ed's part made me anxious and agitated. I knew, no matter what happened between him and me, the worry would always be in the back of my mind, waiting to sneak out and scare the hell out of me at unexpected, inopportune moments.

"What are you thinking, Pink? That she was right? Do you really think I would cheat on my wife?"

"I don't know you well enough to make a call. Obviously, if I'm willing to sleep with you, I must trust you, and I do like you Ed. A lot. But after what George did to me, I'm gun-shy. No way I ever want to be in that position again. You have no idea—"

"Wanna bet?" he interrupted. "Did Sam tell you I caught them together, in *my* bed?"

"No, he didn't ever mention that." Small wonder there was so much animosity between them.

"So don't trot out your hurt feelings of betrayal from George and expect me to make up for an asshole who couldn't keep his pecker in his pants. Either you trust me, or you don't, but who I am has nothing to do with him. You got it?"

"Got it." I watched him come toward me. "Are you mad?"

"No, I'm horny as hell, scared shitless for you and I'd really love a cold beer right now."

"I'd love to help you out, Ed, but I really need to make that call."

"Are you gonna tell me why you're calling Owl?"

"I wasn't planning on it."

When he was near, he reached out and smoothed my hair behind my ear. "I don't want to leave you here alone, Pink. Come home with me."

"No, Ed. I've got two days to find out who's selling off Marvel's salvage pipe and I intend to do it any way I can. You're bound to hold me up."

"Maybe I can help."

"Maybe you could, but you won't. You're just like everyone else because you think it's stupid for me to be so determined about this."

"I don't think it's stupid," he allowed, "but I don't really understand. In the grand scheme of things at Marvel, those pipe sales are small potatoes."

"Lowell and the execs are greedy liars, but whoever's selling that pipe is actually a thief. Maybe a murderer. You're the one who said that prostitute was killed because she was mistaken for me."

"Exactly why you shouldn't keep digging. He might not make a mistake next time."

"Ed, I've gone through just about every negative emotion in the dictionary since I blew the whistle, and now I'm down to being righteously pissed-off. I'm so close to finding the guy, there is no way I'm backing off."

"What do you intend to do when you figure it out? Confront him? Call the cops? The FBI?"

I hadn't thought about that, my goal always focused on finding the guy. "It depends on who it turns out to be."

He took a deep breath and let it out slowly, as though he was waiting for a measure of patience. "No way you'll give up?"

"No way."

"Then I'm going to help you." Moving closer, he snaked an

arm around my waist and leaned down to kiss me again, but before his lips touched mine, the phone rang and he let me go.

I looked at caller ID and recognized the area code as Washington. I answered after the third ring, watching Ed take a seat at the tacky table and reach for Skeeter's canceled check.

"Pink? Are you okay?" Steve sounded very distressed. "I just got a call about what happened this afternoon."

"I'm fine."

"Thank God. I gotta tell you, I'm about ready to come get you and keep you under lock and key until the next hearing."

"Don't worry, I promise not to get knocked off before I get the disk."

Steve was quiet for several heartbeats, then said softly, "You know damn good and well that's not fair."

"Isn't it? After all, without the disk, the whole investigation will take at least a year, well past the next election. With the disk, you and all the other committee members get instant gratification. You can publicly hang the Marvel execs and look very good to all those voters." I ignored Ed's severe frown, as well as his slicing motion against his neck. In a very strange way, I was almost as pissed-off at Steve as I was the Marvel execs. Everyone wanted something out of this, and it seemed none of it had anything to do with the victims, all those employees who would lose their jobs, and all those investors who would lose their money. "I'm sorry if that offends you, Steve, but I call 'em how I see 'em."

"On the contrary, I'm not the least bit offended. And you're right about me wanting the disk so we can move ahead with this thing, but it's got nothing to do with the voters. Haven't you figured out, I have enough confidence in myself that I don't need any dog and pony shows to win elections?"

"Well, yeah, you do seem pretty sure of yourself."

"It's because I'm a sensible, reasonable man who doesn't waste taxpayers' money that I will get reelected. Getting my hands on that disk will save literally millions of dollars over the next year. As for worrying about you, it's got absolutely zero to do with the damn disk. Maybe you believe that, maybe you don't, but that's the way it is."

I wasn't entirely sure how to respond to that, so I just said, "I see."

"No, Pink, I don't think you do."

"Then maybe you need to draw me a picture."

"First of all, I feel responsible for you the same way a prosecuting attorney is responsible for his star witness. Secondly, I'm a man, and an Italian one at that, so sitting here in the middle of all this political bullshit, instead of coming down there to look after you is bugging the hell outta me. And third, I'm way beyond ready to see you somewhere besides CNN, or sitting in front of the finance committee."

Again, I didn't know what to say, especially because Ed was sitting right there, hanging on every word.

Steve didn't appear to notice my lack of response. "So you can believe my only interest in you is the disk, but you're dead wrong."

"All right, Steve. Thank you."

"Will you please be careful?"

"I will, I promise."

"Would you mind saying something besides pleasantries?"

"I wouldn't mind at all, but this isn't a good time."

"Why? Do you have company?"

"Yes. My attorney. We're going over some things."

"Your attorney keeps odd hours. Can I speak to him?"

Oh, my. That was so not a good idea. But what could I say?

"Okay, Steve." I handed the phone to Ed. "Senator Santorelli would like to speak to you."

Ed scowled, but took the phone and switched into lawyer mode. "Evening, Senator. What can I do for you?" He was quiet a while, listening, then said, "Yes, we'll have the disk by then. Thursday at two is fine." He fell silent again, his dark eyes meeting mine, reflecting nothing of his thoughts. "She hasn't mentioned it, no." Another pause. "That's not exactly ethical, Senator." He stood and walked away from me. "Obviously, my main concern is for my client, so I think you owe me the assurance that whatever she chooses to do won't in any way affect the outcome of this hearing." Obviously agitated, he paced around the coffee table. "Immunity can be retracted. If things don't work out, I have to know she won't be indicted for any wrongdoing."

I sat down and wondered how life could suck and be wonderful, all at once. Two men, equally compelling, and both interested in me. I actually had a choice. Amazing. Especially after all the pathetic men I'd dated after George.

"I see," Ed said, stopping in front of the television. "Thanks, Steve, and I appreciate your candor. We'll see you on Thursday." He ended the call and tossed me the phone. "Pink, I thought the guy only wanted to seduce you, but I was wrong."

"What do you mean?"

He sat down on the couch and stared up at the cottage-cheese ceiling. "I think he's head over heels in love with you—or thinks he is."

"No way!"

He turned to look at me. "How do you feel about him?"

"I told you, he's a nice guy, and funny, and if I hadn't met you, I'd probably be a lot more interested."

"You don't have to say that, Pink. I'm a big boy, and if you want to pursue the senator thing, I don't blame you."

I got up and crossed over to sit next to him. "You threatened to kill Sam and Bobby Tom for invading your territory. Are you willing to step aside for another guy because he's a senator?"

Ed didn't put his arm around me like I expected. In fact, he actually shifted away a bit. "You may as well know, right up front, I don't plan to marry again, and even if I did, I don't want kids, I don't want a honker SUV and a membership at the country club and all the trappings so many people get buried under in this town. If you think any of those things are what you want, or may want down the road, I'd say Senator Steve's your man, and I wouldn't want to get in the way of that."

He shook his head slowly and returned his gaze to the ceiling. "I like you, Pink, and I'd be happy to beat the crap out of guys like Sam and Bobby Tom because I know what they're after, but that senator is all about wanting to court you, or something like that, and it's just not the same at all."

I wanted to ask Ed why he didn't want children, but I decided I'd already been nosy enough for one night. Maybe later I'd ask him and he'd explain. "Suppose I don't want to go steady with him?"

"How do you know?"

"All I know is I can't hang out with more than one man at a time, and for now, you're the only one I want to hang out with."

Ed did put his arm around me then. In fact, he put both arms around me and pushed me backward, until he was on top of me. "*Ding Ding,* Ms. Pearl. Correct answer. Now it's time for 'Double Jeopardy.'"

Chapter 15

I never did get around to calling Owl. By the time Ed and I stopped making out on the wagon-wheel couch, it was half-past eleven, way too late to call. Ed agreed the only way to figure out who opened the bank account was a little bit of hacking by an expert, and Owl was definitely the expert for the job. He offered to go with me to see Owl, first thing the next morning.

He left at midnight, against his will, but I told him there were still reporters hanging around occasionally and I didn't need anyone reporting my attorney stayed all night with me. I had enough problems. Besides, I wasn't ready to give it up with Steve. I don't know why. Maybe just because I really liked him, and didn't want to hurt his feelings. When he found out about Ed, I wanted to be the one telling him, not some perky chick on CNN.

I slept with the Bobcat on my nightstand, but it wasn't

much defense against the Dog Doo Stalker's 2:00 a.m. phone call. He called the cell phone, I guess because he thought my apartment phone was tapped. I answered, instinct telling me exactly who was on the other end. "It's been a while," I said as a greeting.

"I've been busy," he replied in his Drano voice. "Looks like you have, too. Sorry Jaworski went off on you like that."

"Thanks. Your concern is touching."

"Only because he's stepping on my toes. You're mine, Pinkie, all mine. When it's time, I'm gonna skewer your pus—"

"Yeah, yeah, I know all about it. Just curious, but why did you kill Sparky?"

"He was getting ready to come over to your side. Thought if he squealed like you did, he could get off the hook. I couldn't let him do that, just like I'm not gonna let you."

So Sparky had a change of heart, a turn of conscience, and died for it. I shivered, there in the dark. "Are you the one selling the pipe?"

"No, but I can't afford for the guy who is selling it to be outed."

"Why?"

"Because he knows who I am. Just leave it alone, and answer a question for me. Have you heard from Merry Thornton?"

"No, but why would I? She and I aren't friends anymore."

"Why is that?"

The turn in conversation freaked me out. What did all this have to do with Merry? I sat up in bed so I could focus a little better. "She thinks I'm having an affair with her husband."

"Could that be because you walked out of The Bar with him?"

"Could be."

"So are you?"

"No." I drew in a deep breath. "Why this sudden interest in Merry? Do you know where she is?"

"I have to go now, Pinkie. Remember, stay away from the pipe deals, and if you know what's good for you, don't take that disk to Washington." He hung up.

Still sitting in my bed, in the dark, I thought of several things, all at once. Why had he asked about Merry? And how did he know about me walking out of The Bar with Bobby Tom? He knew about Bobby Tom because he was hiding in plain sight. He had to be somebody I knew, somebody right in my face, somebody I would never suspect. As for Merry, I couldn't quite figure that one out.

I laid the cell phone back on the bedside table and lay down, staring up at the dim light from the parking lot against the ceiling. What could Merry know that was a danger to the stalker? In spite of her relationship with Ollie Shanks, Merry wasn't the sort to pay attention to anything related to business. If Ollie blatantly double-dealt Bert, right under Merry's nose, she wouldn't catch on. Merry was all about clothes and lake houses and gossiping with the neighbors. So what sort of threat could she pose to the Dog Doo Stalker?

I fell asleep wondering about it, and woke up still wondering. While I got dressed, I replayed the whole conversation in my head, and by the time Ed arrived, I was no closer to figuring it out than I'd been just after I hung up.

Dressed in those killer jeans and one of his faded T-shirts, Ed looked mighty fine. He came in with a sack and handed it to me. "What's this?" I asked, peeking in the bag, spying three donuts. "Oh, my God, Ed, I think I love you. I've bought donuts at least five times for the office, and I've yet to eat one." I drew one out and started to eat it, but stopped so I could tell him about the early morning phone call.

Ed poured himself a cup of coffee and sat at the table, looking thoughtful. "Maybe Merry saw something she wasn't supposed to, something with this guy's name on it."

"I can't see how. Bert buys the old pipe from Skeeter, and unknowingly buys the new pipe from Ollie, but you said yourself, none of the Marvel execs names are associated with Domino. It doesn't make any sense."

"Maybe he was being facetious. Maybe he knows exactly where Merry is and wanted to see if you do, too."

"I don't think so, Ed. He sounded like he really wanted to know. Almost like he was concerned about her."

Looking surprised, Ed set his coffee mug down. "Who would be concerned about her? Certainly not Bobby Tom."

"How would you know?"

"He came to see me yesterday and hired me to represent him when she gets back."

So much for me not recommending Ed to Bobby Tom. He went to him anyway. "No, he wouldn't be too concerned, but it's moot anyway because no way Bobby Tom is the Dog Doo Stalker."

"How can you be sure? Maybe he holds lots of Marvel stock. You know the stalker could be someone outside of Marvel, who stands to lose a lot when the company folds."

I remembered then, the letter Bobby Tom showed me, from Merry's dad. "When Bobby Tom came to hire us to trace assets, he showed me a letter he got from Merry's dad, right before they got married. It detailed some shares in Marvel he was gifting to Merry."

"So Merry's dad owns Marvel stock. Maybe a lot of it."

Thinking back to my high school days, I conjured up a mental picture of Merry's dad. Tall, thin and sort of a nervous guy, he worked for the city manager's office and it always seemed like he and his wife were at odds with each other. Being a kid, I never paid much attention, and Merry didn't talk about it, but I did recall a few trips we took with the school and Merry didn't go because her family couldn't afford it. "Could Merry's dad be the Dog Doo Stalker?"

"Did you see him that afternoon at The Bar?"

"I don't remember seeing him, but the place was packed."

"Let's go see Owl, then we'll pay a visit to Merry's dad."

"What will we say? I mean, we can't just come out and ask if he's the stalker."

"I'm representing his son-in-law, and you're tracing their assets. We both have a vested interest in finding Merry. We'll ask him if he's heard from her and while we're talking, we'll gauge his reactions, see if he looks nervous or scared."

We left in Ed's 4-Runner and headed for Owl's house. "Have you seen Owl since high school?" I asked curiously.

"Saw him a few months ago at Bettina's. He's really into the Indian thing now, and he went off on me about his Apache relatives. It was interesting for a while, but I lost track when he started telling me about the spiritual side of things."

"Ed, how very un-P.C. of you."

"I guess, and don't get me wrong because I think that's great for a guy to get into his roots, but Owl got pretty preachy about it and that turned me off."

"Is he married?"

"Not at the moment. He was, but when he got into all this Apache stuff, she got fed up and left."

"I always liked Owl in high school, even if he was a geek."

"Yeah, he's an okay guy, but I'm warning you, don't ask him about the Apache thing, or we'll be stuck for hours. Just give him the check and state your business."

"Does he work out of his house?"

"He does now. I asked and he said he was getting more into contract work for other software firms."

We were headed north. "Does he live in Green Tree?"

"No, he's got a couple of acres out by the polo grounds."

I always forget about the polo grounds. That's because I never ran with the seriously rich Midland kids, the ones who went off to boarding schools back East and were debutantes and married other filthy rich kids. The ones who rode horses with English saddles and either played or watched polo matches. I was more into every-man sports, like football.

Owl's house was a rambling stucco, with tall yuccas at the corners and a couple of desert willows in the sparsely green yard. The willows were in full bloom, their feathery, soft pink blossoms giving an air of beauty to what would otherwise be a pretty boring house.

"Look," Ed said, pointing toward the back, "he's got a teepee out there."

"Wow. It looks authentic, doesn't it?"

"I'm sure it is." Ed parked and got out, then came around to my side. "If he asks us to take a look at it, say no. Say we have to be somewhere in thirty minutes."

I frowned up at Ed. "Maybe I want to check it out."

He returned my frown. "Suit yourself, but don't say I didn't warn you."

It took several doorbell rings and knocks before Owl answered the door. In jeans, a white shirt and pigtails in his black hair, he looked good. But he still wore the thick glasses that earned him his nickname. "Hey, Owl," I said, sticking my hand out to shake his. "Remember me? Whitney Pearl?"

Instantly, he engulfed me in a bear hug. "Of course I remember you!" He loosened his hold, but didn't let me go completely, his round-eyed gaze moving across my face. "You look good, Whitney. I've been following the news about you, and I'd just like to say, I think it's really rotten the way you've been treated. It takes a lot to do what you did."

"Thank you, and I'm glad you feel that way because that's why Ed and I are here. We need your help with something."

Owl let go of me and reached over to shake Ed's hand. "Good to see you," he said with a smile.

Ed mumbled the same and we followed Owl into his house, decorated in Santa Fe–style twig chairs, Saltillo tile and blush stucco walls. He led us into the living room and we all took a seat. "So tell me what I can do for you," he said pleasantly.

"Well," I began, "it's not exactly legal, but you could say we're fighting fire with fire." Briefly I explained the problem and all the while, Owl nodded, as though he understood.

When I was done, he said softly, "I can't help you. I've given up any illegal activity because it sullies the spirit."

"I'll pay you five hundred dollars," I offered.

"Please, Whitney, don't insult me this way."

"Very well then, I'll make it a thousand."

"Okay," Owl said without batting an eye.

I guessed he didn't mind sullying his spirit for a thousand bucks. "How long will it take?"

"About ten minutes, but I can't do it right now. You'll have to give me until this afternoon."

"No problem," I said, handing him the canceled check, along with a business card. "All of my numbers are on there, but I'll most likely be at the office."

Owl blinked as he read the card. "You work for your mom?"

"After I was fired, it was the only job I could get."

"Perhaps you should spend some time out in my teepee. I can help you overcome your blocks, Whitney."

With a quick glance toward Ed, who was scowling ferociously, I politely declined. "Maybe later."

"Yes," he said, also darting a glance at Ed, "maybe later."

We left then and I could tell Ed was relieved I didn't go for the teepee sit. On the way to see Merry's dad, he said, "A thousand dollars is a lot of money, Pink. Do you always blow large wads of cash like that?"

"Only when there's a full moon."

I could tell he didn't like my flippant answer, but I didn't much care. It was my money and I'd blow it how I wanted. That's one of the perks of being single.

On the street where Merry's parents live, in a ranch-style not too far from the one I grew up in, the curbs along either side were packed with cars. We got to the door and rang the bell. I could hear a lot of voices inside, and within a minute, the door swung open. An older woman stared back at us. "Please come in," she invited. "It's such a tragedy, isn't it?"

I had no clue what she meant, so I simply nodded.

"Merry was such a sweet girl, I just can't believe she'd do something like this. Is it any wonder Allan died? The poor man had heart trouble, and all this business with Merry was just too much for him to take." She waved toward a book. "Please sign the visitor book. I know the family will want to know who all stopped by, later when this is behind them." Then she faded into the crowd.

I looked up at Ed and he shrugged. "I'd say that rules him out as your stalker, wouldn't you?"

"Let's get out of here," I whispered, suddenly overcome with strong karma. Last time I felt that way, Skeeter's wife cussed me out and Caroline lost her job. I knew something wicked was headed our way and I was determined to get out before it got there.

As quickly as we came in, we left, and hurried back to Ed's car, but even while we drove back to my apartments, I couldn't shake the icky feeling of impending doom.

"Are you okay?" Ed asked as he pulled into the parking lot.

"No. I've got bad vibes about something."

"Bad vibes?"

"Never mind, Ed."

He stopped next to the Ford and said, "You need to get a car and quit using Sam's field car."

"I know. I guess it's really rude to keep it so long."

"It's got nothing to do with being rude. I just think you shouldn't be driving such a butt-ugly car. What color is that, anyway?"

"Sort of a cross between lavender and sky-blue."

"It's an eyesore."

"I'll buy a car as soon as we get back from Washington." I waved goodbye, then went to get into the old Ford, wondering when the other shoe would drop.

As soon as I got to the office, Gert reminded me to go resign. That chick never misses a beat.

Just as I expected, Mom wouldn't accept my resignation. In fact, she never really took me seriously at all. Instead, she got annoyed and said, "Stop wasting time, Pink, and don't be so dramatic. If I want you to not work for me, I'll let you know. In the meantime, go get some billable hours, willya?"

I went back to Gert's office and gave her the bad news. She looked ready to cry and I said, "Tough breaks," before I went back to my cube.

Lying on my desk were three envelopes, all from the producers I'd requested Mrs. Colder's transfer orders from. I was excited as I opened the first one, anxious to have proof of

Bert's duplicity. I'd turn the orders over to Sam, who'd give them to the sheriff, and Bert would get sent up the river for stealing half of Mrs. Colder's royalty interests.

I scanned the order copy, my gaze finally reaching the assignee name.

That's when the other shoe dropped. The name on the transfer order wasn't Bertram Shanks.

It was Edward Ravenaldt.

Chapter 16

I knew I'd never get anything done that day, not until I found Ed and asked him what the hell his name was doing on Mrs. Colder's royalty interests. Not even a lecture from Sam about billable hours and my complete lack of any could get me off high center. I needed to go out to Thorn Pipe and start digging through Bobby Tom's records, but I couldn't do it, not with the Ed thing hanging over me like a black thundercloud, threatening to rain all over my parade.

When I couldn't reach him by phone, I took off in the old Ford and searched all over, including his office, the courthouse, his house and even the post office. His assistant was down south, in Terrell county, gathering information for Ed's class-action suit against the Shankses, so she was no help. Obsessed, I wouldn't give up looking for Ed. It was as though everything I'd hung my hopes on now hung on the answer to one simple question: How did Ed's name get on those transfer orders?

By lunchtime, I knew I had to give up. Ed wasn't anywhere that he should have been, which meant I had no prayer of finding him. I grabbed a sandwich and headed back to the office.

While I attacked it, my mood even leeching into my eating, Mom came into the break room and sat down. I offered her a bite and she declined. "How's it going?" I asked around a bite.

"Okay, I suppose. How are you?"

"I'm okay." No way I was going into the Ed and Mrs. Colder thing with Mom. Not until I had an explanation from Ed.

"Your aunt Fred says Mrs. Bohannon will be back late tonight. Are you going over to get the disk tomorrow?"

"First thing."

"Good. Then you're going to Washington on Thursday?"

"That's right." Something was up. Mom looked a little antsy, and her twenty questions seemed weird because she knew all the answers before she asked. "What's up, Mom?"

"I got a call from Skeeter Dawson's wife just a while ago, complaining about you."

"Oh." I kept my concentration on the sandwich. "Is she a friend of yours?"

"She's a client of mine."

Eh-oh. "Still?"

"Barely." Mom leaned back in the chair and stared at me. "Pink, what were you doing over there?"

Once Mom has the scent, there's no use trying to hide. Come hell or high water, she'll get to the bottom of things. I knew that. So I opted not to even try to lie. I told her about the cleared checks, and about Caroline.

This did not make Mom happy. All through the rest of my sandwich, I got a lecture. She wrapped it up with the lucky speech. "You're damn lucky the Dawsons didn't call the police and have you arrested. You're even more lucky they didn't call the state board this morning. If you get your license revoked, you'll be in a world of hurt." She watched me wipe my hands on a napkin. "What about the woman who got fired?"

"What about her?" I asked, feeling guilt wash over me again.

"Are you going to try and find her another job? It's the least you can do, Pink."

"I know, Mom, but I don't know people in Midland. How can I know who needs a maid? Or a bookkeeper?"

"You could ask me. I know a lot of people in this town."

"Okay, so I'm asking."

"It depends on what she wants to do—clean or keep books."

"She says she makes more money cleaning."

"Only because she never worked for anybody decent."

"Like?"

"Like me."

I dropped the napkin and stared at Mom. "Are you serious? You'd hire Caroline?"

"I could use another bookkeeper, especially since Ashley keeps taking time off with her sickly kids, who aren't really sick. Obviously, I need to interview Caroline before I make a decision, so how about you go find her and ask her to come up?"

"You're not doing this just for my sake, are you?"

"No, Pink. I'm running a business here and I don't do anything based on emotion."

"Okay, Mom, I'll find Caroline. Thanks."

"Thank me if I hire her."

With something constructive to do, I left the office again and went in search of Caroline, but she must have been hiding out with Ed because I couldn't find her, either. While I was out, I looked for Ed again, but came up empty, so I decided it was high time I went out to Bobby Tom's and got started. Driving out to the Thorn office, I wondered if he'd heard from Merry. Surely she would come home for her father's funeral. Besides, she couldn't stay away from her children forever. Okay, I guess she could, but even considering her obvious problems with fidelity, I didn't think she was the type to abandon her children. Not permanently.

When I got to the office, Bobby Tom came out to greet me, then asked me to follow him back to his office. He looked grim and I steeled myself for whatever he had to say.

Looking across his desk at me with those beautiful cornflower-blue eyes, he said, "It doesn't look like I'm going to need you to trace assets after all. Merry called me yesterday, after she got word that her father passed away, and said she would agree to any settlement I proposed."

That surprised me. "Why would she do that?"

Bobby Tom looked like he might blow a gasket, clenching his hands into fists as he leaned forward. "Because she's going to marry Ollie Shanks as soon as our divorce is final. I told her I want the kids, that they're not going to live under the same roof with that jackass, and she agreed."

"No way!"

"She did. She really did. You know, Whit, I would wish like everything that I never married her, except for the kids. They are really great, and I can't regret them." He shook his head, his expression disgusted. "When I think about what all this is doing to them, I could kill her."

"That wouldn't make it any better, Bobby Tom."

"I know," he said, looking like it pained him to give up the idea, "but I guess her backing out of the picture completely is almost as good."

"Maybe for you, but she's their mother, and even though

I'm disappointed in Merry for the way she's acted, I don't think she's a bad person."

Bobby Tom looked at me like I was speaking a foreign language he didn't understand. "Not a bad person? Whitney, she's been carrying on a flaming affair, right under everyone's nose, and she skipped town because she was afraid she'd be arrested for murdering a whore! If that's not bad, I'd hate to see your definition."

"But she didn't murder anyone."

"That's not the point."

"No, the point is that she's the mother of your children, and even though she's being a sleaze, that doesn't make her a bad mother, especially in their eyes."

Suddenly, he looked very tired. Leaning back in his chair, his gaze traveled around the room. "I guess you're right. It's just such a bummer, the way things have turned out."

"Where has she been since she left?"

"I don't know and she wouldn't say. I do think she was with Ollie because I could hear a man's voice in the background."

"Is she coming back for her dad's funeral?"

Bobby Tom shook his head. "Merry hates funerals, and she wasn't too keen on her dad. I don't think she'll come back until her name's cleared of suspicion."

"Well then, if there's nothing for me to do here, I guess I'll head back to the office."

"Did I tell you I hired Ed Ravenaldt for the divorce?"

I didn't see any point telling him I knew because Ed told me, so I answered, "No, you didn't."

"Are you seeing him, Whit?"

"Sort of, but not for long."

He stood as I stood and followed me toward the door. "Why is that?"

Turning my head to look at him, I could only say, "He's not my type." I just wasn't into liars and crooks.

By the time I got back to the office, it was almost four o'clock. I went to my cube and found three more transfer order copies, all delivered by a local courier. I sat there at my desk and stared at Ed's name on all those orders and wanted to cry. How could I have misjudged him so much? Was I doomed to zero in on lying, cheating men? I thought about my own father, and even though he was a mean SOB, he had more integrity than anyone I knew. Lurch might be mean, but no way he was a liar.

I'd been there drowning in misery maybe thirty minutes when Tiffany buzzed and said I had a visitor. Feeling so apathetic, I wasn't even curious who it was, I got up and went toward the front. Owl stood there, holding a manila envelope, looking well pleased with himself.

"Hey," I said, "come on back to the conference room."

He followed and as I took a chair, I noticed Gert was on full-alert, her curious stare focused on Owl like a radar. Hmm, why hadn't I thought of that? Owl was a computer geek—a nearsighted one. He was cool because he was Native American, but all the same, he was definitely tipping the geek meter. I wondered if Gert was into Native American spirituality. Probably not, but maybe Owl could get her interested.

"What did you find?" I asked, as he handed me the envelope.

"Looks like a guy named Roy Kipper."

My heart fell all the way to my toes. "Oh, no. I really like Roy." I pulled the printouts from the envelope and looked them over. There it was, in Arial letters, "Roy Kipper." "This is really blowing my mind. Roy's a good egg."

"Maybe he's just running scared because Marvel's about

to bite it. From his birth date, I figured out he's sixty-two, which puts him close to retirement. Probably has all his retirement tied up in Marvel stock, which is worth half what it was a month ago." Owl looked thoughtful. "What are you going to do about him?"

"I don't know. To tell the truth, I expected it to be one of the Marvel execs, not a nice guy like Roy."

"Maybe you should just talk to him, tell him to lay off and you'll keep this under your hat. If you go to the cops, or the feds, they'll lock him up and throw away the key." Owl glanced at the printouts. "Desperate people sometimes do strange things, Whitney."

"I know," I said, my mind turning over the situation. I thought about my late night call and how the stalker responded when I asked if he was the one selling the pipe. He'd said no, but he couldn't afford for the seller to be outed. Maybe one of the execs put Roy up to it. Maybe they took the money and gave Roy a small cut for doing the dirty work. That had to be it. Roy was just too nice a guy to be a thief, no matter how hard up he was. "Thanks for doing this. I'll get you a check." As I left the conference room, Gert waved me into her office.

"Is that Owl Nunez?" she asked a little breathlessly.

Narrowing my eyes, I nodded. Gert looked way hot and bothered and I might have laughed, except she was so obviously trying not to be obvious. "He did some computer work for me, and I have to go get him a check. Why don't you go in and keep him company while I'm gone?"

Immediately, she shook her head, no. "I'm too busy."

Taking a step closer to her desk, I lowered my voice and said, "Never figured you for a chicken, Gert."

"What are you talking about?"

"Don't be coy because it doesn't suit you at all. Are you gonna pass up opportunities when they slap you in the face?"

Gert scowled at me. "I only asked a simple question."

I shrugged as I turned to leave. "Suit yourself."

While I was at my cube, writing the check, I wondered if she'd go for it. I was sorely disappointed when I went back and saw her door closed, and Owl in the conference room—alone. I had to get her hooked up with somebody, but it wasn't gonna be easy if she insisted on crawling back into her shell every time an eligible male came around.

I handed Owl the check. "Thanks again."

He took it as he stood. "Anytime. If you ever need computer work, I'm your man." His gaze went to Gert's closed door across the hall. "Was that Gert Luebner?"

"Yeah. You know Gert?"

"I remember her from high school, but I haven't seen her in years." Owl blinked at me. "She's still homely."

This, coming from a geek? Something about that got my back up. As much as I disliked Gert, I also felt sorry for her, and had an odd sense of protectiveness toward her. Maybe just because she's a woman, and I think women should stick together. "How very unkind and chauvinistic of you, Owl. Gert happens to be maybe the smartest woman I know, and just because she puts her priorities in places other than looking hot so men will want to sleep with her, it doesn't make her a worthless person."

"Ouch," he said with a sheepish grin. "I guess I deserved that."

"I guess you did." I eyed him speculatively. "After I get home from the hearing in Washington, how about you come over for dinner and I'll ask Gert and you two can get reacquainted."

The guilt trip worked like a charm. He nodded and said with resignation in his voice, "Okay, Whitney. Just call me."

I watched him leave, my mind already forming a plan of attack. Because the more I thought about it, the more I was convinced Owl and Gert were perfect for each other. All I had to do was figure out how to get Gert to try makeup.

Making my way back to my cube, I wondered if Roy was still in Midland. Deciding to take the bull by the horns, I picked up the phone and called Neil Dollar. "I've got some information I'd like to hand off to Roy Kipper and wonder where he is."

"He's out at the yard."

I thanked Neil and was about to hang up when he asked, "Are you going to Washington on Thursday?"

"That's the plan."

He was quiet for a bit, then said, "Good luck."

Bemused by that, I hung up, grabbed my purse and took off in search of Roy. Unfortunately, no one was at the Marvel yard and I spent the next hour hunting for Roy. He was hiding out with Ed and Caroline, I supposed.

I had to stop for gas after spending so much time out looking for people I couldn't find, and while I stood at the pump, gassing up the Ford, I saw Caroline drive up. I waved and she stopped in the next bay. "My mom wants to talk to you about a job," I said.

Caroline shot me a look. "I don't need no mercy job."

"Good thing, since Mom's a barracuda and doesn't hire people because she feels sorry for them." Except me, but hey, I'm her kid. "She's got a bookkeeper who's out of the office more often than not and she says she can't find a decent employee to take up the slack."

"Don't matter," Caroline said, losing her frown, but still not looking too happy, "'cause I bet she don't pay shit."

"Mom says you haven't ever worked for anybody decent

and that's why you didn't make as much doing books as cleaning."

"How much you reckon she'll pay?"

"It'd be easy to find out. Go see her."

"Is she there now?"

"Yep." I cast a look at Caroline's tight, knit pants and her T-shirt. This one said Queen Bitch. "But you better not go up there dressed that way. Mom's real big on looking professional."

Caroline looked at my clothes. "I ain't got nothin' like that."

"Follow me to my place and you can borrow something."

"You don't have to suck up, Pink. I fergive you."

"Thanks, but I wasn't sucking up. You did me a favor, so I owe you one."

She got into her car and waited for me to finish, then followed me home. Within thirty minutes, I had her outfitted in a nice khaki skirt, a button-down, blue cotton blouse and some Cole Haan mules. I fixed her hair in a loose ponytail, took off half her makeup, and—voilà!—she looked like a bookkeeper.

"Damn, I look classy, don't I?" she asked, turning this way and that while she looked in the mirror.

"Very nice," I agreed. I gave her directions and sent her on her way, then called Mom and gave her a heads-up. "Her language is horrible," I said, "but she's a hard worker, Mom. Give her a shot, okay?"

Mom said, "If she passes the test, I'll hire her."

"Test?"

"I make people take a test before they come to work for me."

"You never gave me a test."

"Pink, you're my daughter and you couldn't find a job. You didn't need to pass a test."

"Oh."

"I guess this is the part where I'm supposed to give you an ego stroke and tell you I didn't hire you because I felt sorry for you, that I've always wanted you to come to work for me."

"Skip it, Mom. I really hate it when you lie." I slammed down the phone and wished all over again that I could have found another job. I love Mom, but she can be really nasty sometimes.

I was severely depressed as I got back in Sam's Ford and went off in search of Roy. Everything was turning to shit. Seemed like I took one step forward and three back. I parked outside the Marvel office building, which also happened to be Ed's, and watched the entrance to the parking garage, waiting for either Ed or Roy to come out. With sweat rolling down my back and chest, listening to Stevie Ray Vaughn, I thought about Merry and wondered if she'd come out of hiding for her father's funeral. Then I thought about Roy, and wondered who put him up to selling the pipe.

It was close to five when Roy drove out of the garage in a rental. I followed him at a distance, all the way to El Corazon, and sat in the car while he went inside. Forty-five minutes later he came out, a toothpick dangling from his lips as he crossed to his car. Just as I expected, he drove to the downtown Hilton, across the street from the courthouse. As he parked in the lot behind the hotel, I pulled in behind him and got out. "Hey, Roy!" I called.

Turning, he spotted me and smiled. "What's up?"

I came close, so I wasn't yelling, and said, "Roy, I don't know exactly how to tell you this, but I know it's you."

He looked confused. "What are you talking about?"

"The pipe sales, Roy. I know you're the one who opened the Marvelous Energy bank account, and I know how much money you've deposited. But here's the thing, if you'll stop, I won't tell anyone, because I know someone had to have put you up to it. I like you, Roy, and it breaks my heart to know—"

I never finished my sentence because Roy shoved me so hard, I went backward, landing on my ass. Then, before I could ask Roy why he did that, he was on me, his hands around my throat, his pudgy red face close to mine.

"I told you to back off, didn't I? But you just wouldn't do it! Dammit, I don't want to do this, but you leave me no choice. Why'd you have to turn that information over? Couldn't you just leave well enough alone? I've watched my retirement fund dwindle away to almost nothin', and it isn't fair! Not after all I've done for this company!"

His hands tightened painfully around my neck, and for the second time in two days, I stared death in the face. Something told me this time wouldn't end like the last one did. I was a goner. Fighting did no good because Roy's considerable weight pinned me to the hot asphalt. His sweat dripped on my face and I blinked as I prayed, making all sorts of outrageous promises to God.

"Didn't finding Sparky in your bathtub scare you? Didn't you get that I meant business? I went to all the trouble of luring him to your apartment, leaving him there with a dog turd, thinking surely to God you'd get the message that I wasn't fooling around, but you're a true blonde, aren'tcha?"

That's when I realized nobody put Roy up to selling the pipe. And he was definitely the Dog Doo Stalker. I was about to die at the hands of a madman who had a dog doo fetish, in a parking lot. I wished I could talk, because even though he was about to kill me, I always thought Roy kinda liked me, and maybe I could talk him out of it. But with stars dancing before my eyes and my vocal chords compressed, I couldn't do anything but drag wheezing, stingy breaths into my collapsing lungs.

"He wouldn't leave it alone, just like you. Kept asking about that pipe, and wondering what happened to it. Then he point-blank accused me of selling it and keeping the cash. I couldn't have that. Besides, he was the one behind all the screwy accounting at Marvel. Seems to me like I did everyone a favor, getting rid of him."

I was close to losing consciousness, but he dragged out the misery, waiting to finish me off, I suppose, so he could browbeat me some more for ruining his retirement fund.

"You shoulda been where you were supposed to be last week, instead of shopping. Just like a damn woman. It was your fault I got the whore instead. Followed you to that dress shop, watched you go in and hid in the back seat to wait for you to come back out." His usually amiable face twisted into a grotesque mask of fury. "How the hell was I to know it wasn't you or your car? They were both black, and she looked just like you from behind!"

His hands tightened and I knew this was it.

Oh, God. How could such a nice man be a cold-blooded murderer? All for lousy money. I was on to a prayer where I promised God I would go save all the starving babies in India when suddenly, Roy's hands fell away. I saw Ed haul Roy off of me, then plow his big fist into the fat man's face, knocking him to the ground on the other side of the Ford. Scrambling to my knees, I tried to get up and couldn't, I guess because I'd been deprived of oxygen so long. I crawled toward the sickening sound of flesh pounding flesh and then I saw Ed whalin' on Roy, who was almost unconscious. Ed was so mad, looked so crazy, I sort of cringed backward.

If I didn't do something, Ed would kill Roy. Not that I cared so much about Roy, but I didn't want Ed to get in trouble. Even if I was pissed off at him. "Ed," I croaked, "stop!"

So caught up in taking out all his anger on Roy, he never heard me.

I crawled closer and slapped his leg. "Ed! Stop! Overkill!"

He felt my hand and stopped to look down at me, then reached for me and dragged me up against him. "Jesus, Pink, are you okay?"

I nodded against his shoulder, then burst into tears. Damn PMS.

The whole Tell the Cops My Story scenario was getting to be routine. I watched them take Roy away on a stretcher, accompanied by a uniformed cop who would stay with him until he could be charged with murder, attempted murder and grand larceny. I was still sniffling, as much for Roy screwing up his life as anything else, and the detective kept asking me if I needed to go in the ambulance and get checked out at the hospital. Finally, I said in a rocky voice, "I have PMS, okay? Willya leave it alone?"

He didn't ask any more after that. When he was done asking me all his questions, Ed put me in the 4-Runner and took me to his house, in spite of my protests. I was dying to ask him about Mrs. Colder's transfer orders, but I couldn't speak very well, and a small part of me didn't want to face it just then. I was tired and bummed out and all I really wanted to do was go to sleep.

Which is exactly what I did, in Ed's big bed, with Ed right there in a chair beside me.

When I woke up, it was dark, I was naked and he was still there. "Why am I naked?" I whispered.

"Because you looked uncomfortable," he replied.

I glanced around, and heard low voices from the other side of the bedroom door. "Who's here?"

"Your mom, and Caroline, and Sam."

"Is Mom freaking out?"

"Only a lot. I'll go get her," he said as he started to get up.

"No, Ed, not yet."

He sank back down to the chair and reached for my hand. "She's worried about you, Pink."

"In a minute. First, I have to ask you a question." Swallowing and flinching because it hurt, I shook my head. "Never mind. Maybe later."

He leaned over and kissed my cheek and I caught a whiff of his Ed scent. I couldn't believe I wasn't going to ask him. How unlike me. But I just didn't have the energy to get up and leave if his answer wasn't what I wanted to hear.

And what did I want to hear? That there was a perfectly logical explanation and he wasn't a crook. But I didn't see any way he could explain it logically, so I knew I'd have to leave as soon as I asked and understood that my instincts really were out of whack, and I really had picked a skanky lawyer to sleep with and hang out with and maybe fall in love with.

Dammit.

"How did you happen to be there?" I croaked.

He gave me an ironic smile. "You can thank Sam for having that butt-ugly car. I was just coming out of the courthouse when I saw the car turn onto Main street. I wondered where you were going, so I followed." His smile faded and he held my hand tighter. "Jesus, Pink, I probably lost ten years off my life."

"So did Roy. Where'd you learn to beat the shit out of somebody like that?"

"School of Hard Knocks. My older brothers kicked my ass a lot."

"Thanks, Ed," I whispered.

He went to get Mom then, and she and Caroline and Sam all came in to stand around the bed and ask questions and pat me and say they were sorry. Mom said she hired Caroline and they appeared to be good buddies already, just like I knew they would. Caroline is a worker bee and Mom loves worker bees. When they were all gone, it was just me and Ed again. He stripped down to his boxers and climbed in with me, scooping me next to him and shushing me until I went back to sleep.

The phone rang at eleven and I woke up to hear Ed talking to Steve. "She's had a bad time, and she's asleep, so I'll have her call you back tomorrow, after we go get the disk."

He gathered me close again and I drifted back to dream world, where life is good and dogs never shit.

Chapter 17

Early the next morning, Ed took me back to the scene of the crime so I could get Sam's car and go home to the apartment and clean up and change clothes. I called Mrs. Bohannon to tell her we would be over in a while, then got into the shower. While Ed waited for me on the wagon-wheel couch and watched the reports by CNN from the Midland courthouse steps, where a beat-up Roy was being arraigned, the tech guy from the police department showed up to dismantle the recording equipment they'd set up on my phone.

As soon as I was ready, Ed switched off the TV and we headed for the door, but the tech guy stopped us before we could leave. Pointing at the phone, he said, "Somebody has patched into this. We're not the only ones who've been listening in on your phone calls."

"Probably Roy Kipper," Ed said.

The tech guy shrugged. "Probably."

A few minutes later, Mrs. Bohannon answered the door, looking perplexed. "Why are you here, dear?" she asked me. "Mr. Maloney said you were having car trouble and you sent him for the disk, that he'd be sure you got it."

Son of a bitch if Mrs. Bohannon wasn't more ditzy than she'd been when I was in third grade.

Turning away, I grabbed Ed's arm and we ran, yelling goodbye to a shocked and awed Mrs. Bohannon. At the car, Ed said, "Must have been Maloney who patched into the phone."

I called Steve on the cell and caught a lucky break when he was in his office, instead of a meeting. "You're not gonna believe this, but Maloney beat us to the disk. I was hoping you'd have his home address."

"Hang on," he said. I could hear papers rattling, then he was back on the phone. "Here it is. He lives in an apartment on Midland Drive." He gave me the address, then said, "But he may be at the office, Pink. I'll call the local FBI and they'll meet you there, to make sure he hands it over."

"Okay, I'll call you later." I hung up and told Ed.

"Let's split up," he suggested. "You take my car and I'll borrow Mrs. Bohannon's."

"Where should I go?"

"Since the FBI will be there, you go to the office and I'll go to his house."

I got into the driver's seat and took off, driving way over the speed limit, determined to beat Maloney before he could break the password on the disk and erase it.

When I got to the building where the IRS has their Midland office, I jumped out of the 4-Runner and hauled ass upstairs, to the fifth floor. The FBI hadn't made it yet, but no way I was waiting on them. I asked at the front desk to see

Ronnie, and of course I was told I'd have to wait. I pulled out the Bobcat and the IRS lady decided maybe I didn't have to wait after all.

Storming down the hall, I yelled at the top of my lungs, "Erase that disk, Maloney, and you're goin' to the Big House!"

I looked in each office as I passed, and found him almost to the end of the hall. He sat at his desk, hurriedly typing, an evil grin on his ugly, fat face. "Too late!" he cried.

I pointed the Bobcat at him. "Step away from the computer before I blow a hole in you."

His gaze jerked toward me and his smile died. Then he ducked down, dragging the keyboard with him. "You won't shoot me," he called from beneath the desk, the sound of tapping keys a backdrop to his voice.

He was right, but no way in hell I'd admit it. I pointed the little Bobcat at a hat lying on his credenza, and suddenly realized, it was a Kid Rock hat. The guy who smoked cigars by the duck pond was Ronnie Maloney! He'd been hanging around, spying on me, all along. The night Lucky surprised me, he'd been out there, probably waiting for the reporters to leave so he could pick the lock on my cheap-ass door and put a patch on my phone. Bloody bastard. I fired and missed the damn hat, but nailed Ronnie's CPA license. The glass shattered and fell to the floor.

"You coulda killed me!" he shouted.

"I said, *step away from the computer.*"

Still, he typed.

Utterly frustrated, raging mad, absolutely determined to get that disk away from him, I faced the last option and knew I had to do it. Raising my arm, I cupped my left hand beneath my right, took aim, and shot the fax machine. I was enormously gratified by how it exploded into a zillion pieces, then smoked.

The tapping stopped. "You shot my fax machine!"

"Damn straight, and the freakin' computer's next, so I suggest you get out from under it before it blows."

Ronnie scrambled to his feet and backed away from me and the Bobcat. Reaching over, I popped the disk out of the computer, then turned and walked out.

He yelled after me, "It's too late! The disk is empty!"

Turning back, I said, "You better hope that's not true, because this is now considered the property of the justice department and you're guilty of tampering with evidence."

"She's right, Maloney," a man said from behind me. "I'm with the FBI and authorized to arrest you if that disk isn't intact."

Looking desperate, even in defeat, Ronnie's shoulders slumped and he said, "It's all still there."

The next day, Ed and I had to leave Midland at the butt-crack of dawn, fly to Houston and lay over for three hours, then finally on to D.C. As senate finance hearings go, I thought it went well. Ed sat there next to me, in a navy suit and a red tie and gave me good, solid Ed-like lawyer advice and I handed over the disk, along with all the copies I'd made, and answered questions for what seemed like ten hours, but was only two.

Seeing Steve again was a trifle weird, I guess because he was back in his serious senator mode, a stranger from the funny guy I'd talked to so often on the phone. A couple of times, I made eye contact and there was definitely something there, but I don't think anyone else noticed. The only time anything might have struck an odd note was when he asked me about Lowell's attack. "Did you have any idea he might be violent?"

"None," I replied. "I've known Mr. Jaworski for a very long time, and I've never known him to be anything but courteous and professional."

"Ms. Pearl, some people aren't what they seem."

"Yes, Senator, I've become well aware of that in the past few months." The other senators were all staring at Steve, but he didn't appear to notice. Or if he did, he didn't care.

"In the future, I caution you to be more careful."

A lecture? Totally bizarre for a finance committee hearing. What could I say, except, "Thank you, sir, I will."

Ed leaned over and whispered, "Change the subject. Tell them about the memos and direct them to look at the copies."

I cleared my throat. "If you'll direct your attention to the memos included in your copies, you'll see where the Marvel CEO agreed to a five-year consulting contract, in exchange for the firm's blessing on the audit."

Barbara Clemmons asked, "How much would the firm earn from the contract?"

"In the neighborhood of fifty million dollars."

"How much of that money would you have received?"

I shot a startled look at Ed. He leaned over to whisper, "She hates you, Pink, so don't get sucked in. Tell the truth."

"I worked on a salary, Ms. Clemmons, and would have received the same amount, regardless of the contract. Besides, I was an auditor and had nothing to do with the management consulting side of things at the firm."

"How did you get a copy of this letter?"

Again, I looked at Ed. He whispered, "Spill your guts because they already know the answer. She's trying to set you up." He looked into my eyes, leaned closer and added, "No fear, Pink. Remember, you're in the right and have nothing to hide."

Sitting up a bit straighter, I looked right at Barbara and said clearly, "I broke into Mr. Jaworski's office, found the letter in his files and scanned it onto the disk."

"You admit to breaking and entering?" she asked in a

shocked voice, as though I'd just confessed to a string of serial murders.

"It's my objective to be completely honest."

"So to cover your own interests, you broke into your boss's office and stole a classified document?"

I sighed and looked at the evil witch, deciding she wasn't going to get the best of me. I'd been stalked, attacked, maligned, fired, humiliated and shot at. Barbara Clemmons couldn't have lived five minutes of my life over the past two months without caving in and having a nervous breakdown. How dare she sit in judgment of me? "Other than my life, I didn't have any interests. It just wasn't in my grand scheme of things to go to prison for a bunch of greedy bastards who gave no thought to anyone but themselves. But I'm funny that way. If that makes me a criminal, I don't really give a rat's ass."

The gallery of spectators behind me started clapping. They stood and yelled, "Go, Pink!"

Barbara Clemmons glared at me, but she didn't ask any more questions. I glanced at Steve and noticed he was looking down at his copies, hiding a smile.

The rest of the hearing was much more sedate and boring, although there was someone in the crowd who occasionally yelled out, "Atta girl, Pink!"

Just after four o'clock, we were dismissed. Ed took me to eat at a famous Washington watering hole, where the pastrami sandwiches are monstrous and the beer's bitingly cold.

When I was halfway through my sandwich and thinking no way I could tackle the other half, I decided it was time to get the story from Ed about Mrs. Colder. Watching him polish off his beer, I asked, "Why is your name on all of Mrs. Colder's transfer orders, giving you one half of her royalty interests?"

He set the still icy mug down, looked at me and said, "So

no one else can take them away from her. First of next year, I'm taking the other half."

Cool as a cucumber, he sat right there and admitted to stealing a dotty old lady's royalties. I was speechless.

"How did you happen to get that information?"

"Mrs. Colder hired me to look into why her monthly royalties were down so much, even with the price of crude at a ten-year high."

"Why didn't you ask me? I could have saved you a lot of work and Mrs. Colder a lot of money in fees."

Astonished, I watched him continue to eat, as though he hadn't just admitted he was a crook. "Gosh, how stupid of me. I should have known you stole her royalties, but there I was thinking you're an honest man."

He slowly set down his sandwich, leaned back in his chair and frowned at me. "You think I stole from her?"

"What else can I think? They're not in trust, but in your name, with your social security number."

"In trust, they could still get taken away from her. If I'm a court-appointed custodian, if I have Power of Attorney, under any possible scenario, someone can take her interests if they get a good enough lawyer. The way I did it, no one can contest it. Mrs. Colder signed those transfer orders, which were witnessed by three people and notarized. If that isn't proof enough, a handwriting expert will back it up."

"Ed, she's older than dirt and not all there. Don't you think that's taking advantage of her?"

"She's all there, and no, I don't think so at all because it was her idea."

"If it was her idea, why did she hire me to figure out what happened to her interests? She was positive Bert Shanks was behind it."

"That, I don't know. You'll have to ask her yourself." He picked up his sandwich and continued eating, obviously assuming the subject was closed.

Like hell it was closed. "Ed, I want to go home."

Again, he set down the sandwich. "What about the room at the Watergate?"

"I've changed my mind."

"Bullshit."

"No bullshit. I just don't think I want to sleep with a man who would cheat an old lady, especially one who saved my life—twice."

He drew his cell phone out of his pocket, punched in some numbers and waited a bit. Then he said, "Dolly, this is Ed." He watched me, his dark eyes hard. "I'm here with Pink, and she's mad because she thinks I stole half of your royalty interests." He held out the phone. "She wants to talk to you."

I took the phone and said, "Hello, Mrs. Colder."

The old lady's voice practically cackled, as though she'd just heard a very funny joke. "Are you going to get a *room* at the Watergate?"

"I beg your pardon?"

"You heard me, girlie! Are you and Ed *gonna have an affair,* or not?"

With a heavy sigh, I said, "I don't think so."

"*Why?* Because you think he ripped me off?"

"That's exactly why."

"You're a real sharp tack, Pinkie. I didn't figure you could get the goods on Ed, but now you have, so I'm gonna tell you a *little secret.* You ready?"

"Yes, ma'am."

"Ed's my godson, and someday I'm gonna *kick off* and

leave him all I got. Those babies of mine are spoiled rotten, and I love 'em, but not a *damn* one of 'em has got any sense. They'll lose every dime before I'm *cold in the ground.* Ed's a real man and doesn't spend money like it's nothing. He'll be *in charge* of everything and he'll dole it out as he sees fit. We decided to transfer those royalties so there won't be so much in *my estate* when it's time for me to go."

"If that's true, why did you hire me to look into your royalties? Why make me think Bert stole them from you?"

"First off, I wanted to see how smart you are, and I wanted to give your mama some more business 'cause *I like* Jane Pearl. I also wanted to see what you'd do when you figured out Ed had the interests."

"What did you expect me to do?"

"I hoped you'd be ticked, and you are, but if you'd gone ahead and slept with him anyway, I wouldn't want nothin' else to do with you. Since you told him to *bug off,* you're okay."

"Okay for what?"

"For Ed."

"You mean, this whole thing was a setup so you could do some matchmaking?" I watched Ed's eyes widen.

"That's about the size of it. Are you *mad* with me, girlie?"

"Only a lot."

"That's okay, because I'm *not the one* who likes you, but you need to forgive Ed, because he didn't know anything about it, and because he likes you a lot. I can tell."

"Okay," I agreed, watching the waitress set another beer in front of me, thinking this was maybe the weirdest conversation I'd ever had.

"Have fun, Pink. You deserve it." She hung up then and I handed the cell phone back to Ed.

"Everything okay?" he asked, looking very satisfied.

"It's totally weird and wacked out, but yeah, it's okay."

"Then drink your beer so we can go get naked."

Ed made a liar out of Mrs. Colder and blew a gigantic amount of money on a suite at the Watergate. I went in the bathroom that was big enough to herd cattle in and showered.

Feeling very naked, looking very forward to hot sex with Ed, I opened the door and saw him sitting on the small sofa in the living room of the suite. All he had on were his faded, holy jeans. No shirt, no shoes, no rules. He looked better than any man had a right to. His dark gaze swept my body and he grinned. "You look like some kinda hot girl, you know that?"

He got up and came for me, then grabbed my hand and led me toward the bed. But he stopped before we got there and kissed me, his big hands wandering all over, ending up with my breasts in his large palm. "Anybody ever tell you that you've got amazing breasts?"

"No, but how can breasts be amazing? They just sort of sit there and do nothing."

Kneading them with his hand, he said, "You'd have to be a guy to get it, I guess."

"Ed, I'm very glad I'm not a guy right now."

"Hmm, me, too." He kissed me again, and his hand fell to my hip, where his fingers slowly made their way to the middle of me and I gasped when he dipped inside. "Did you ever do it backward?" he asked against my mouth.

"Once, in an elevator."

"Did you like it?"

"I was too nervous about getting caught."

"Are you nervous now?"

"Not hardly."

Before I could say anything else, Ed spun me around and bent me over, until my palms were splayed against the snowy white sheets of the bed. I heard his zipper slide open, I heard the condom wrapper tear, and I heard Ed say a lot of very nasty things about what he intended to do to me. I might have been embarrassed if I wasn't so turned on. He bent low, his solid chest warming my back, his five-o'clock shadow grazing my cheek, and whispered, "You like wearing khaki and cotton and sensible shoes and you think you're real conservative, don't you?"

Gasping with impatience, I answered, "I'm a CPA. Of course…I'm conservative."

"I got news for you, Miz Pink. Your little ass fits in those skirts like skin on a grape, and those nice button-up shirts you wear leave nothing to this man's imagination."

I was about to tell him to stop teasing me or I'd start without him when someone knocked on the door.

"Shit!" Ed said against my neck. "Let's not answer it."

"Fine by me," I agreed.

The knock sounded again, louder, accompanied by a deep, male voice I'd grown to know well. "Pink! Are you okay?"

Ed whispered, "I'm gonna kill the son of a bitch."

I hung my head and said, "Get in line."

"You better answer him, or he'll get security to open the damn door."

I turned my head and hollered, "Gimme just a second."

"No problem," Steve answered.

Ed moved away from me and I swear to God I wanted to cry. What did a girl have to do to get laid?

Shoving one of the white terry room robes into my hand, Ed whispered, "Put this on. I'll be in the bedroom." He left me there, strode to the opposite door and disappeared.

Feeling very uncharitable, I went to the door and opened it. "Hello, Steve," I said, managing a smile.

"Mind if I come in for a minute?"

I glanced outside and seeing no lurking reporters, I stepped back and waved him in. "What's this all about? I thought we decided to wait for a couple of weeks." I noticed he was dressed in jeans almost as faded as Ed's, and a blue chambray shirt that looked like it came straight from a rancher's back. His perfect hair didn't look nearly so perfect, like he'd ridden over with the windows rolled down. Coal-black and shiny, it was messy. Steve looked awesome. Or maybe I just thought so because I was still turned up hotter than the broiler on my toaster oven.

His gaze moved all over me and he smiled. "Did I get you out of the shower?"

"Uh, yeah, just a while ago." I motioned toward the little sofa, but he shook his head.

"I can't stay. I'm actually on my way home, to California, but I wanted to stop by and see how you're doing."

"I'm okay, Steve, thanks."

"You did well today, Pink. I was proud of you."

"I just told the truth. Can't screw that up too much."

Surprising me, he moved closer, wrapped his arms around me and kissed me. I'll never be able to live it down, and I can only blame it on hormones, but I kissed him back with way too much passion for a woman with another man in the bedroom. He tasted like a breath mint, smelled like the men's cologne counter at Saks, and felt like a solid wall of warm male. Everything in the universe faded into oblivion and I kissed him like we were Adam and Eve, solely responsible for the creation of humanity.

Finally, he raised his head. He was grinning at me. "I'll call you. Soon, Pink. Real soon."

Then he was gone and I stood there, staring at the door, wondering if I'd completely taken leave of my senses. I heard the bedroom door open and turned to look at Ed. He leaned against the jamb and said in a dry voice, "Why is it that every time I turn around, you're kissing other guys?"

The past two months all caught up to me then, and I burst into tears. "Ed, I wish I knew the answer. Do you hate me?"

"No. I actually like you quite a lot." He walked past me, into the bathroom, then returned with a handful of tissues. Leading me to the bed, he made me lay down. He sat there beside me and handed me tissues while I bawled like a big crybaby.

"Are you mad at me?"

"Maybe a little, but I figure you've been under a lot of pressure, and that makes you do things you wouldn't ordinarily." He dried more of my tears and said, "Truth to tell, I happen to know you dig my chili more than any of them, so it all works out in the end."

"How do you know that?" I asked around a hiccup. "Am I that obvious?"

"Yeah, but don't worry. I'm probably just as obvious."

"Ed, do you still want to have sex?"

"Only a lot."

I sat up. "I'm going to wash my face, okay?"

"I'll be right here."

With renewed enthusiasm, I headed for the bathroom, only to find Lady Fate in there, laughing her fool head off. My bout with PMS was over and Ed's and my sex life was put on hold. Again.

The next morning, we checked out of the Watergate and went back to Midland. I was seriously bummed about the way things worked out, but it all got better when I stepped off the plane to a welcome home party that included Mom, Caroline, Sam and even Mrs. Colder. They took me and Ed to the office and we had lots and lots of donuts.

While I scarfed one down, Sam came close. "How are you?"

"I'm great, Sam. Everything worked out okay, didn't it?"

He looked at the donut. "Fine, Pink, just fine."

"It wouldn't kill you to tell me I did a good job."

"It's not my style to reward people with flattery."

"Oh? Then how do you reward people?"

"By giving them better assignments."

I perked up at that. "Like how much better?"

"Like a bad oil deal."

"Really?"

"Really. So wrap up that round heart attack and come to my office. We'll discuss it."

I looked across the room at Ed and he grinned at me, just before he turned and walked out. He would be back, I was sure. We still had a lot of unfinished business to take care of.

And above all, I've got a very good head for business. That's because I'm a CPA.

* * * * *

COMING NEXT MONTH

#41 SOPHIE'S LAST STAND by Nancy Bartholomew

Threats, stalkings, exploding cars—Sophie Mazaratti had had enough! And the formerly mild schoolteacher was taking matters into her own hands. Her sleazy ex-husband had sicced both the mob and the FBI on her, and the detective handling her case was making her rethink her vow of celibacy—but no one would stop Sophie from getting her life back on *her* terms....

#42 TARGET by Cindy Dees

Athena Force

Army intelligence captain Diana Lockworth had uncovered a plan to assassinate the president-elect of the United States—but no one believed her. She had only twenty-four hours to figure out who was behind the plot, where they planned to strike—and how to stop them. With the hours ticking away, Diana had to get the president himself on her side, and rely on her own ingenuity to save the day....

#43 THE AMAZON STRAIN by Katherine Garbera

Dr. Jane Miller had made her career by creating vaccines for lethal viruses, but she hadn't counted on having to travel to the Amazon Basin to administer the latest cure herself. Racing through the jungle to prevent a deadly outbreak, she soon learned that other people had their own agendas—and they'd do anything to stop Jane from reaching her goal....

#44 PARALLEL LIES by Kate Donovan

Her father had trained her to be the perfect spy. But when he died tragically at the hands of an assassin, Sabrina Sullivan had given up her dream of working for the CIA and entered a quiet life with a new identity. Now her sister had been kidnapped—and Sabrina suspected her father's killer was involved. Coming out of hiding to take on the secrets and lies from her former life, could she trust the man who'd replaced her father, or was she working with the enemy?

SBCNM0405